You Must Remember This

You Must Remember This

Mary D. Brooks

Renaissance Alliance Publishing, Inc.
Nederland, Texas

Copyright © 2001 by Mary D. Brooks

All rights reserved. No part of this publication may be reproduced, transmitted in any form or by any means, electronic or mechanical, including photocopy, recording, or any information storage and retrieval system, without permission in writing from the publisher. The characters herein are fictional and any resemblance to a real person, living or dead, is purely coincidental.

ISBN 1-930928-57-2

First Printing 2001

9 8 7 6 5 4 3 2 1

Cover art and design by Mary D. Brooks and Marcella R. Wiggins
Illustrations by Lúcia A. de Nóbrega

Published by:

Renaissance Alliance Publishing, Inc.
PMB 238, 8691 9th Avenue
Port Arthur, Texas 77642-8025

Find us on the World Wide Web at
http://www.rapbooks.com

Printed in the United States of America

Acknowledgments:

I want to take this moment to thank LJ Maas for her fantastic imput, her support and encouragement for this novel. Thanks LJ!

To Marcella, Amy and Lucia for being there to encourgage and support.

Last but not least I would like to thank Cathy LeNoir for believing in me and fulfilling a dream.

— Mary

This book is dedicated to my dear friend, soul sister and one heck of a decent human being...

> Merci mon cher ami
> Lise Desmerais

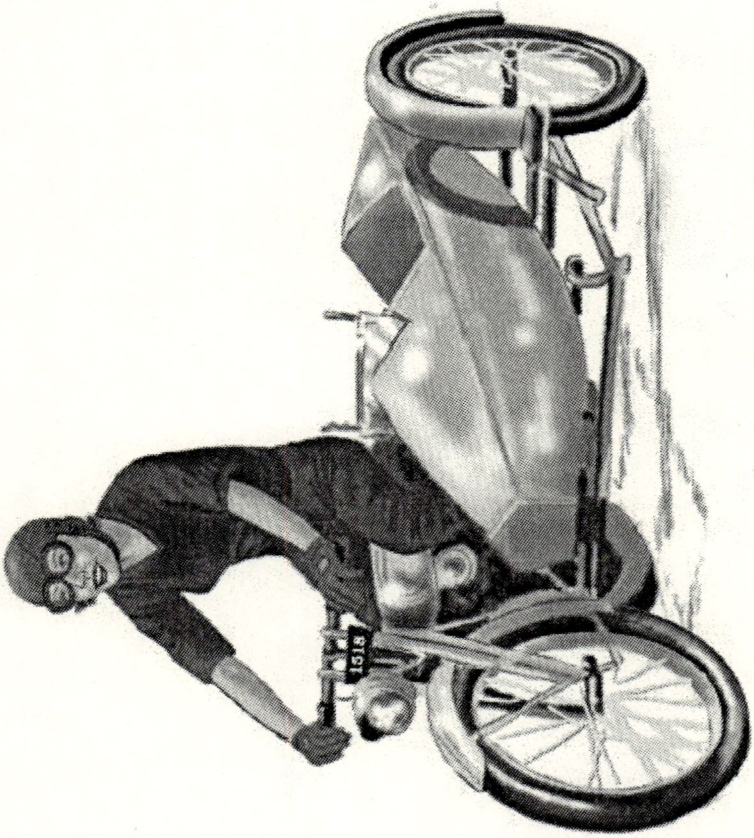

Chapter 1

The sounds of crashing came from the bedroom, and Eva Haralambos popped her dark-haired head out of the kitchen door. The noises were coming from the bedroom. More crashing was followed by a screech and then another thump.

"ARGH! I'm going to be late!" Zoe's voice drifted out of the bedroom.

Eva shook her head as she went to investigate. Zoe wasn't a morning person, and now that she had had most of the summer to laze about, it was going to be difficult to convince her to get up early. Eva had tried to get her partner out of bed as soon as the bell on the clock started to ring that morning. Zoe would not budge and had flung the clock out of the bedroom instead. They would undoubtedly have to buy another alarm clock, since they had a tendency to stop working when Zoe violently reacted to their insistence that she rise. Eva grinned as she watched Zoe hop out of the bedroom on one foot, unable to find her other shoe. Zoe's dark bangs fell across her eyes as she turned to see the wall clock, and she fell to the ground, grunting.

Morning in the Haralambos household was anything but serene and peaceful. Today was a momentous day for both of them. Eva was going to start her new job at the translation section of the Immigration Department, and Zoe was starting classes at university toward her art degree. Eva had told her about her educational experiences, and Zoe wanted to be able to have that in common with her partner. It had taken Zoe little time to decide what she wanted to pursue, and she was looking forward to university life, just—not quite so early in the morning.

"You know, if you had gotten out of bed when the alarm clock went off, you wouldn't be rushing." Eva stated the obvious as she held an inviting mug of tea in her hand.

Zoe looked up at her partner with a sheepish grin. "It's not my fault we went to bed so late."

They had spent the previous night at their friend Earl's home playing poker, which had gone really well until Eva started to lose. She had to recoup the matchsticks she'd lost to Earl. Dave, Earl's partner, and Zoe got out of the game early, and they watched the remaining two play. The contest had gone well into the morning when Zoe dragged Eva away, promising Earl a rematch.

"He got all my matchsticks!" Eva objected.

"Oh yeah, we were going to go bankrupt," Zoe said as she tied her laces, got up and gave her smirking partner a quick kiss, and went into the kitchen.

"You're late."

"I know. Registrations start at 10 am," Zoe said as she grabbed the toast from the counter top and began munching.

There was a knock on the door, and Eva turned around and went and opened it. Elena Mannheim stood outside, wearing a harried expression on her face as she tried to juggle her notebooks and her bag.

"Morning, Elena." Eva welcomed the young woman inside. "Come in. The tortoise isn't ready yet."

Elena smiled at her friend as she quickly hurried over to the sofa before she dropped her notebooks on the floor. "Phew, I couldn't wake up this morning," she said as she flopped down on the sofa.

Zoe came out of the kitchen with a piece of toast in one hand and her cup of tea in the other. "Hey, El," she said as she munched on her breakfast.

"Hi, Zo. Aren't you ready yet?"

"Nope. I'm just having breakfast, want some?"

"I already had breakfast! I think someone was late getting up today," Elena teased her friend as she watched Zoe hurriedly eat her breakfast.

"I didn't see you banging on my door to get me up. Were you out with Freddy last night?"

"In a manner of speaking," Elena said quietly as a blush tinged her cheeks. "Come on, we're going to be late!"

"Okay, okay. The university isn't going anywhere!" Zoe mumbled as she put the mug in the kitchen. She was met outside the kitchen door by Eva.

"I love you, gotta go. I can't wait to hear about your first day," Zoe said and tried to give Eva a quick kiss; but her partner held her for a moment, then smirked and kissed her thoroughly. Zoe picked up her notebooks and her bag and rushed out the door, crashing into her mother-in-law, Alberta.

"Sorry, sorry. Gotta go," Zoe said quickly, gave Alberta a kiss on the cheek and bolted down the stairs with Elena in tow.

Alberta Haralambos stood at the door and watched them fly down the stairs. She loved her two stepdaughters dearly, and Zoe had occupied a very special place in her heart in the short time she had known her. She reminded the older woman of her sister who had died when she was 19 years old—full of life, and with energy to burn. Alberta went inside and closed the door to the flat. She looked around at the messy lounge room and began to tidy up.

"Eva, are you ready?" Alberta called out as she picked up the cushions that were on the floor.

"In a minute," Eva's voice called from the bedroom.

Alberta sat down on the sofa to wait. Her gaze was immediately captured by a painting of a young woman reading, the curtain lightly draped over her shoulder as if a breeze had blown it on her. Alberta hadn't seen the painting before, and she stood and walked over and looked at it intently. The woman's face displayed a look of concentration as she read. The bottom of the painting was signed "Zoe Lambros." Zoe had drawn Eva so beautifully, Alberta was quite impressed by it.

Eva came out of the bedroom, putting on her sweater. She noticed Alberta was looking at the drawing. "Morning, Ally." She greeted her stepmother with a kiss on the cheek. "She's getting really good," she said and looked at the artwork. "She's very talented."

"Hmm. How long did you sit for it?"

"A couple of days," Eva replied as she picked up her lunch and put it in the briefcase. She had enjoyed just sitting there reading and occasionally looking up at Zoe as she was trying to get her image on canvas. She loved watching Zoe draw and would sometimes look up and see a furrowed brow with the tip of her tongue sticking out while she concentrated on a difficult area. "How's Dad this morning?"

Since leaving the priesthood to marry Alberta, Eva's father, Panayiotis, missed the church and being involved with the various church activities. Eva had introduced him to Father Eleftheriou when they went for worship on the Sunday after he arrived. The local priest and her father instantly hit it off and became good friends, which didn't surprise Eva since they so were so much alike. Panayiotis enjoyed singing and had a good voice. He was going to begin working with the local Greek Orthodox church as a psalmist, the lay minister who sang out the various bible texts when required during worship, and helped out the priest during the week with church business. When Father Eleftheriou suggested the psalmist job might be something Panayiotis would like to do, he was overjoyed.

"Oh, he's looking forward to starting work. He was quite excited," Alberta chuckled. "I think we'd better hurry, or we'll miss our bus."

Eva closed the door to the flat, and they made their way down the steps and into bright sunlight.

"I've been thinking of sitting for my driver's license," Alberta said as they stood at the lights to cross the road and watched the cars pass.

"I didn't know you could drive."

"Oh, yes...I used to drive the tractor on my brother's farm before the war. I got my license just before signing up. Do you know how to drive?"

"No, never learnt how. I guess it would be easier to get a car. Zoe would like to learn, but I'm not sure if Sydney is ready for Zoe on wheels," Eva laughed. Her partner would enjoy the freedom of having a car; she already loved to tinker with Earl's. She would have to talk to her partner about it.

❖❖❖❖❖❖❖

As the bus made its way though the busy, rush hour traffic, Eva looked out the window. They had managed to find seats next to one another just before the bus became "standing room only," which was a common occurrence during the rush hour. Eva sighed as she recalled having experienced many days of standing on tired, sore feet. She watched her fellow passengers and played the game Zoe had invented–trying to match the person to a job.

Sometimes Zoe came up with the strangest of occupations, which amused Eva.

"I think a car would be good right about now," Alberta leaned over and muttered. She was being struck in the shoulder by a woman's handbag.

Eva grinned, leaned over her stepmother, and poked the bag out of the way. The owner of the bag gave her a pointed look and made a rude noise before moving herself and her handbag further down the bus.

Ally burst out laughing as she shook her head.

Eva went back to staring out the window as the bus went down City Road and past the entrance of Sydney University. She wondered how Zoe's day was going. It was going to be different for her partner who had never experienced anything like university life. She remembered her time at the Berlin campus. She'd had a great time once she got over her jitters. She had met so many different people and learned so much. It was also the place she had met Greta and come to terms with who she was.

She sighed. She hadn't thought about Greta for a long time and felt a little guilty that she hadn't been faithful to the memory of her first love.

She had registered at the office and spent the rest of the day taking a slow tour of the campus where she would spend the next few years. Mamma was so proud of her and had taken photographs just before she left. Her stepfather had been silent and only grunted his assent to the pictures, but she knew he was proud of her in his own way. The young girl was overawed as she stepped out around the university grounds. She felt like she had a grin plastered on her face all day.

Tired from walking around, she noticed that some of the students were sitting on the grass, and she followed their example. She took off her sweater, put it on the grass, and sat down. Enjoying the spring weather, she turned her face to the sun, then frowned as a shadow fell over her. She opened her eyes and looked up.

"Hello," Eva said to the shadow. The shadow moved and plopped down beside her.

"Hello. You must be new; you have the new, fresh look about you," Greta Strauss said and offered her hand. "I'm Greta."

"Eva Muller," Eva replied. "You don't look like you're new."

"Oh no. I'm an old hand at this. I just came here today to lend a hand at the registration office. You know, answering questions and that sort of thing," Greta replied and smiled at the dark-haired girl.

"Oh," Eva said and smiled back.

Greta was a tall young woman. Her auburn hair flew about uncontrollably, and she had long ago lost the fight to keep it in any semblance of order. Greta had an easy smile and laughing eyes, which made Eva feel quite relaxed in her presence.

Eva smiled to herself. It was a pleasant memory compared to what happened later. She had been so young. She was a different person back then. If Greta were present now, Eva was sure she would be most surprised at the woman she had become.

She was drawn out of her trip down memory lane when Alberta tapped her on the shoulder as they neared their stop. The bus conductor smiled at the two women as they got off and headed into the John Curtin Memorial Building that housed the translation section.

When Eva found out where she was going to be working, Zoe had insisted they discover what the building looked like. So they had taken a bus into town, going over the route; and then they did a little window shopping, much against Eva's resistance.

The elevator opened and a young woman in a blue and white uniform popped her head out. "Going up!" she announced as a few people entered the elevator.

As the doors closed, Ally turned to her companion. Eva wore a frown and bit her lower lip. "Are you all right?" Ally asked.

"Oh yeah. I'm just a little nervous," Eva mumbled.

Alberta smiled at her stepdaughter and squeezed her hand. The elevator stopped on the 9th floor, and they got out to be greeted by the sight of an overcrowded waiting area. Eva's eyebrows rose into her bangs when she looked around her at the refugees that were sitting huddled together and talking. She smiled when she realised the voices were in different languages. It was like a mini Tower of Babel, she thought to herself.

She followed Alberta to the reception counter where a harried young woman was answering phones, and they stood patiently until the receptionist had finished.

Looking up, the receptionist was quite startled to be met

with piercing blue eyes. The woman's dark hair framed her face, and Debbie thought it was quite a striking combination. Looking at the woman next to the first, who was smiling a smile that reached her dark brown eyes, she asked, "Can I help you?" hoping they understood English.

"We're here to see Adam Eden," Alberta told the young woman, resisting the urge to grin at the name. She'd had a good laugh at home when they had received the letter from him, informing them of the date and time of their job commencement.

"Thank God! You're the new interpreters?"

They both nodded and received a huge grin from the young woman. "My name is Debbie. As you can see, I'm the receptionist. What language area will you be in?"

"This is Eva, and I'm Alberta. I'm in the Greek section," Alberta replied

"German and Italian," Eva offered as she smiled at Debbie.

"Excellent. I need to learn how to ask our clients to sit down, so when you have a free moment and when I can get unchained from this desk, will you teach me a few phrases?"

Both women smiled and agreed as Debbie led them down a corridor which housed several offices, tapped lightly at the end office, and entered. "Be seeing you around, ladies," she said, excusing herself.

Alberta and Eva looked at each other and then stared at a vacant desk. Before they could decide what to do next, a middle aged woman came into the office and sat down. They introduced themselves and got a wide smile in return.

"If everyone appears to be happy to see you two, it's because we are. My name is Edith Andrews; I'm Mr Eden's secretary. We are severely short staffed, and as you can see outside, our clients are getting rather restless."

"It's always nice to be needed," Alberta quipped, and was rewarded by a short chuckle from Edith.

"We need you desperately," Edith responded as she knocked on the inside door which led to Adam Eden's office. "Adam, Alberta Haralambos and Eva Haralambos are here." She showed them inside the office and gave them another smile.

A middle-aged man in his fifties sporting short salt and pepper hair, with more salt than pepper, came around his desk and extended his hand. "Welcome, ladies. My name is Adam Eden. Welcome to the translating department. Please, have a seat."

He waited until Alberta and Eva sat down, then circled

around his desk and took his own seat. "So. I gather you came through our waiting area? It's a mini jungle out there. Now, Alberta, you will be in the Greek section; we have plenty of work there today. And Eva..." He stopped and began to laugh. "I'm sorry, Eva. All we need now is someone called snake to join our little group, and it would be complete."

Eva gave Adam a grin. She liked the man. He was easy going and didn't have the typical airs and artifices that middle managers usually acquired.

"I know that's a bad joke, but once you've heard all the bad jokes, you tend to create new ones." He chuckled and Alberta and Eva joined in. "Now, getting back to where you will be going. Our German area needs about ten more interpreters than what we have. I understand you grew up in Germany?"

"Yes. I grew up around Hamburg and then Berlin," Eva explained.

"Ah, Berlin, beautiful town. I was there before the war. I guess it's in ruins now. What a shame," Adam sighed. He loved Germany and had spent time picking grapes and working around the farms. "Okay, now where were we before I took a mental holiday?" He chuckled. "Ah yes, most of the clients are Jewish, you don't have a problem with that?"

Eva was taken aback, but bit back her retort. "No, I don't have a problem with Jewish people."

"That's good. Two of our previous translators were quite, how shall we say...racist. I won't tolerate racism here. We are here to help people, and since the majority of our clients are refugees, I think we need to show a little patience and a great deal of tolerance."

He looked at Eva and Alberta and gave them a sheepish grin. "I'm sorry. I do tend to get carried away. Your workload is going to be rather heavy over the next few days, not because we want to see how good you are," he gave them a grin, "but we had the *Patris* docked yesterday. We have to process everyone so they can start their lives, but hopefully we will get some slow days. Have I scared you enough?"

They both shook their heads. "Very good," he said to them and looked down at his files. "Your immediate supervisor is Richard, but he is away today. You'll get to meet him tomorrow. He's in charge of the section where both of you will be working. Edith will show you the staff cafeteria, which has some very interesting meals, and give you the slow tour of the place. I guess after that you may want to familiarize yourselves with the various government departments that handle refugee matters. As much as I would love to get you two working, I think you need some time to get to know how we do things before I throw you into the deep end."

He escorted the women to the outer office, and Edith led them outside once again.

It was a whirlwind of a morning as Edith patiently explained how things worked and where they should go. Each translator had their own little office where they could meet the clients and assess their various problems and needs.

Some time later, Eva sat in her office and looked at the volumes of information in front of her and smiled. This was a lot more interesting than packing biscuit boxes every day. It was going to be a challenge, but she did enjoy challenges. She couldn't wait to tell Zoe when she got home.

Chapter 2

Sydney University was a large institution. Zoe had received quite a number of brochures and information leaflets about various campuses in the Sydney area, and she and Eva had looked at each of them and what they offered. Zoe was quite taken with the biggest university, and they settled on that one after they had taken a short bus trip to see it.

She looked around as the students sat on the grass, talking and getting to know each other. Elena was beside her and tugged her arm.

"Does this intimidate you a bit?" Elena asked.

"Yeah," Zoe mumbled as they walked into the student registration office.

A severe looking older woman sat at the desk looking very unhappy. Zoe looked at Elena and shrugged. "I'm here to register," Zoe said quietly.

"You don't say," the woman replied, giving her a sour look. "What's your name?"

"Um...Zoe Lambros."

"You're Greek?" the woman asked as if it were a disease.

"Yes," Zoe replied. She had been intimidated by the woman at first, but now she was getting annoyed at the woman's tone. "Do you have a problem with me being Greek?"

Elena rolled her eyes and tugged on Zoe's jacket. "Not now, Zo," she whispered.

"Got too many Greeks here," the woman muttered and

opened the registration book. "Says here you're doing an art degree?"

"Yes, ma'am," Zoe said respectfully giving Elena a grin.

"All right. Here is the schedule and what you need to know." She handed Zoe a bundle of papers and a book. "If you have any problems, you will find a list of people in there that you can ask for help."

"Thanks," Zoe said as Elena gave her name and received the same information. They walked back out into the sunlight.

"Racist cow," Zoe mumbled.

"Zoe, you're not going to make life easier for yourself if you get annoyed at everyone that is racist."

"No, I guess not."

They walked several minutes before deciding to claim a patch of grass that wasn't already occupied. Zoe put her notebook and the various leaflets down next to her. She closed her eyes and turned her face to the sun.

"Oh, this is nice. So, El, what's with you and Friedrich?"

Elena fidgeted with her papers. "I like him a lot, Zoe. He's funny and smart."

"Friedrich is funny?" Zoe joked and received a playful slap on the arm.

"He is. He is quite funny and makes me feel comfortable. He is so sweet and gentle. He lost his family in Germany, too, and we've been talking a lot."

"So has he kissed you yet?" Zoe asked and closed her eyes again. She didn't want to make her friend uncomfortable by staring at her.

"Yes," Elena admitted with a sweet, shy smile.

Zoe grinned at her. "About time, I'd say. Then what happened?"

"You are nosy, aren't you?"

"Hey, you asked me about Eva."

"Yeah, and I got way too much information when you were drunk!" Elena laughed as she remembered Zoe's amorous behavior when they had gone to a party and her friend had a little too much to drink. She recalled an exasperated Eva trying valiantly to control Zoe's hands, and she couldn't get the image out of her head of Zoe straddling a prone Eva on the floor. "You love her a lot, don't you?"

"Yes." Zoe said with conviction.

"I think I could love Friedrich that way, but I may have a

problem." She looked at her friend shyly and then revealed, "I'm not a virgin."

Zoe's eyes went round at the revelation. She had never seen Elena go out on any dates and just assumed she wasn't ready. They hadn't really discussed it.

"Um, would you like to walk with me? I would feel more comfortable in talking about it in a less public place."

"Sure," Zoe replied, picked up her books and followed Elena down the jacaranda lined path, the purple blossoms giving the walkway a serene look. They walked quietly for a few moments.

"You know I was at Bergen Belson during the war?" Zoe nodded. Elena had told them about the concentration camp when they had first met, but she hadn't mentioned it since. Zoe didn't want to ask her and unintentionally cause her friend any anguish.

"My mother was there, too, for a short time." Elena went quiet, and Zoe just walked next to her. She took her hand and gave it a tiny squeeze. Elena turned to her friend and smiled. "You know, Zoe, you are my best friend; and I've wanted to tell you this for a long time, but I didn't have the courage."

"You know you can tell me anything, El."

"I know, but can I ask a favour?" Zoe nodded. "Can you please not tell Eva. I know you two discuss everything together but, well...I would feel more comfortable if you didn't tell her."

"Okay."

"It's not that I don't like Eva...I do...but..."

"Elena, I give you my word I won't tell Eva."

"Okay."

They walked a little further in silence. Elena's head was bowed as if she was trying to pluck up the courage to continue her story. They stopped near a bench and sat down, the trees giving them some privacy.

"When I was fifteen...um..." Elena stopped. She bit her lip and waited until she was ready to go on. Zoe took her hand and held it. "On my fifteenth birthday, one of the guards came into the barracks and took me outside. He said the commandant wanted to see me, since it was my birthday. He took me to his office, and then he left."

Zoe waited patiently for her friend to continue. She had an idea of where this was going, and it horrified her.

Elena looked up at her friend, then back down at her hands. "He...um...he raped me," she said quietly. Zoe didn't say a word as she wrapped her arms around her friend and hugged her. "He told me that was my birthday present," Elena added. Silent tears ran down her face as the memories came flooding back. Zoe held her as her own tears silently tracked down her cheeks.

"I'm so sorry, El," Zoe whispered. They embraced for a few minutes. Zoe tenderly wiped the tears from Elena's face.

"You're my best friend, Zoe, and I wanted to tell you but..."

"You can tell me anything, El. You know that. I will never betray your trust."

"Do you think Friedrich will still want me?"

"He would be a total jerk if he didn't. You are a gentle and loving woman, Elena. It wasn't your fault that you were raped. You are not to blame," Zoe said gently and kissed her friend on the cheek. "Are you going to tell him?"

"Well, he's going to know when we...you know...I have to tell him."

"Do you think you are ready to have sex with him?"

"I know I've fallen in love with him. And I want to."

"Let your heart tell you what to do, El. When I first met Eva, my head was telling me to kill her while my heart was telling me to love her and care for her. I listened to my heart, and I don't think I've regretted it for a single moment since."

"You wanted to kill her?"

"Yeah," Zoe chuckled. "Long story. Go with your heart."

They sat in silence as Zoe held Elena. Elena was relieved in some ways that she had talked to her friend about it. Zoe was a soft hearted person that Elena loved a great deal, and she trusted her.

"You are my best friend, and if he ever hurts you, I will get Eva to thump him," Zoe said, eliciting a chuckle from her friend.

❖❖❖❖❖❖❖

Eva opened the door to the flat and put her briefcase down. She smiled when she saw Zoe asleep on the sofa, several books scattered around her and on the floor. She knelt beside the sofa and brushed away Zoe's bangs.

"Zoe," she whispered, kissing her softly.

"Oh, nice," Zoe mumbled. She opened sleepy green eyes and smiled. "Hi there."

"Hi. University that tiring?" Eva teased as Zoe made room for her on the sofa. Zoe laid her head on Eva's lap and looked up.

"Ah, no, I had a headache, so I thought I would grab a few minutes snooze time."

"All gone?" Eva indicated her headache, and Zoe nodded.

"So tell me, what was your first day like?" Zoe asked, gazing up at the strong profile.

"We can compare first days if you like. Want to go to dinner and a movie, Miss Zoe?"

Zoe grinned. "Wow, you mean, go on a date?"

"Yep."

"With who?" Zoe teased.

"Only me."

"Hmm..." Zoe considered. "Well if it's the best that I can do," Zoe teased back and tickled her partner. "So what's at the cinema anyway?"

"*Casablanca*, with Humphrey Bogart and Ingrid Bergman."

"Sounds great. Why don't you go and get changed, and I'll tidy up in here."

"It's a date," Eva replied and gave Zoe a quick kiss before walking into the bedroom to change.

❖❖❖❖❖❖❖

The full moon lit up the walkway as two figures moved quietly up the path. The smaller of the two bumped into the taller figure causing them to giggle as they entered the building foyer. Elise Jenkins was taking out her cat when she spotted the pair walking down the corridor

"Hello, girls, did you have a nice evening?" Mrs Jenkins asked as the two women walked towards her. Mrs Jenkins was the middle-aged woman who owned the block of flats with her husband, Albert. The previous night had given her a new insight into her tenants at number 12, one she'd never expected.

Elise had a bundle of washing in the basket she held as she made her way to the laundry room. She heard voices and looked at her watch. It was very late at night, and she wasn't expecting anyone to be down there. She could see the occupants from the stairwell, and she grinned. Eva and Zoe were sorting out laundry and joking with each other. Elise liked the two women immensely. She was totally surprised when the younger of the two leaned up and gave Eva a kiss. Elise's eyebrows went into her hairline. She continued to watch as Eva and Zoe were playful with each other, having a duel with a wet towel–which made Elise smile. Zoe was decisively losing that battle. They finally settled down, and Eva said something to her younger friend that Elise couldn't hear. Zoe gave her a quick kiss and then left the laundry, not seeing Mrs Jenkins in the shadows.

Elise wasn't sure whether to announce herself or what to do. She had caught the couple–yes that's what they were, a couple–in a very private moment, and she didn't want to intrude by putting her nose in it. She sighed. She was going to have to go into that laundry.

"Good evening, Eva." Elise greeted Eva and put the basket down. Eva turned and gave her a smile. The older woman began to sort her laundry, and then she stopped. "Can I ask you a personal question?"

Eva leaned against the tub and nodded.

"How do I put this...Zoe isn't your sister, is she?" Elise asked, watching Eva's face.

A smile crept over the younger woman's face. "No."

"I didn't think so. I never met sisters as close as you two are," Elise said, and then chuckled at the expression on Eva's face. "Don't worry, child, I'm just surprised—although I shouldn't be. I've never seen you have any men friends come in, apart from Earl; but I've known Earl since he was in diapers. He's a good boy, but he isn't interested in girls."

"You know about Earl?"

Elise chuckled. "Of course. His mother and I are good friends!"

Eva sat down on the bench and looked sheepishly up at Elise who was now chuckling.

"Um..."

"Don't worry, I won't reveal your secret to Mr Jenkins, or anyone else."

"Thank you."

"Now that I think about it, I should find it extremely funny that Zoe kept coming up with reasons for you not to date!" Elise said with a chuckle. Zoe had come up with amazingly inventive reasons for Eva not to date her nephews.

"Yeah, Zoe can be quite creative," Eva agreed with a laugh.

She had spent the time talking to the young woman and enjoyed her sense of humour. She liked both of them a great deal, and they were quiet tenants except for that one evening when the whole building was buzzing with the news of their attempted murder.

"It was wonderful, Mrs Jenkins," Eva replied in answer to her query about their evening.

"Good, good. You young people need to get out and enjoy life. Good night, girls," she said and went into her flat.

Zoe shook her head and walked with Eva up to their flat, waiting patiently for her partner to open the door. Eva was about to escort her wife into the flat when she saw Elena walking up the stairs with a young man. She motioned to Zoe to look behind her. "So where have you been, Miss Elena?"

Elena and Friedrich reached Elena's flat, hand in hand, and they stopped. Elena gave Eva a huge grin. "We went and saw *Casablanca*," she said as she threaded her arm through Friedrich's, who gave her a shy smile in return.

"That's where we were!" Zoe remarked, and the two friends shared a laugh. "Where were you? We didn't see you."

"Um...we were at the back," Elena said quietly.

"Did you see any of the movie?" Eva asked and got her answer when Elena went a bright shade of pink.

"So you missed the bit where Rick kissed Ilsa on the tarmac, and then they flew away like superman, high into the sky," Zoe exclaimed, teasing her friend.

Elena stuck her tongue out at her friend, which only made Zoe laugh harder.

"How's the head, Friedrich?" Eva asked the young man. Friedrich had come to their aid when he and his partner realised that Eva's stepfather and his friend were holding Eva, Zoe and their friend Earl at gunpoint. In a case of misplaced defense, he got whacked in the head with a cricket bat which had been Earl's hastily procured weapon.

"Getting back some of the lost neurons," Friedrich replied and joined in the chuckles. He spent most of his free time with Elena, and he had come to know Eva and Zoe pretty well and enjoyed their company.

"I hear kissing helps to bring them back," Zoe teased, which got her a slap on the rear from Eva.

"Well, I guess we will leave you two lovebirds alone; it's been a long night," Eva said as they waved and entered their flat.

As Eva closed the door, Zoe wrapped herself around the taller woman and looked up into the blue eyes that reminded her of the Aegean Sea.

"Want to increase my brain power?" Zoe asked, waggling her eyebrows. She stood on the tips of her toes and kissed Eva.

"You should be a genius by now," Eva said, then they both laughed. "Did you like the movie?" Eva asked as they walked into the living room and sat down on the sofa where she cuddled the young woman.

"Oh yeah, it was so romantic!"

Eva looked at Zoe with a quizzical look. "Did we see the same movie?"

Zoe swatted her on the arm, which got her a hug.

"Sing it to me again?" Zoe pleaded. Eva had sung her the song *As Time Goes By* as they walked home. The warmth of the evening, with the sounds of the cicadas in the trees, added to the wonderful night they were both having. It was a celebration of Eva's new job and Zoe starting her Arts degree at the university the following day.

"Why, I can't remember it, Miss Zoe. I'm a little rusty on it," Eva replied taking a line from the film and grinning.

"I'll hum it for you," Zoe replied remembering the lines uttered by Ingrid Bergman in the film, and she began humming the song, a little off key, which earned her a lopsided grin from her partner. "Sing it, my sweet Eva."

Eva smiled and caressed Zoe's cheek.

"*You must remember this. A kiss is still a kiss,*" Eva sang and bent down and kissed Zoe tenderly. Her eyes shone brightly as she gazed lovingly at her wife.

"*A sigh is just a sigh.*"

Zoe sighed and fell back into her embrace.

Eva hummed the next verse, then sang "*They still say, 'I love you.' On that you can rely. No matter what the future brings; As time goes by.*"

Eva finished and looked into Zoe's emerald colored eyes and smiled.

"I love you," Zoe softly whispered as Eva picked her up and stood. She gave Zoe a crooked grin as she cradled her in her arms.

"Eva! Your back." Zoe protested.

"What back?" Eva replied with a twinkle in her eye as Zoe snuggled against her. "I bet Rick wanted to do this to Ilsa," Eva whispered in Zoe's ear as she walked to the bedroom and closed the door with her foot.

Chapter 3

"This is nice," Zoe mumbled, her head lying on Eva's chest. They had both awakened before dawn and stayed in bed cuddling together, neither of them wanting to get up. The window was open, and a light breeze ruffled the curtains as the sounds of a typical early morning in the city drifted in. The milk truck could be heard as it made its usual stops along the street, softly squeaking to a halt and idling nearby. A moment later the tinkling and clanking of glass bottles began as the milkman started his deliveries for that morning among the flats. Very soon, the bakery would start its deliveries of fresh breads and pastries, as the early morning rituals blended into the new day. The street lights were still on in the predawn darkness, flickering dimly through the moving curtains into the dark bedroom.

"Did you like the campus?" Eva asked her partner, playing with Zoe's dark locks.

"Apart from the racist administrator? Yeah. It's big, though. Elena and I got lost a couple of times." Zoe smiled and put her arm around her partner. Eva chuckled as she got a mental picture of Zoe trying to find her way around the huge campus and getting lost. She had teased her wife many times about her inability to follow a map.

"Stop that," Zoe mildly rebuked her laughing partner and slapped her gently on the belly, which only caused Eva to laugh more. "It really wasn't my fault this time. Elena took a left turn when she should have taken a right."

"Zoe, you could lose your way in Larissa," Eva mumbled. Zoe gave her a mischievous grin and proceeded to tickle the older woman. Eva squealed and fought off Zoe's hands "Okay, okay, stop. I'll stop teasing you," she promised, backing down. Zoe gave her a triumphant grin and put her head back down on Eva's chest.

"Don't mess with Zoe Lambros, or else."

"I wouldn't dream of it," Eva replied, for which she got another playful slap on the belly.

"How did you go yesterday?" Zoe looked up and asked.

"Ally and I walked into one of the busiest places I've ever been in. People everywhere. It was nice, though. You remember the story of the Tower of Babel?"

"Oh yeah, where everyone used to speak the same language, and God didn't like that Nimrod guy and made people speak different languages."

"Yeah, well this place sounds like it. They had the *Patris* dock yesterday, and it was bedlam. It was busy, busier than I expected. There's a ton of information to remember, but I think it's going to be really good. The people are nice, very friendly."

"I hope you don't have to deal with any 'Jacks,'" Zoe mumbled, referring to Eva's previous supervisor at the Westons factory. Jack had made Eva's life extremely difficult. He was a churlish racist and generally crude man who took delight in getting Eva to do the heavy lifting and causing her partner's recurring back problems to flare up. "You know, Jack would have made a great Nazi," Zoe mused as she traced the tiny scar on Eva's shoulder.

"I don't think there are any 'Jacks' there. But there is a Debbie. She's the receptionist and a really nice person. She does all the heavy lifting."

Zoe gave her a quizzical look. "Heavy lifting in an office?"

"Yeah, all those files she carries." Eva said as Zoe groaned at her bad joke.

"You know your jokes are getting worse than Earl's." Zoe complained, as she directed a mock scowl at her laughing partner. "I don't care if she has to lift things as long as you don't have to. I don't want you to hurt your back again."

Eva looked down at Zoe's dark head resting on her chest and grinned. "Nah I don't think so. I think the heaviest thing I'm going to be lifting in that office is my cup of tea," Eva said and chuckled.

"Do you know the only thing I will miss about you not working at Westons?"

"No, what?" Eva asked, and looked down at Zoe who was engrossed in blowing a piece of fluff across Eva's chest. "Zoe."

"Oh." Zoe looked up at her with a smile. "I'm going to miss not being able to escort you home."

Even though Zoe hated getting up in the morning, she would do so when Eva worked nightshift. She would get up early in the morning and take the bus and wait for Eva to finish her shift. They would take the bus home together and stop off at the bakery and pick up some raspberry tarts for breakfast. It was moments like these they both cherished.

"You can escort me home if you like. The university is only 10 minutes away. I can always wait to carry your books back."

"I would like that. You know, if I had a car I could come and pick you up," Zoe said, wondering if Earl would give her lessons. "That's, if I had a car...and if I had a license to drive this imaginary car..."

"I don't see why you can't. I checked with the Roads Authority, and they told me you had to be 18 and six months in order to be eligible. Well, if I've done my math correctly, that would mean you can sit for a learner's permit tomorrow."

Zoe looked up and beamed. "You mean, I can get a car? Wow! What colour would you like?"

"The colour of your eyes," Eva whispered and got a kiss. "Do you think the world is ready for that?" she teased.

"Ah, Miss Eva, the world will never be ready for me," Zoe replied and nuzzled Eva's neck. "Hmm. Smells like cookies here, need to investigate."

Eva wrapped her wife in her arms, and they both started laughing.

❖ ❖ ❖ ❖ ❖ ❖ ❖

Zoe sat in the kitchen eating breakfast and reading *The Woman's Weekly*, a magazine she found one day while she was waiting for Eva's shift to finish. She had bought it and was soon quite addicted to the serial that appeared every week.

"Oh no!" Zoe's anguished cry rang out, causing Eva to drop her briefcase and rush into the kitchen, fearing her partner may have hurt herself. She found Zoe's nose in the magazine.

"What's the matter?"

"Derek is leaving her!"

Eva rolled her eyes. She sat on the stool near Zoe and looked at the magazine. "Who's Derek?"

Zoe looked up and frowned. "Derek is Maggie's boyfriend, and now he's gone back to Jane, but he can't decide if he wants Maggie or if he wants Jane."

"So, hasn't he left already?" Eva asked as she made herself a cup of tea. They'd had this ongoing discussion about the serial ever since Zoe told her about it. Their animated discussions caused a smile or two on the bus from the conductor who joined in the conversation when he remarked his wife read the serial every week as well.

"He did, but he came back and then he went again."

"And now he's gone for good?"

"Yeah," Zoe said and went back to reading. "Sort of. He can't decide who he wants."

Eva was about to suggest that Jane should leave Derek alone when she went into the lounge room to answer the knocking at the door. She opened it to reveal a grinning Earl with a box under his arm.

"G'day, my favourite interpreter." he greeted Eva, and gave her a kiss.

"You're in a cheery mood." Eva remarked as she directed him into the kitchen.

"Hey, Wiggy." Zoe greeted Earl with a wave as she went back to her serial.

"Don't tell me she's still glued to that story."

"Yeah. Derek left Maggie to be with Jane, but Derek loves both Maggie and Jane."

"I reckon Jane should dump that low life. Oh hell, now you're getting me involved." Earl protested as Eva gave him a grin.

"To what do we owe the pleasure of your company this morning? Not that I'm not happy to see you," Eva said as she sipped her tea.

"You are in the presence of the newest supervisor of Westons." Earl proudly proclaimed, which got him a whoop from Zoe and a hug from Eva. "I found out last night. I think Jack is going to have kittens when he finds out. I bring you gifts."

He opened the box to reveal seven large mangoes. He knew Eva loved them, and he went by the fruit market and picked some up in celebration. Eva had helped him when he needed her most, and their friendship had blossomed.

"Mangoes!" Eva said as she picked one up and sniffed at it.

Zoe looked at her partner's enraptured face and grinned. "She is so easy. Give her a little fruit, and she's yours for life," Zoe teased.

Eva stuck her tongue out and went to the sink to peel the fruit. "Congratulations, Earl. You've worked hard. Which section are you going to be in?"

"Cookies."

"Ah, my favourite." Zoe looked up and waggled her eyebrows at Eva which got a puzzled look from Earl.

"Ah, let's not forget my partner in crime. If it wasn't for your full blooded kis...er..." Earl stopped as soon as he saw Eva's eyes roll. Zoe looked up with a frown.

"Eva kissed you?"

"Ah...yeah..." Earl stammered.

"She has good taste in men," Zoe said and went back to reading the magazine. Eva put her arms around her partner and whispered in her ear, "You're wicked."

Zoe turned and gave her partner a smirk and a quick kiss. She looked up at Earl and chuckled at his puzzled look. "Eva told me about it."

"Damn it, woman, you gave me a heart attack. You told me I shouldn't mention it to Zoe."

"I don't have any secrets from Zoe, Earl," Eva replied and backhanded him in the stomach. "I think I forgot to mention that I told her. Sorry."

"You two could drive a man to drink," he muttered and sat down, giving Zoe a playful cuff across the head.

"Hey, speaking of driving, I'm going to get a car," Zoe said brightly. A look of mock fear crossed Earl's face.

"Oh no! I'll inform the traffic authority to remove all the light poles–"

"Cut that out! Can you teach me?"

"Me? Teach you how to drive?"

"Yeah."

Earl met Eva's eyes over Zoe's head, and he grinned. "Sure, Stretch, I'll teach you, but you promise not to hit any old ladies or anything like that?"

"Promise. Thanks, Wiggy!" Zoe jumped up and put her arms around his neck and gave him a kiss on the cheek.

"Hey, now that I'm here, I'll give you a ride in to work,

check out your new job...if you want me to?" Earl suggested and looked expectantly at Eva.

"I would love to show you around," Eva said, handing him cup of tea.

"Can you drop me off at the uni?" Zoe asked as she heard the knock on the door.

"Sure," Earl agreed as Zoe went to the door and Elena came in.

They rounded up Alberta and Elena and headed out. They left Elena and Zoe at the university gates and traveled to the Immigration Department. Earl filled them in on the latest news from the factory, making Eva laugh when he did an excellent mimic of Jack falling over a pallet of cookies.

❖❖❖❖❖❖❖

"You should drop by more often," Daisy, the elevator operator, said as she stopped the elevator on Eva's floor.

"Oh, I'll be around, since my girl is working here," Earl said, putting his arm around Eva's waist.

Earl missed the crestfallen look Daisy had on her face as the doors shut. Eva poked Earl in the side as they got off the elevator, shook her head and took his hand and led him out to the busy waiting area.

"Wow," Earl exclaimed as he looked around him. All the chairs were taken, and more people were sitting on the floor or standing. Little children were running around and playing. "Is it this busy all the time?"

"Nah, they tell me this is the quiet period," Eva replied, then laughed at Earl's face. "Yeah, it's the busy season. The *Patris* came in a few days ago, and this is the latest batch of immigrants."

Eva led him to Debbie's desk as the receptionist's head popped up from behind a filing cabinet.

"Debbie, this is my good friend, Earl Wiggins. Earl, this is Debbie, our overworked receptionist."

Debbie gave Earl a huge grin. "Hi there, Earl."

"Hi, you're not working my girl too hard are you?" Earl smiled as he continued to wrap his arm around Eva's waist.

Debbie blinked a few times and realised that Earl must be Eva's boyfriend. She mentally chastised herself for attempting to flirt with him. *He is cute,* she thought to herself.

"Oh no, she had an easy day yesterday. Today the fun begins," Debbie teased.

"Can't wait," Eva replied. "I'll just show Earl around, and then I'll come and pick up the files."

They walked down the corridor together, Earl placing his arm around Eva's shoulders as Debbie watched them walk into Eva's office. Debbie sighed and went back to her work.

"Hey, nice office." Earl said and plonked himself down on the client chair. "It needs some posters and stuff. I'll get you a couple. And you need a photo for your desk...Dave took this great shot of all of us at your birthday party. I'll bring it to you."

Eva stood with her hands folded across her chest and grinned at him.

"What?"

"You know Debbie is going to spread the word that you're my boyfriend."

"Of course," Earl said smugly.

"You are incredible." Eva leaned down and kissed him.

"I am incredible, aren't I?" Earl replied and puffed out his chest. "So many kisses from you and Zoe today, I think I could get used to this."

"Hey, thanks for volunteering to teach Zoe to drive," Eva told him as she took off her sweater and sat in her chair.

"As long as she doesn't kill me or run over any animals, it's going to be great."

They both chuckled. Earl had missed Eva being there at work with him, and he took the opportunity to fill her in on some of the factory floor politics.

❖ ❖ ❖ ❖ ❖ ❖ ❖

Eva kissed Earl goodbye at the elevator and watched as he gave her a wink before the doors closed. She turned to find a grinning Debbie with a stack of files in her arms.

"The fun begins." Debbie teased as Eva walked down the corridor and into her office.

She spent the morning interviewing clients, all with their various concerns. She was finding she was enjoying the job even more than she thought she would. After the fifth client had gone, there was a quiet knock on the door and Debbie stuck her head in.

"Oh, so there you are. We thought maybe we lost you

between Mrs Strauss and Mr Hermann," Debbie said. "Morning tea is at 10.00 and we didn't see you come out, so I thought I would come in and rescue you." Debbie entered the office with a cup of tea and placed it in front of Eva.

"Oh no, I'm still here," Eva replied. Giving Debbie a sidelong glance, she picked up the tea cup and took a sip. "Thank you, that's nice. Did you want to ask me something?"

"Well...yes and no. I'm on my tea break, so I thought I would come in and see how you were getting along...you know."

"I see," Eva replied and continued working, marking the file with her notes about the client and the actions she had taken to get them accommodation.

"I think Mr Hermann was quite taken with you, he wanted to know if you are married and could he send flowers."

Eva chuckled. Mr Hermann was her fifth client of the day. He was a Jewish survivor of the concentration camps, and he was charming and gracious. She'd enjoyed talking to him. They had spent a bit of time talking about Berlin University where he had lectured in history before Hitler forbade Jews from teaching.

Debbie sat there looking at Eva with an expectant look on her face.

"So, I guess you drew the short straw?" Eva asked, knowing the office wanted to know all about the new girl. She had been expecting it. When she started at Westons, one of the girls cornered her and asked her personal questions. She wasn't forthcoming with her answers and soon developed a reputation as aloof and cold. It wasn't until the incident in the cool room when she and Earl became friends that she had become aware of the interrogation all new staff were subjected to.

"Yeah, and since I'm a natural born busybody, it was a good choice. Mr Hermann did want to send you flowers. He told me you should expect some later today."

Eva laughed. She liked Debbie and her easygoing manner. "What would you like to know about me?"

"Oh good, you're going to play the game. I've had to play question and answer games with all the new people. You're easy."

"Didn't say I'll answer them," Eva responded and laughed at Debbie's crestfallen look.

Debbie groaned. "Why can't things be so much easier? Oh, all right. Let's start with the easy bits. What's your full name?"

"This sounds like an interrogation." Eva said with a mock

frown.

She got a snort in reply. "Ve have vays of making you talk," Debbie said in a very bad German accent, which only made Eva laugh even more. She put down her pen and folded her hands on the desk.

"So much for my interrogation skills. So are you going to answer it?"

"What was the question?"

Debbie rolled her eyes. "What are your first and middle names?"

"Oh, that's the question," Eva responded and sat back with a smug look on her face. "Eva."

"That's it? No middle name?"

"Nope. Just Eva. My mother was poor, and she couldn't afford to give me a middle name." Eva repeated a joke she'd overheard Earl telling at the factory.

Debbie groaned. "Oh that was bad. Very bad. Moving right along, Eva, just Eva. Okay, how old are you, date of birth and where were you born?"

"I'm 26. I was born on the 10th of January in Vienna, Austria."

"Vienna, what a beautiful city! Oh, your birthday was only a couple of weeks ago. Happy birthday!"

"Thank you."

"So tell me, Miss Haralambos—by the way, that is a very difficult name to get my tongue around. That doesn't sound German...that's Greek, isn't it?"

Eva nodded.

"And are you going to tell me how you got the name?"

"My father gave it to me," Eva said drolly and watched as Debbie rolled her eyes.

"How tall are you?" Debbie asked, leaving the previous question alone since Eva appeared not to want to go explaining about her surname. "Please tell me you're over 6' because I've got 2 pounds riding on this."

"You bet 2 pounds on how tall I am?"

Debbie laughed. "Eva, most Aussies will bet on two flies on a wall as to which fly would get up the wall quicker. So naturally we took an office betting pool to find out how tall you are. Deirdre thinks you are 5'10", Alexander thinks you're 5'11", Edith thinks you're 5'9". We didn't have time to poll everyone else."

Eva laughed at their antics. "And you?"

"I think you're 6' because my brother is about your height."

"Close. I'm 6'2"."

"Wow. That's tall. Yes! I win that round." Debbie exclaimed. "Moving right along here, so are you and Earl engaged?"

Eva grinned. "He hasn't proposed yet."

"Well, if I know my men, I would say the guy is head over heels in love with you."

Eva laughed. "You think so?"

"Oh yeah. He had the 'she's my woman' look about him."

"Earl is a sweetheart."

Debbie sighed and then gave Eva a huge grin. "Does he have a brother?"

"A sister," Eva replied, and watched Debbie as she took a sip from her tea.

"That's too bad. So you don't live with Earl?"

Eva wasn't sure how to answer that question or whether to leave it. She liked Debbie, and she was sure Zoe was going to pop her head in later in the week. They always introduced each other as flatmates, which satiated most people's inquisitive natures.

"No, I live with Zoe. She's my flatmate. You'll probably see her up here at some point. She's about 5'5" with short brown hair and green eyes."

"I look forward to meeting her." Debbie stood and went to the door. "Thanks, Eva, you're a good sport. I think that's enough interrogating for today."

Eva watched the door close and shook her head slowly before taking the next file off the pile.

Chapter 4

The jacaranda trees provided a little shade in the hot sweltering weather as Elena sat cross-legged on the ground munching away at her lunch. She was watching Zoe try to figure out where her next class was going to be. They had spent the morning finding the library, which Zoe found absolutely fascinating, and then going through the various books. Zoe was sprawled on the grass with a map of the university in front of her.

"Eva reckons I can't read a map."

"You can't." Elena's muffled reply came as she took another bite from her lunch.

"Elena, you are not a comedienne."

"I can read maps, though," her friend replied with a smug grin.

"Be quiet and eat your lunch," Zoe muttered as she went back to the map. "Hey, you want to go to the beach later?"

Elena sat quietly eating her lunch and ignoring Zoe until she looked up and saw Zoe's annoyed look. "You told me to eat my lunch."

"Since when do you do what I ask? Do you want to go to the beach afterwards?"

"Sure. Can I bring Friedrich?"

"I don't see why not. Earl said he had the whole week off, so we can go in his car. You bring Friedrich, Eva will be home by 5:30, and we can grab Father H and Ally."

"Um...excuse me, are you Zoe Lambros?"

Zoe turned and found herself staring at a pair of legs. She looked up and squinted. The sun was behind the woman, and she couldn't see her face. "Yep, that's me."

"Oh, finally I found you! My name is Kiriakoula Evagenlopoulos, and I belong to the Hellas Club." After introducing herself, Kiriakoula sat down next to Zoe.

"I would never have guessed that," Zoe said and got a nudge from Elena. "What's the Hellas Club?"

"Yeah I know my name does tend to give it away, doesn't it? Well, it's a club where all Greek students get together and we help each other. Would you like to join us?"

"Depends on what I have to do to get in," Zoe replied and looked at the girl as she leaned out of the shadow. She did indeed have black eyes and the blackest hair Zoe had ever seen. Her skin was pale, which made her look like something from a scary film. Zoe decided she wasn't going to let that slip out. "This is Elena," she said, introducing her friend.

"Are you Greek?" Kiriakoula asked Elena, who shook her head.

"I'm German. Elena Mannheim, pleased to meet you." Elena's outstretched hand was ignored as Kiriakoula gave her an odd look.

"Oh," the young woman said and looked at Elena before turning her attention back to Zoe. "We only allow Greeks into our club."

"Elena is an honorary Greek," Zoe replied, giving her friend a grin.

"We don't fraternize with the enemy, or Jews," Kiriakoula replied. Her smile turned into a scowl.

Zoe's smile vanished as she regarded the young woman in front of her. "I don't consider Elena the enemy. She's my best friend."

"Well, she's German."

"Yes, that's quite obvious. And you think all Germans are the enemy?"

"*Ame, to pistevo me oly ti karthia mou,*" Kiriakoula responded in Greek and got up. "*An thelis na eise me tous germanous tote then ise Elinitha.*"

"*Na pas sto thialo, strigla!*" Zoe retorted.

Kiriakoula gave her a disgusted look and walked off, leaving a furious Zoe in her wake. It was only Elena's crash tackle that kept her on the ground and prevented Kiriakoula from getting flattened.

"No! Stay put," Elena urged her friend as various students looked at them.

"I'm going to squash her big ugly head into a pretzel. Racist bitch," Zoe yelled out, unable to move since Elena had decided she was going to sit on her until Zoe's anger dissipated.

"What did she say to get you all ready to squash her into a pretzel?"

"Get off me, El," Zoe muttered.

"No. Not until you cool off."

"I've cooled off."

"Yeah, I believe that," Elena replied. She cupped Zoe's face with her hands. "Zoe, you can't fight racism by squashing faces into pretzels. Although it might be fun trying, it doesn't solve the problem."

"It's going to make me feel good," Zoe insisted.

"Quite true, but you could get expelled, and that wouldn't look good for your first day. Anyway she probably has had bad experiences with Germans. If I let you up, do you promise to behave?"

"No," Zoe replied and pouted.

"Come on, Zoe, please?"

Zoe continued to pout, and then rolled her eyes when she saw Elena's pleading look. "Okay."

"Promise?"

"Yes, now get off me."

Elena got off Zoe slowly and watched as her friend sat back up. She still scowled and looked at the direction where Kiriakoula had gone.

"What did she say?" Elena asked and got total silence from her friend. "Zoe?"

"She said that she believed in her heart that Germans were the enemy, and that if I didn't believe that then I wouldn't be a true Greek," Zoe muttered.

"You know that's not true, Zoe. Forget her. What did you tell her?"

"I told her to go to hell and called her a bitch."

"Did it make you feel better?"

"No. If I squished her face like a pretzel, it would have," Zoe mumbled insistently as she got up and helped Elena up to go to their next class.

❖❖❖❖❖❖❖

They wandered through several corridors before coming to the right class, with Elena feeling a little vindicated since she was the one that found the room.

"Don't say a word," Zoe grumbled as she they entered and sat down in the front. The class filled up quickly as the students took their seats.

Zoe watched a casually dressed young woman walk to the front of the class and lean on the table that held books and drawings. She tried to see what they were, but couldn't. She looked around the room, hoping she wasn't going to have the racist Greek in the same class, and was relieved when she didn't see her. The lecturer moved and held up her hands to quiet them down. She wasn't a tall woman; she had dark brown hair and blue eyes which Zoe found fascinating, since they were the same shade as Eva's.

"Welcome to my class. My name is Lucia de Nobrega; you can call me Lucia. I see we are going to have a big group this time around. If you joined this class to learn to create what is in your mind's eye, then you are in the right place. If you came to look at naked bodies, I believe the biology class is in the Carslaw Building." Lucia smiled as she saw the reaction from her students.

The students chuckled. Zoe and Elena looked at each other and grinned. They were going to have fun here.

"In a moment, we will go around the room and get each of you to introduce yourself and tell why you chose this class. Now before we do that little exercise, let me give you my philosophy about art and artists. Whether you draw or paint or write, an artist gives of him or herself fully. Giving of yourself is usually done most comfortably with loved ones, but here you will learn to express yourself through your art. How do you do this? You have to lose all kinds of prejudice. You cannot have a prejudice and be a great artist. You don't come here to learn how to be a bad artist; you want to reach inside yourself and become the best that you can be. Being prejudiced will blur your vision; it won't allow you to look beyond what you think you know and how you view it," Lucia said as she gazed at her students.

"Secondly I want you to lose your inhibitions. I'm not saying you have to run around naked across the campus—"

The room burst out laughing. Elena poked Zoe in the ribs.

Elena was quite sure Zoe would do it if she was dared to. Their attention was riveted back on their lecturer.

"That's a nice little visual, isn't it? Now I want you to be free about yourself and what you look like. Look at yourself in the mirror and create some funny faces, dance in your own home while singing—you can sing off key as long as the neighbors don't call the police." Lucia got another chuckle from her class and continued, "If you allow yourself to look silly and act silly, you will find that your inhibition will be lost. Everything you are feeling will be expressed in your art. You have to *give* a little part of yourself to your artwork. Okay that was a mouthful, wasn't it? Now, while I take a break, you can each tell me about yourself and why you are here."

Zoe listened carefully as her classmates introduced themselves. Elena had her turn, and then it came to Zoe. She got up and looked around the room.

"Boy, I'm glad this is not a class for public speaking," Zoe muttered and got a laugh from the class. "My name is Zoe Lambros. I've been in Australia eight months, and I'm living out my dream of learning how to draw and be an artist," she finished quietly, and sat down with a slight blush.

❖ ❖ ❖ ❖ ❖ ❖ ❖

"Eva, can you please take Mrs Marangos?" Debbie asked as she stuck her head in Eva's office. "Sorry about this. We try and get her seen quickly, and Alexander has a difficult couple."

"Sure, Debbie. Have you got her file?"

Debbie grimaced. "We sent it down to filing, and they've misplaced it."

Eva blinked. She was so used to Debbie being on top of everything, even in the two days she had been there, that she found this disconcerting, but she pushed it to the back of her mind and nodded. She followed Debbie to the front desk where an old woman stood, a cane in her hand and hunched over.

Eva introduced herself and escorted the older woman to her office. "How are you today, Mrs Marangos?"

"Ah, not so good, my child," the old woman responded, shaking her head. Eva smiled, despite what Mrs Marangos said. She reminded Eva of Despina in a small way. "My little red box is missing."

"Little red box?"

"Yes, my little red box. It was outside my house, and now it's gone; and I don't know where it's gone to." the old woman wailed.

Eva was at a loss concerning what this little red box meant. She went over to the woman and held her as she started to cry. "Don't worry, Mrs Marangos, we'll find your little red box," she said, holding the sobbing woman. "Can you tell me a little about it?"

"It's red," the old woman said through her sobs.

Eva was stumped. "Was it round or square?"

"It was red, and it was long."

"Red and long," Eva repeated, having no idea where this conversation was going to go.

"Yes."

"Was it in your garden?"

"No. It was outside my house."

"Outside your house, and it was red and long," Eva repeated again, trying to think of something that was red and long and outside. She had no clue.

"My little red box is missing, and it's so important I find it."

Eva sat there completely stumped. Mrs Marangos looked at her and began to wail again, seeing the lost look on the interpreter's face.

"I put my brother's letters there, and now they won't get to him." she wailed.

Eva needed to speak to Debbie, surely she would know about this since she had a file somewhere. Eva looked up as a soft knock on the door was followed by Debbie entering quietly and giving Eva the file.

Eva smiled and tried to look through the woman's file as discreetly as she could to find any reference to red boxes. She wasn't having any luck, and the woman was staring at her.

"You're not interested in helping me?"

Eva looked up from the file, looking like a child caught with her hand in the cookie jar. "I am, Mrs Marangos. I just need some more details." Eva closed the file and smiled at the woman before getting up, "Mrs Marangos, I'm going to go outside and get you something to drink, okay?"

"Yes, thank you, my child."

Eva closed the door and scratched her head. She was trying to think of what this little red box could be as she walked up to the reception area and only looked up when she got there. A sea of faces greeted her as half the interpreters were doubled up laughing.

"Oh gosh, Eva, you should have seen your face as you came out of your office!"

Eva looked around at the grinning faces and realised she had been the victim of a prank. "I was set up, wasn't I?" Eva asked quietly.

Debbie nodded and burst out laughing. Eva shook her head and joined in. She held up her hand to quiet her colleagues, remembering that Mrs Marangos was sitting in her office. "Uh, I have Mrs Marangos in my office, I need some water, and what is this little red box?"

The question got another round of chuckles from the assembled group before Debbie put a glass of water in her hand and explained, "It's the mail box. The post office does that sometimes. Usually they leave it outside her house, but they must have moved it again. Mrs Marangos is a little senile, so we try and help her when we can."

Eva chuckled. "Red, long box...I guess that's my initiation here, right?"

Debbie grinned and nodded.

"I get it now. So what do I tell her?"

"Tell her that the little red box will be put back in a week or so, but there is another red box just up the street and she can put her letters in there."

"Okaaay," Eva replied and walked away chuckling to herself.

❖ ❖ ❖ ❖ ❖ ❖ ❖

"Eva!" Mrs Jenkins waved at Eva and Ally as they were headed up the sidewalk towards the flat. She was coming down to them as quickly as she could, and Eva had to stop herself from laughing as Mrs Jenkins broke into a sprint.

"I wonder what she wants?" Ally whispered. "I hope it's not another date for you."

"She knows about me and Zoe."

Ally didn't have time to respond as Mrs Jenkins stopped in front of them, a little out of breath.

"Good afternoon, Mrs Jenkins."

"How are you, Elise?"

"I'm fine, thank you. Eva, you may have a problem."

"Oh?"

"Your pet is screaming its head off in your flat!" the older woman said as she took her handkerchief from her pocket and dabbed the sweat off her face. "It's so hot today."

"My pet? I don't have a pet."

"You don't?"

"No."

"Oh, I'm not sure what it is, but it's screeching, and it scared Mrs Deakin in number 7."

Eva looked at Ally and shrugged. She hoped Zoe hadn't brought home any pets. Her young partner was always trying to talk her into adopting a cat or a dog. She turned when she heard Earl's car stop, waved, and turned back to Mrs Jenkins.

"I'm sorry, Mrs Jenkins, but I'm not sure what it is. I'll go and have a look."

"Yes, please do that. Mrs Deakin's ticker isn't all that strong."

Eva had a bemused look on her face as she watched Mrs Jenkins walk away. She didn't know what was going on, but the day had been one for surprises and it seemed as if she was going to get another one.

"Hey, Earl," Eva greeted Earl as he walked with them to the flat. As soon as they entered the foyer, they heard screeching and what sounded like very bad singing, but Eva couldn't be sure.

They arrived at her door, and she unlocked it. The three of them watched in absolute fascination as Zoe, clad in shorts and t-shirt, waltzed around the lounge room singing—or what passed as singing—at the top of her voice with Elena, who was also clad in t-shirt and shorts.

"Is this some form of new therapy?" Earl yelled, trying to be heard over the din.

Eva went over to the record player, shut it off, and stood there looking at the pair.

"Hey, Eva!" Zoe bounded up and kissed her partner. "We were inhibiting."

"Uninhibiting," Elena corrected her.

"You were scaring Mrs Deakin." Eva replied as Ally and Earl came in.

"Mrs Deakin can't hear a single thing. We weren't that loud."

"Well, Mrs Jenkins heard you and so did we, from the

foyer."

"Oh," Zoe said as she sat down on the sofa.

"What was that about?" Ally asked Zoe.

"Our art teacher told us in order to be great artists, we have to lose our inhibitions and be silly. So, in order to do our homework, we have to sing and dance."

"And scare old ladies," Earl added and got a slap on the arm from Zoe. "Ow, stop that, Stretch, or I'll dunk you in the deep end."

They laughed as Earl and Zoe got into a tussle. Zoe was hauled up and carried into the bedroom, and the screams of "Save me, Eva" were drowned out by giggles and "Oh, uncle, uncle."

Eva laughed as she went inside the bedroom to rescue Zoe from Earl's teasing clutches. She was happy with how the day turned out, and her nerves about starting a new job had also settled upon meeting Debbie and the rest of the closely knit group.

Chapter 5

Eva spent the morning trying to help a Greek couple get settled in their new flat. She was rewarded a few hours later by the delivery of the gooiest Greek baklava anyone had ever tasted. Everyone was eating it as the doors opened and Mr Hermann came in with a bunch of flowers and a huge grin on his face.

"Ah, Fraulein," the old man greeted her. Eva's eyebrows went into her hairline as the old man went down on bended knee. "Oy, I'm not as young as I used to be," he grumbled and then looked up into Eva's sapphire coloured eyes. "Thank you, you have been most sweet," Mr Hermann told her as he smiled. "And if I was 20 years younger, I would ask you out," he teased before Eva helped him up.

The day seemed all the more special because of the appreciation expressed by her two clients, Eva mused to herself as she worked away at her desk. She looked up when there was a knock on the door, and Debbie stuck her head in.

"You're going to starve, and I'll have Earl berating me for not looking after you." the receptionist said with a smile. She came into the office and around Eva's desk. "Come on, shoo, go to lunch."

"Uh..."

"Don't 'uh' me. The clients will be here when you get back."

Debbie pulled Eva out of the chair and gently shoved her out the door, much to Eva's amusement.

"Okay, I'm going, I'm going."

Eva walked down the corridor and noticed Ally standing at the reception desk. "You sent her after me, didn't you?"

"Oh no, not me. She came to my office and bullied me out—"

"Will the two of you go to lunch, already." Debbie exclaimed giving them a mock glare. She grinned when they walked away.

❖❖❖❖❖❖❖

An hour later the two women came back to a very quiet waiting area. A few clients sat on the plastic chairs waiting for their appointments, but the usual din of the waiting area had been replaced with the whirring of the ceiling fan.

"Anything exciting happen while we've been gone?" Eva asked Debbie who, for once, was not attached to the other end of the phone or trying to do ten things at the same time.

"It's pretty quiet. Doesn't happen often, so savor the moment." Debbie smiled broadly. She looked down at her ever present appointment book. "Eva, you have a Mrs Wagner coming in soon, and after that..."

"After that?"

"Nothing. You're free for the afternoon." Debbie exclaimed, showing a shocked Eva the book. "The clients over there are for Ally and Deirdre."

"Lucky me," Ally said with a grin, picking up the files and giving the two women a tiny wave.

Eva picked up Mrs Wagner's file and walked down to her office. She spent a few minutes looking over the notes Debbie had made about the reason Mrs Wagner had an appointment. She put the file aside and went to her bookcase and took out a book on family law.

Sitting down, she opened the book and began reading. She didn't realise the time until there was a knock on the door and Debbie came in. "Mrs Wagner is here," she announced, and ushered the woman inside and closed the door.

Eva stood to welcome her client and looked up and blinked. *It had been so many years. Could this woman be...? But no, Greta was dead. Wasn't she? This woman had the same long auburn hair, the same hazel eyes as her former lover...the same regal bearing in her features. She was thinner and older but...*

The woman stood at the threshold. She wore a light summery dress with soft sandals and a sweater which was casually draped across her shoulders. Her eyebrows had gone into her bangs.

Eva fell back down on her chair in shock. She couldn't even begin to believe that the woman standing in her office was Greta. It couldn't be Greta.

"G...Greta?" Eva stammered.

Greta Wagner was rooted to the spot. She hadn't moved since she entered the office. Her shock at seeing Eva was as great as if someone had punched her. Eva. The lover she thought had disappeared, the friend she spent nearly two years with, was standing in front of her—a little older, and her hair was cut into a bob. She had loved Eva's long hair. But the crystal blue eyes were as magnetic as they had been when they were both in their teens. "Eva?"

Greta came around the desk and Eva looked up from where she was sitting, still unable to believe what was happening. She was mute, her feet planted on the ground, unable to move.

"My dear God, it is you!" Greta cried out and knelt in front of Eva and embraced her. "Oh, dear God. I don't believe this," Greta muttered as she took hold of Eva's hands. "You don't believe this, do you?"

Eva shook her head, which caused Greta to laugh.

"You're supposed to be dead." Eva said when she found her voice.

"Dead? Why would you think I was dead?" Greta asked as she pulled the other chair around and sat near her former lover.

"Reinhardt told me he beat you and put you on a train headed God-knows-where—"

"Reinhardt? Jurgen Reinhardt? Why would he beat me?"

"B..b..because he found out about us."

"Good grief, he didn't beat me; he didn't even touch me. He lied to you, Eva. That man couldn't tell the truth if his life depended on it."

"You're alive," Eva said in wonder. "Where did you go?"

"Where did I go?"

"After we burnt the synagogue," Eva said quietly.

"Oh! After Jurgen and the boys decided they were going to throw some rocks, and you took off. Is that what you mean?"

Eva nodded.

"Well, I followed them and got up to all sorts of mischief. It was quite a night. You missed out on all the fun. I then went home, and the next day I was to meet you, but you didn't show up. I thought maybe you had forgotten about my trip to Hamburg."

Eva shook her head. "What trip?"

"My cousin was getting married. You don't remember?"

"No," Eva said quietly.

"Oh...now I wonder if I didn't mention it. No matter. When I came back, you were at your uncle's place in Austria."

"You went to my...father?"

"I tried, but he was busy; so I asked Jurgen where you were, and he told me."

"You asked Jurgen?" Eva couldn't believe she was having this conversation. She couldn't believe the lies she had been told by Reinhardt. All the lies. She exhaled a breath she hadn't even noticed she was holding in.

Greta leaned over and wiped away Eva's tears and cupped her cheek with her hand. "Eva, I can't believe it's you. I think we need to sit down and have a good heart to heart. Would you have dinner with me tonight?"

Eva sat there trying to get her thoughts together. "Um...I can't tonight—"

"I know, you need to get yourself together. How about tomorrow night? I can come over to your place, and we can get reacquainted?"

Eva nodded.

"Excellent, we can catch up on old times."

Greta smiled and rubbed her thumb across Eva's cheek. She couldn't believe her luck. Her marriage to that buffoon Heinrich was all but dead, and her former lover was back in her life. *Things couldn't get any better*, she thought to herself.

❖❖❖❖❖❖❖

Eva was in a daze. It was a good thing her stepmother had gone to meet her father in the city. The last thing she wanted to do was talk to anyone except Zoe. She had helped Greta with the information she wanted, quite amazed she was able to function at all. She had spent the remaining time trying to come to terms with what had just occurred. It felt like her whole world had crashed around her.

For over eight years she'd believed Greta was dead, her

father being responsible for having sent her to her death. All the abuse and humiliation she'd suffered at his and her uncles' hands, the abject loneliness she'd felt at being viewed as a deviant, and the constant threat of more violence came crashing back into her conscious mind. Her back ached from the stress.

She felt like she had been punched in the head. Emotionally, she was a total wreck. When it was time to leave, she had mechanically signed off and said her good-byes to Debbie.

"Hey, are you okay?" Debbie asked. She was worried because Eva had been extremely quiet for the rest of the afternoon, not even venturing out of her office for the afternoon tea break. Eva had spoken to Debbie only to inform her that Greta was coming in the next day and to put her in the appointment book.

"Yeah, just tired," Eva responded and walked out. She couldn't even remember how she caught the bus home. She walked the few meters from the bus stop in a daze as she went up to the flat and opened the door, dropping her briefcase to the floor.

"Zoe? Are you home?"

There wasn't any reply, and Eva went and sat on the sofa and closed her eyes. "Oh God," she exclaimed. Eva wished her partner was there. She needed her so much that her chest ached. She picked herself up and went into the bedroom.

"You disgust me!" he spat. *"Do you know what that will do to my reputation? They will send me to the front for this. And you, do you know what they do to perverts in concentration camps?"*

He folded the belt strap, popping it for effect, and leaning over her so close she could feel his breath, he hissed, "Is it true?" But Eva could not speak, her words frozen in fear. "Answer me damnit!" he demanded. Eva remained motionless, which only served to explode the rage boiling inside her father.

What followed was the worst, most cruel beating she had ever received. The leather belt, used so mercilessly against her back, left welts too painful to touch. But that pain was nothing compared to the mental anguish she now suffered. She had been beaten into the bottomless pit of guilt and shame and, as she lay there sobbing, blood covering her back and legs, her father's words: "bastard child," tortured her until she wished she were dead.

She could feel every lash as it cut into her back and her legs. The pain never ending, the torture had only begun.

BASTARD CHILD! DEVIANT! Her father's words echoed in her mind.

"NOOOOOOOOOOO!" Eva screamed and bolted upright. Her breath came in shallow gasps as she wiped the sweat from her brow.

Zoe raced from the kitchen as soon as Eva started screaming, and she dropped to her knees in front of the bed and held her.

Zoe had come home from cricket practice and had found the flat in darkness, which was a surprise as Eva hadn't told her she would be late coming home. She'd removed her white cricket uniform which had turned green from the many times she had run and fallen on the oval chasing balls all over the park. She took them to the laundry and was heading back when she noticed that Eva's briefcase lay on the floor and not in its usual place. She had been surprised, since Eva was a very neat person. Going into the bedroom, she had seen her partner lying on top of the blankets as she slept. A frown marred her features, and Zoe had knelt and kissed her gently and covered her with a blanket. She had stood watching her for a few moments and then went and had a shower. It was while she was fixing herself something to eat that she heard Eva screaming, and she bolted from the kitchen and ran into the bedroom to find her partner sitting up and looking extremely pale.

"It's all right, love. I've got you." Zoe held her as Eva sobbed. "I've got you," she repeated in reassurance. She held onto her partner who was overcome with emotion. Zoe was also shaking. Eva's nightmares had dissipated since Egypt, and it had been a year since she had woken, drenched in sweat and screaming.

"Hold me," Eva asked as Zoe got into bed with her and held her shaking partner. She kissed her and tried to soothe her as she rocked her in her arms. To many people, Eva was the strong one, the one most thought had the most control over her emotions, whereas Zoe wore her heart on her sleeve. Zoe knew differently.

Zoe wondered what had happened that had caused Eva's nightmares to return. She would wait until the morning to ask.

❖❖❖❖❖❖❖

Zoe woke with a start. She had an uneasy feeling. She turned to look for Eva, but her partner was not in bed with her. She got up and put on her slippers and walked out of the bedroom into darkness. She could see Eva sitting on the sofa, her strong profile outlined in the light from the open curtain. Zoe sighed. She didn't know what happened the day before, but Eva's nightmares returning only meant trouble. She padded quietly to Eva's side.

Eva looked up and gave a tired smile. "Hi."

Zoe knelt beside the sofa and took Eva's hand. "Hey, are you okay?"

"No."

Eva opened her arms and Zoe snuggled on her lap, giving her a big hug and a kiss. Zoe tilted her head sideways and looked at Eva's reddened eyes and tearstained face.

"Want to tell me what happened yesterday?"

Eva sighed deeply.

"Did someone hurt you?"

Eva shook her head. "No."

"Evy, I love you and all, but I'm not a mind reader."

"Would you still love me if I had died back in Greece?" Eva asked quietly. "If I had left you, alone–"

"I would love you 'til I die," Zoe said. Back in Greece she had thought about life without Eva and pondered that very question when Eva was lying in the American medical tent hospital back in Larissa. She had lost her family and friends, and the idea of losing Eva made her physically ill.

Eva held Zoe closer. She couldn't put into words how she felt, and she buried her head on Zoe's shoulder.

"Eva, you're scaring me. What's the matter?"

Eva took a deep breath. "Do you remember I told you about Greta?"

Zoe frowned. They had discussed what had happened during the night Eva's mother was killed, and that Greta was her lover. Zoe hadn't wanted to push her for more information since that night was the start of her journey into pain and anguish.

"You told me a little about her. She was your first lover, and she left you alone..." Zoe stopped talking as she realised that Eva's question about dying in Greece and Greta's abandonment in Germany were connected. "Were you thinking of Greta? It's not your fault, love. It's not your fault she was killed."

"She's not dead," Eva whispered. "She walked into my office yesterday."

Zoe was stunned. There was no other way to describe how she felt, but one look at her partner and it was obvious Eva was shocked as well. She didn't know how she would react if she were in that position.

"Wow," Zoe said quietly. No wonder her usually unflappable partner was so unsettled. She now understood why Eva had the nightmare. Even though she didn't know the woman, she disliked Greta for what she was putting her wife through.

"You know, Zoe, as she walked into the office, I was about to introduce myself. I froze. I stood there like I had been punched. What's that cricketing term Earl uses all the time?"

"Hit for a six."

"Yeah, I was hit for a six. I didn't know what to do. She wasn't sent to a concentration camp. Reinhardt lied to me. She had gone to her uncle's place in Hamburg, and she thought something had happened to me when I didn't reply to her mail." Eva stopped. She had been sitting in the dark going over what she was going to say to Zoe, and she couldn't stop the tears. Zoe looked at her with so much love that the tears started anew. "I love you, Zoe. You own my heart, my body and my soul, and I don't think I could ever go on without you."

"I'm not going anywhere, love. I'm staying put. I hold your heart, your body and your soul, and you hold mine," Zoe replied brushing away Eva's tears. "I made a promise to you on the ship that I would love you and care for you. I vowed before God that you are my partner for life."

"Partners for life," Eva whispered.

"I want to spend the rest of my life waking up to you, loving you, and being there for you," Zoe said. She tangled her fingers in Eva's hair and brought her head down and kissed her passionately.

They gazed into each other's eyes. Eva kissed her gently and held her tighter, then repeated what she had told Zoe so many times before. "You are the love of my life, why would I need to search for what I already have?" She believed it, but Greta's return had unsettled her greatly.

"I know this is hurting you, but, do you still love Greta?"

"She was my first love, Zoe. I can't deny I have feelings for her. She was the first one to make me feel special...I'm not the same person I was back then." Eva stopped trying to express what she was feeling. "I love her, but not the way I used to...not the way I love you. Do you understand?"

"I think so."

"Never doubt my love for you, Zoe. Yesterday threw me for a loop. I never expected her to walk into my life again..."

"I understand, love. I do. Are you going to see her again?"

Eva nodded. "She wants to have dinner and talk."

"Okay," Zoe said as she tried to recall all she had to do later that day. "I'm going to come over to your office in the afternoon. Do you want me to do that?"

"Yes, please." Eva was relieved. Having Zoe with her was all she wanted. She had feelings for Greta, but those feelings weren't love, just deep affection for a friend. "I would love for you to be there." Eva smiled. She would love to show Zoe the office and have her close when Greta turned up.

"Well, that's settled then," Zoe declared and gave her a kiss. "You think a warm bath would be nice?"

Eva nodded.

Zoe got off Eva's lap, took her hand and helped her partner up. Zoe turned and put her arms around Eva. "I'm sorry I wasn't here yesterday when you came home." She hugged the taller woman. "Together, we will work this out." Unbuttoning Eva's crumpled shirt, Zoe let it drop to the floor, then put her arms around the slender waist and looked up into a tired face. "I love you."

Chapter 6

Zoe blinked her eyes open and groaned. The alarm clock was pealing loudly, and she couldn't reach it to shut it off as it was on Eva's side of the bed. Eva was curled up into a ball under the comforter, and Zoe didn't want to disturb her to turn off the ringing bells. She was about to get out of bed and go and turn it off when a long arm reached out from under the comforter and flung the new clock out the door. It crashed into the sofa and landed on the floor with a thud, the bell falling off the ringer. Zoe sat on the bed with a bemused expression on her face and turned to her partner who was looking at her with sleepy blue eyes.

"Now we have to go and buy another clock," Zoe mumbled as she leaned over and kissed Eva good morning.

"The department store loves us," Eva consoled sleepily. She pulled back the comforter and wrapped it around Zoe who cuddled up next to her.

"How are you feeling?"

Eva sighed. "As if I was run over by a truck and then the driver backed up and ran over me again."

"I wish I could do something to make you feel better," Zoe said, tracing the worry lines on Eva's brow.

"You did it, love. Last night you were here for me."

"Do you want to go in today? Can you call in sick?"

"It wouldn't look good for my third day at work to call in sick, Zo. I'll be okay."

"Well, I have classes this morning, but I cancelled my driving lesson with Earl last night. I'll see you at lunch time. Okay? Earl is going to give me a lift to see you and then come and pick you up so you can get home in time to prepare for Greta's visit. How does that sound?"

Eva nodded. "You've got things under control. Does Earl mind playing taxi?"

Zoe grinned. "Nope. I'll make you some *yimesta* for when I come to your office for lunch."

Eva smiled. Zoe was going to make her favourite food— large green and red peppers scooped out and filled with rice and minced meat with mixed herbs. Zoe was in full protective mode, and Eva found she was relieved to have Zoe close by and lending her support. She would thank Earl for taking the time to ferry them about when she saw him.

❖❖❖❖❖❖❖

David Peterson was a happy man. His meeting with his boss had gone very well. He was given a commendation for the job that was done with Muller and Rhimes, which he was asked to pass on to Friedrich, as well. In addition, two more suspected war criminals had been arrested. He was given additional files on new German immigrants which he needed to cross check with the wanted list.

He opened the door to the office and got smacked in the face with a crumpled piece of paper.

"Good aim, Freddy. I think the bin is over there," he said and pointed to the empty bin near the desk. Around the bin were a dozen crumpled pieces of paper. "Oh no, you're not attempting yet another love letter are you?"

"Shut up," Friedrich Jacobs muttered to his friend, going back to his letter to Elena.

"Wouldn't it be quicker to just tell the girl?"

"I can't," Friedrich mumbled.

David sighed and sat down opposite his friend. "Mate, this is one time I can't help you. Just tell her you love her."

"What if she doesn't love me?"

"Oh bloody hell," David muttered as he shook his head. "Do you think she's interested in you?"

"Uh, yes."

"Where is the problem?"

"Unlike certain people, who shall remain nameless, I am

trying to find a woman to marry and have a family with; and I think I have."

"Yeah? I don't see the problem, Freddy."

"For life."

"Sounds like a death sentence," David snickered, then stopped when he saw the chagrined look on Friedrich's face. "Sorry, mate. Elena is a nice girl."

"I know." He crumpled another sheet of paper and threw it. It landed next to the other discarded pieces.

"Here." David placed a list and a stack of files in front of his friend. "This should take your mind off love letters for a while."

"What's that?"

"The latest immigration list. The bossman wants us to cross check them with the wanted list."

Friedrich rolled his eyes. "As if they would put their real names down!"

"You know some of them are that stupid. Pete found three last week. Same first name, surname and age. No wonder they lost the war. You take half, and I'll take half; and we can go through them to see which boofhead used his real name."

Friedrich looked at the long list of names and sighed. "Then what?"

David grinned. "Then, Freddy, we get to see happy snapshots. Just imagine thousands of photographs." Friedrich made a face, but took the first sheet with the names on it.

❖ ❖ ❖ ❖ ❖ ❖ ❖

"Come on, Zoe!" Elena yelled out from the foyer. She checked her watch for the fifth time and was quite agitated by the time Zoe came bounding down the stairs.

"Okay, okay I'm coming," Zoe muttered as she stopped at the last step and had an idea. She pursued her lips in thought. "Hey, El, one more minute okay?"

Elena scowled at her friend. "Okay, but hurry up. I hate standing up in the bus."

Zoe went further down the corridor and knocked on Panayiotis' door.

"Hi," Zoe greeted her father-in-law. "Can I speak to you for a minute?"

"Absolutely, you want to come in?" Panayiotis asked, still

holding the door open.

"Um, Elena is waiting for me. I think Eva needs you this morning."

"She does? Is something wrong?" the former priest asked.

Zoe looked down and grimaced. "Yeah."

"Are you two fighting?"

"No. No, I mean, I think it's best if Eva tells you about it."

Panayiotis frowned. Zoe had always found it easy to talk to him, so he wondered why she was acting so strangely. "Alright, I'll go and see her now."

"Thanks," Zoe said, giving him a kiss before running back down the corridor and out the door.

"What was that about, Pany?" Alberta asked, standing by her husband as he closed the door.

"I don't know. Zoe was acting very strangely. She said Eva needed me."

"How very odd. What do you think it is?"

Panayiotis shrugged. "I'll find out in a few moments, I guess. Are you going to work with Eva today?"

"No, I need to go to the Circular Quay office today, they are short staffed down there. I'm taking the train." She looked down at her watch. "Actually I'm going to be late if I don't leave right now."

"Okay," he acknowledged as Alberta kissed him, picked up her bag, and walked out. It was going to be a busy day. He went into the bedroom and picked up his Bible. He had dressed in his black robes to go the church today and smiled at himself when he passed the mirror. He hadn't worn the black robes for over a year. It felt good to be back in the garb he had worn for so many years.

He closed the door to his flat, walked up the stairs to Eva's apartment and knocked. He was disturbed to see his daughter's tired face.

"Morning, Father. Come in." Eva ushered him inside. "Want a cup of tea?"

"Oh, I just had one. Eva, you look like you've had a very rough night. Are you alright?"

Eva smiled. "Did Zoe come to you?"

"My child, if Zoe hadn't come and I had seen your face today, I think I would have guessed there was something wrong," her father said as he put his arm around her shoulders. Eva melted into his embrace, resting her head on his shoulder. "Want to tell me about what's bothering you and what's got Zoe acting strangely?" They walked to the sofa and sat down, the former priest taking Eva's hands and holding them as he watched Eva intently.

"In 1937, I had a friend...well she was someone who I absolutely loved with all my heart."

"A lover," Panayiotis said matter-of-factly, which got a smile from his daughter.

"Well, she was a friend first, and then we fell in love," Eva clarified. "Greta was—"

"Is this the same Greta that got Muller so demented?"

"Yes, the same Greta." She gave her father a small grin at his description of her stepfather and then continued. "Well, she was the first person...uh..."

"You had sex with," her father furnished.

"Father, do you have to be so blunt?" Eva protested.

"Why? You didn't have sex with her?" Panayiotis asked in mock surprise.

"Actually, I did."

"Well what do you want to call it? Horizontal dancing?" Panayiotis gave his daughter a huge grin when Eva poked him in the leg.

"Well, she was my first lover. I thought she had died because Reinhardt went to Muller and told him about us."

Panayiotis nodded. He had spent many years as a priest listening to his congregation as they came to him with their troubles, trying to find a solution. It wasn't an easy task, and many times he found himself worrying and lying awake at night. He thought that if he applied what God said in the Bible, most problems would be overcome. What he couldn't solve by applying God's word, he would find other ways of helping.

"You blamed yourself for her death?"

Eva nodded. "For many years I thought that if I hadn't fallen in love with her, she wouldn't have died, mother wouldn't have died and..." Eva stopped and closed her eyes to compose herself. She opened them again to see her father's concerned face, his blue eyes glistening.

"Oh, my sweet Eva, you don't know what would have happened if you had chosen not to do the things you did. We all have doubts about our actions. What if I hadn't gone on the train, if I had escaped like you, Zoe and Thanasi wanted me to? What would have happened? I would have been safe, but I wouldn't have met Alberta. My life would have been different."

Eva nodded. She had tried to persuade her father not to go on the transport train to Thessaloniki because the Resistance was going to bomb the line. She tried everything she could think of to stop him, but he went on the train and the line was bombed. Eva didn't believe in fate, but she had tried very hard to come up with any other explanation as to how her father had survived and then met Alberta on the hospital ship.

"Father, Greta turned up yesterday in my office."

Panayiotis' bushy eyebrows shot up. He hadn't been expecting that revelation. "My God," he whispered. "What happened?"

"She said that Reinhardt lied to me. She hadn't died. She had gone to her uncle's place or something like that. My mind was numb, so I only half remember what she said." Eva recalled feeling utterly shocked and her body refusing to move. It was if she had been planted and taken root in the floor. "She wants to pick up where we left off. Though she's married now to some man, she wants to divorce him."

Panayiotis looked at his daughter and asked, "Do you have feelings for her?"

"Father, I do have feelings for her, but I know that it's not love. I don't know how to explain it, but it's not the same. I love Zoe, and I don't want to have a relationship with Greta. Well, not a sexual one."

"Does Zoe know?"

Eva nodded. "I told her. I didn't know how she would react, but she was quite calm about it."

Panayiotis shook his head. Zoe always found ways to amaze him. If he had been told about what had happened, he would have predicted that Zoe's reaction would be anything but calm.

"I was worried about what Zoe would say. If she would think I wanted to—"

"Are you worried about yourself—that you might want to resume this relationship with Greta? Or are you worried about how Zoe will handle it?"

Eva looked at her hands and sighed. "I don't love Greta the way I used to, Father. I'm not the same person I was when I was eighteen. I keep thinking to myself that there are two Evas who are nothing alike. I thought about this last night: the person who I was died the night that mother died. I don't know what to call it, but it was as if I became another person."

"You went through a pretty traumatic time. Every experience in our lives changes us—some for the better, and some not so positively. Even Jesus was changed when he was on earth."

"Dying does that to you." Eva grinned at her father's grimace at her attempted humour.

"Lucky for us, something good came from it," he replied and gave her a hug and a kiss on the top of her head. "Now, what are you going to do?"

"Greta wants to have dinner and talk."

"Oh."

Eva nodded. "Zoe is in full protective mode. I don't think dynamite could blast her out of the flat tonight. Not that I want her to be gone. I want her near me."

"Can I make a suggestion?"

"Always."

"Tell Greta you want to continue your friendship, but not the sexual aspect of it. You are married; and you have vowed to God and to Zoe that you would love only Zoe. I'm sure once she knows about your marriage, she wouldn't want to interfere with your happiness."

"Father, what if she doesn't—"

"You get Zoe to go into attack mode," Panayiotis joked to ease the tension. "Let's take one step at a time and deal with what comes up. How does that sound?"

"I hope I don't have to get Zoe to go into attack mode."

They chuckled as Panayiotis gave his daughter a hug. "Let me know how it goes. I have to go and see Father Eleftheriou about some painting of the pews."

"Are you happy, Father?"

"I am more than happy, Eva. I have two beautiful daughters, a wife that loves me, a God I trust. What more could a man ask for? I'm blessed." He gave her a smile and cupped her cheek with his hand. "I want you to be happy and to live your life with love and happiness. You love Zoe and she loves you. Nothing else matters as long as you love each other, okay?"

Eva nodded and looked down. She loved her father with all her heart, and his support of her marriage was one of the things she adored about him. He lifted her face and met her eyes. "Love conquers all things, no matter what we go through. If you have love for each other, there is nothing that can destroy what you have with Zoe."

"I love you, Father," Eva whispered as she hugged the taller man.

"I love you too, Eva. Put your trust in God and He will help you. Take this matter up in prayer with Zoe before you meet Greta for dinner. Ask Him for His guidance. Before I go would you like to pray with me?"

Eva nodded. He led her to where the crucifix hung on the wall, and they both knelt.

❖❖❖❖❖❖❖

Eva arrived at the office looking more upbeat than when she had left it the previous night. When she saw Debbie, she would have to apologise to the hard working woman for having acted like a hermit. She stepped off the elevator to a quiet waiting area, which surprised her.

"Good morning, Debbie."

"Ah, good morning, Eva. Are you feeling better today?" Debbie asked. She had been concerned about the way the older woman looked. She had a mind to go into the office and have a good old sit down with her, but she felt a little shy in doing that since she didn't know Eva well enough.

"I am, thank you. I am sorry I was rather hermit-like in the afternoon," Eva apologised as she was handed some files.

"Hey, we all have bad days. Usually mine strikes before I get my you-know-what, and I am quiet as a mouse when I'm not yelling." They both chuckled, and Debbie gave Eva a chocolate bar. "I usually find chocolate makes my day ever so much nicer."

"Yum, chocolate." Eva gleefully said as she popped a bit of the bar in her mouth. "Mmmm."

"Hey, another chocoholic! I'll remember that in the future."

"Around lunch time, my flatmate, Zoe, will be coming around; so when you see her, can you please send her to my office?"

"Sure. Zoe?"

"Yeah. Zoe Lambros."

"Will do. You've got Mrs Dieter coming in at 9:30, and then you have Mr Lieberman at 10:30," Debbie read off the appointment book, then looked up. "You don't have any appointments for the afternoon, but Alexander called in sick and he has two appointments. Would you mind covering for him?"

"No, I don't mind. What language?"

"Italian."

"I'll need to brush up on my Italian then," Eva said as she

popped another chocolate in her mouth and waved at Debbie as she went down the corridor to her office.

The morning passed rather quickly as she saw her two appointments and lent assistance when a Greek woman passed out in the waiting area. She spent some time with the woman until the ambulance arrived and took her away.

Debbie looked up at the clock as the elevator stopped on the floor and a young woman with a picnic basket stepped out and looked around. Debbie smiled, realising this must be Eva's flatmate. The young woman wore a t-shirt, neatly creased jeans and gym shoes. *Looks very comfortable,* Debbie thought to herself, wishing she could come in to work looking like that. The young woman came towards her and put the picnic basket down.

"Hi, I'm—"

"Zoe Lambros," Debbie said with a smile.

"Wow, you're good!"

"Eva has been telling tales about me? You are Zoe Lambros, aren't you?"

"Ever since I was born," Zoe replied and stuck out her hand to shake the receptionist's. "You're Debbie?"

"That's me. Eva is expecting you. Just go down the corridor, and it's number 5."

"Thanks. I'm bringing her some lunch."

Debbie hesitated for a moment and then crooked her finger and motioned for Zoe to come closer. "You know, Zoe, I think you need to speak to Eva about lunch. She keeps forgetting to go."

Zoe didn't know whether to laugh or look serious. Eva was known to miss lunch when she was working and focused on a problem. Zoe had asked, pleaded and ordered her wife to stop and feed herself. "Ah...I'll try and convince her to stop once in a while."

"Thanks, Zoe. It was a pleasure meeting you."

"I've heard a lot about you from Eva. Is it true you run the ship?" Zoe whispered to her as she looked around.

"Shhh. They are not supposed to know that," Debbie replied in a loud whisper.

Zoe chuckled as she picked up her basket and walked down the corridor.

"Wish I had a flatmate that nice," Debbie muttered as she looked at her own lunch of salad and cheese sandwich.

Eva looked up at the clock and wondered where Zoe had

gotten to. She was about to pick up the phone and ring Debbie, when she heard a light knock on the door and it opened to reveal a grinning Zoe with her picnic basket.

"Zoe's Mobile Catering Service," she announced as she put the basket down and walked around the desk into Eva's open arms. She sat on her lap and kissed her soundly. "Now for that, I charge extra," Zoe mumbled as she cupped her wife's face and looked into her blue eyes. "Hi, there."

"Hi."

"Debbie wants me to let you know that you should take better care of yourself and eat lunch."

"She ratted on me?"

"Yep, sure did, cupcake. Seriously, Evy, you have to stop and eat."

"I will," Eva promised as she got another kiss. "Thank you for sending my father up this morning."

Zoe smiled. "Did he help?"

"Yeah, I was feeling better this morning; and then he and I spoke for a little and we prayed together."

"That's great, love. I could convince you how much I love you, but I thought you might need a little extra help."

Eva brushed Zoe's errant bangs and looked into the emerald eyes. "You are wonderful."

"Well of course I am," Zoe joked, getting a laugh out of her wife. She reluctantly got up from Eva's lap, picked up the basket and took out two plates and a container. "Okay, Miss Eva, we have *yimesta* as I promised, a little feta cheese and some olives, and I squeezed some orange juice for you."

"Did Earl bring you over?"

"Nope. Mabel did," Zoe grinned and put the food in front of Eva.

"Who's Mabel?"

"Well," Zoe took a forkful of stuffed peppers and fed Eva, who gave her a grin. "I went over to Earl's so he could drive me over, but then I saw her and I fell in love."

"You saw 'her'?" Eva's brow raised in question and Zoe laughed.

"I have wheels! I saw this old motorcycle with a sidecar in Earl's garage, and I fell in love with it. Earl told me that Dave brought it over from Europe, but doesn't want it any more; so I got it."

Eva remembered those motorcycles with a sidecar; she had

driven one herself many times when she was with her stepfather during the war. "Don't you need a license for it?"

"Nope."

"What does Earl want for it?"

"His life," Zoe chuckled. "I promised not to kill him when we start our driving lessons."

They both laughed at that, and Eva made a mental note to speak to her friend about this latest interest of Zoe's.

"Isn't it a bit big for you?" Eva asked as she picked up her orange juice and took a sip. She watched Zoe over the rim of the glass.

"Yeah, it is a little, but it's okay. With the sidecar, it's perfect. And of course, with your long legs," Zoe ran her hand up Eva's thigh, "it's perfect." She waggled her eyebrows and grinned.

Eva didn't know what to say. She leaned over and gave her wife a kiss. "Why Mabel?" Zoe had a quirky habit of naming mechanical objects. She had come home one day to discover Zoe talking to the icebox, that had too much ice in it, and calling it "Percy." So the icebox became Percy, which had Eva doubled up laughing so hard she had tears running down her face. Zoe explained to her that when they had the little chicken farm back in Larissa, she named all the chickens in the chicken coop, and she named the cows and the goats as well. She also had a pet sheep which she called Lamby, until it met its untimely death one Easter.

Zoe shrugged. "I don't know. I saw her, and the name popped into my head. It needs a bit of work. It's a little rusty, and the paint is peeling off; but Earl said he would fix the rust, and I'll paint it hot pink with black trim."

Eva was drinking her beverage when Zoe's colour combination registered, and she snorted the orange juice. Zoe patted her on the back with smirk. "Do you want to come downstairs and see me off?"

"Oh yeah, I want to see the object of your affections."

They finished their lunch with Zoe telling Eva her plans for the bike, how she and Elena could get to classes with it. She put the containers and the dishes back in the basket and then set it down. Zoe got up and pushed the visitors' chairs back against the wall.

"Zoe, what are you doing?" Eva asked, trying to understand why the visitors' chairs weren't in their normal place.

"Well, I gave you some lunch, a little romancing and now," Zoe took out a portable radio and set it on the desk, "a little dancing." She beamed at Eva and held out her hand. "Dance with me, Miss Eva." Eva took the smaller hand in her larger one and led her wife to the middle of the office. Zoe tuned the radio to Eva's favourite station and one of Zoe's favourite songs, *The Way You Look Tonight*, was playing. Zoe grinned

Eva put her arms around Zoe's waist and looked down into Zoe's eyes. Zoe put her hands on Eva's hips as they swayed. Zoe started to sing–a little off key–but Eva didn't care.

"Some day,
When I'm awf'ly low,
When the world is cold,
I will feel a glow just thinking of you,
And the way you look tonight.
Oh, but you're lovely,
With your smile so warm,
And your cheek so soft,
There is nothing for me but to love you,
And the way you look tonight."

Zoe stroked Eva's cheek as Eva took up the next verse.

"With each word your tenderness grows,
Tearing my fear apart,
And that laugh that wrinkles your nose,
touches my foolish heart.
You're lovely,
Never, never change,
Keep that breathless charm,
Won't you please arrange it, 'cause I love you,
Just the way you look tonight."

"I love you, Miss Zoe," Eva said and bent down and passionately kissed her partner, pulling her closer. They danced for a few minutes, just holding each other as Eva relaxed. Zoe rested her head on Eva's chest, and they swayed together to the melody. They didn't realise the door had opened until they heard the cough.

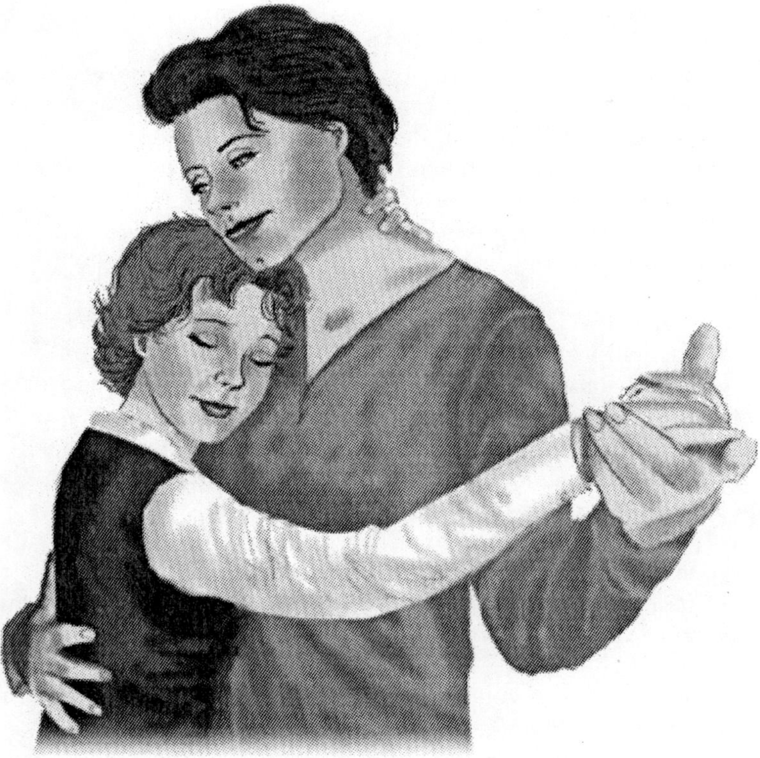

"Oh! Excuse me..." Debbie stammered. She had heard the music and was intrigued. She had knocked and entered to find Eva holding Zoe so close it was impossible to see daylight between them.

Eva opened her eyes and smirked. "Zoe."

"Hmm?" responded Zoe, who had her eyes closed and was enjoying holding Eva.

"We've been busted."

"Huh?" Zoe questioned, looking up at a smirking Eva. She turned around to find a shocked Debbie standing with her hand on the doorknob.

"Oh, majorly busted," Zoe muttered and reluctantly let go of Eva.

"Come in, Debbie." Eva invited the now bewildered woman into her office. Debbie shut the door and sat down in the visitor's chair closest to the door.

"I'm sorry, I didn't mean to intrude. I heard the music, and I was wondering where it had come from."

Eva raised an eyebrow at Zoe who was blushing a bit. "My wife brought it in," Eva said and smiled at Zoe who gave her a quirky grin.

"Your wife?"

"Zoe and I are lesbians, Debbie. Does that offend you?"

Debbie stared first at Eva and then at Zoe. She had never met any lesbians before, but they certainly didn't look like the women her priest had warned them about from the pulpit. She liked Eva a great deal, and the little time she had spent with Zoe, she found her to have a quirky sense of humour.

"No, it doesn't offend me, but you have to excuse me, I've never met any lesbians before. Father O'Donnell keeps raising the issue of homosexuality as a gross sin and paints a picture of lesbians as Jezebels." Debbie realised she was babbling and shut up.

"Well, not everyone approves, and we don't usually come out and tell people unless we know them quite well or—"

"Or we get busted," Zoe finished off and got a smile from Debbie.

Debbie looked concerned. "Does Earl know?"

Zoe looked at Eva with a questioning look. "Earl? Did he do his 'you're my girl' act again?"

Eva nodded. "Earl is one of my best friends, and he does know."

"Oh good, he is such a nice man."

"He is and has a heart of gold."

"Does that mean he is available?" Debbie asked hopefully.

Zoe bit her lip to stop herself from blurting out that Earl was involved with another man.

"No, he is involved with someone," Eva replied.

"Oh, what a shame."

"Debbie, can I ask you not to tell anyone? Most people are against our choice, and it would make life difficult."

Debbie looked between Eva and Zoe. "Tell them about what? Your flatmate bringing you lunch? I don't think that's even worth a mention on the grapevine."

"Thank you." Eva smiled and nodded her head.

"Eva, I like you a great deal. It's not often I make friends with people so quickly. Your secret is safe with me." Debbie got up and opened the door. "I wish I had a flatmate who could cook and dance like you do." She gave Zoe a wink and closed the door.

"I like her," Zoe said as the door closed. She turned to Eva and put her arms around her waist. "Okay, Miss Eva, I have to get going. Earl is picking you up at 5:00. What time is our guest arriving?"

"She said she will be there at 6:00."

Zoe reluctantly let go of Eva, picked up her picnic basket and followed her partner down the corridor. They passed Debbie, and Zoe gave her a friendly wave. They took the stairs down to the basement garage.

Standing next to a white pristine looking car was the oldest motorbike Eva had ever seen. Its yellow paint was peeling, rust taking over wherever the paint left off. The sidecar was covered in scratch marks that had rusted over. She wondered if the whole thing wouldn't fall apart. "Uh..."

"Yeah, she doesn't look much now, but wait until we give her a new paint job," Zoe enthused, running her hand on the motorcycle's body.

"Do me a favour, Zo."

"For you, anything," Zoe said as she gave Eva a quick kiss.

"When you get home, take some money and go and buy a helmet, please?"

"Okay, I can do that," she replied. Zoe put the basket in the sidecar and got on the bike. Her feet barely touched the ground. She gave Eva a grin and started the engine. It spluttered to life for a few seconds, and then died.

"Come on, Mabel." Zoe urged the bike. She started it again. It spluttered for a few seconds, and then came to life. "There ya go."

"Be careful!" Eva shouted above the noise.

Zoe waved, and Eva watched as she rode away. She shook her head and turned to go back upstairs. "Mabel," she said and chuckled.

Chapter 7

Debbie was clearing away files and tidying up the waiting area when she heard the lift stop. She looked at her watch and noticed it was way past the time that Daisy would bring any new clients up. The lift stopped and Earl stepped out, waving goodbye to Daisy. Debbie watched as the tall man pushed the glass doors open and walked in.

"G'day, Debbie, Eva still around?"

"Hi. Yeah, she's still in her office," Debbie replied with a smile and watched as he walked down the hallway. "All the good ones are taken," she said to herself and continued to clean up the waiting area and tidy up the magazines.

Earl knocked lightly on the door and walked in to find Eva tidying up her desk. "Greetings, ma'am, your chauffeur awaits. Are we ready to depart?" Earl put on a very bad English accent and doffed his imaginary hat.

"You are nuts, you know that?"

"What gave it away?" Earl chuckled and sat down on one of the visitors' chairs.

Eva looked up from clearing her desk and putting books away. "Hey, thanks for picking me up."

"No worries. When Zoe asks, Earl obeys," Earl joked. "So, are you enjoying it?"

"Yeah, there's a word I can't translate into English." Eva scrunched up her face as she thought of the Greek word for what she had in mind. "What's the word for when something is just so right?"

"Bonzer," Earl replied with a smirk.

"Bonzer? Okay it's bonzer," Eva grinned. "By the way, Debbie knows about me and Zoe."

"Oh boy. That doesn't sound too bonzer to me. How?"

"She walked in when we were dancing."

"Dancing? What in the world..."

"Zoe brought me lunch, and then she also supplied the entertainment," Eva chuckled, thinking about how much trouble her wife had gone to. "Speaking of which, before we go home can we stop at a florist? I want to buy her some flowers."

"Flowers? Sure," Earl replied. He had frequently seen the two give each other little gifts since he had met them eight months before. They were never expensive, just tokens of their affection for each other. Earl wondered if that kept their marriage stronger. He wasn't sure. "That kid just amazes me sometimes. Okay, so Debbie knows. Is she going to cause trouble?"

"No. She said she wasn't. I trust her."

"That's good. Otherwise, it could get a little on the tricky side."

Earl got up and opened the door for Eva, then closed the door behind him. They said good night to Debbie, who was on the phone, and were about to go out when Earl stopped and turned back. "Thanks," he whispered in Debbie's ear and gave her a kiss on the cheek. Debbie forgot what she was saying and stared as Earl walked out with Eva.

❖❖❖❖❖❖❖

In the car, Eva's thoughts turned to Greta. She wasn't as nervous as she'd thought she was going to be. She thought it had a lot to do with Zoe and what her partner had done to ease the pressure she had been feeling. She smiled because she held a bunch of Zoe's favourite flowers, petunias. She turned to Earl as he was stopped at the lights; he had a faraway look on his face.

"So do I thank you or kill you?" Eva joked.

"Huh?" Earl turned to her, unsure of what Eva was talking about.

"Mabel," Eva stated tersely with a mock scowl.

"Not my fault!" Earl said, throwing up his hands in mock surrender.

"No, it never is. You encourage her, Earl."

"I didn't, honest. After she came over, we were just talking."

"And how did she find the bike?"

"The tarp fell off. Really it did. I had even forgotten it was there. She took one look at the old rust bucket, and she fell in love." Earl laughed. "I can't deny her anything when her eyes light up. She lit up like a Christmas tree, Eva. I've only ever seen her light up like that when you are near. It's something else. I first saw it when she was waiting for you one morning after night shift. It was cold, but there she was on the brick fence, just sitting there, huddled up against the cold and waiting for you. When she saw you, it was like someone had lit a thousand candles inside her eyes."

Earl was cold. He buttoned his jacket and lifted the collar to keep his neck warm as he walked outside into the early morning frost. A light rain fell as the city was coming to life.

"I hate night shift," Earl muttered. He wanted to wait to see Eva off, so he made his way to the brick fence—a meeting place for those waiting for shifts to end. Usually at that time of the morning it was deserted. Earl was quite surprised to see a tiny figure sitting on the brick fence, rugged up against the cold. He couldn't make out the face—all he could see was legs, two arms and a bomber jacket. The beanie on the person's head covered their face. He chuckled at the sight.

He went over to the figure and stood next to it. "Hi, are you waiting for anyone?"

The figure nodded.

"It's cold, huh?"

It nodded again.

"Can you talk?"

"I...I'm cold."

"Oh, yeah, it is rather chilly. So, cold person, have you got a name?"

"Zoe Lambros."

"Nice name. Who are you waiting for?"

"Eva Haralambos."

"Oh, I've seen you before, I think. Well, you had a face then," Earl said with a grin as Zoe lifted the beanie and exposed her face. She gave the big man an impish grin. Earl was captivated by her twinkling emerald eyes. "You have beautiful eyes."

"I bet you say that to all the girls."

"Nope," Earl shook his head. "Only to ones in beanies."

Zoe burst out laughing. "So, do you have a name?"

"I do. Earl Chesterfield Wiggins, ma'am." Earl introduced himself and bowed.

"Oh! I know you. You're Eva's new boyfriend," Zoe teased.

"Uh, I'm not really her boyfriend. She told you about me?"

"Oh yeah, Evy told me that you helped her out. I really appreciate it."

Earl was taken aback. This young woman intrigued him. He wasn't sure why, but she was so easy to talk to. He always had trouble talking to women, despite his reputation as a Romeo. She wasn't anything like he'd thought she would be. "So, Zoe Lambros, what are you doing out here at this god awful time?"

"Waiting for my friend," Zoe said her eyes going past him. Earl turned to see what had captured Zoe's attention, and saw Eva walking towards them buttoning her dark grey woolen coat. He was fascinated as he watched Zoe's eyes light up as soon as she caught sight of Eva. Eva returned the smile—a smile Earl dubbed her 1000 megawatt smile, because it resembled those high powered light globes the factory used.

Eva caught up with them and greeted Zoe with a hug and a quick kiss as she sat on the brick fence. "You're freezing, love," Eva whispered to her and pulled Zoe's beanie down around her red rimmed ears. "Have you met Earl?"

Zoe nodded vigorously. "Yep, I've met your new beau," Zoe teased.

"You approve?" Eva gave her a grin while watching Earl's puzzled expression.

"He's a bit tall, but he'll do," Zoe chuckled. "Well, Miss Eva, let's go home so I can get all nice and warm, huh?" Zoe jumped down from the fence, and Earl was even more surprised to see how short the young woman was. "Thanks for the chat, Wiggy."

Earl laughed. No one had called him that since high school. He had hated it then, but coming from this young woman he found it endearing.

"That woman loves you so much. Dave never once got out of bed at 5 a.m. to come and pick me up, but Zoe did it every morning that you were on night shift."

"I love her, too. I think she's the best thing ever to happen to me," Eva said, remembering all those cold mornings when she got off her shift. Some days when she couldn't bear one more racist comment or Jack's crude behavior, she would find her wife outside, waiting patiently. It lifted her spirits to see her there. Even though she didn't ask Zoe to come down, the young woman did it anyway. The only times she wasn't there was when she had a horrible cold and Eva made her promise to stay in bed. And even then, Zoe was out of bed and waiting on the balcony.

"Well hang on to it, Eva, because I don't think lightning strikes twice," Earl said sadly.

Eva looked at him with concern. She waited for Earl to continue, but the big man concentrated on his driving. She realised Earl had stopped talking about Dave and what they were doing for a few weeks now. She had been so wrapped up with the problems her stepfather had caused them, that she hadn't taken the time to listen to her friend. "I'm sorry, Earl. With everything going on–"

"Eva, you've had a lot on your plate lately. Dave and I have some things to iron out. I wish I had someone whose eyes lit up when I'm around," Earl said quietly.

Eva didn't know what to say to that. "I'm sorry, Earl."

Earl turned to his friend and shrugged. "No one said it was going to last forever."

Eva felt that the best response to that was to just let Earl feel her support and concern. She put her hand on his bicep as he drove. "If there is anything we can do, let us know, okay?"

Earl nodded. "Anyway, getting away from matters of my love life, or lack thereof, and back to your gorgeous and totally insane wife. Tell me how am I supposed to stop Cyclone Zoe when her eyes go super bright when she sees the bike, and she's jumping up and down?"

"Cyclone Zoe is unstoppable," Eva chuckled. She knew firsthand that once she had made up her mind about something, no one could stop Zoe even if they wanted to.

"Exactly. And since I want to live to see my next birthday, I gave her the bike on the condition that I stay alive while I teach her to drive. Although I don't think she is going to want to learn if she's riding the bike."

"Mabel."

"Mabel," Earl snorted. "What kind of name is that for a bike?"

"She calls our icebox Percy, so I guess Mabel is better than that," Eva reasoned. She wasn't sure why Zoe named everything, but it was one of the lovable things about her that Eva adored.

They both chuckled as Earl turned into Eva's street and stopped outside the building. Seeing Mabel parked outside, Earl turned to Eva. "She just fell in love with it. I had to take it out and brush off the cobwebs and hoped a spider wasn't lurking anywhere on the thing." He would always remember the look of total joy on Zoe's face when he did that.

Earl took note of Mr Haralambos working on the bike, removing the old paint, then turned back his friend. "Eva, what you said about talking." Earl hesitated for a few moments. "I will, once I find out where I stand with Dave. I might need a beer buddy to drown my sorrows with."

"You're on. You bring the VB, and we can drown your sorrows. But you're still in the dog house about Mabel."

"Awww, come on. Not my fault. Have you ever tried saying 'no' to Zoe?" he asked, knowing full well that Eva couldn't—and wouldn't—deny anything Zoe wanted. One look from those green eyes, and Eva was lost. Not that he blamed her at all, because he had succumbed to the Zoe charm early on in their friendship.

"No," Eva chuckled. "Why would I deny her anything?"

"So tell me, Miss Eva," Earl teased, using Zoe's favourite nickname for her partner, "how could I?"

"You're not married to her," Eva replied with a quirky grin.

"This is true. But if I was married to her, I would give her everything she wanted. You have a gold mine there, mate."

Eva nodded her head, fully aware of how much of a gift Zoe was to her. "I know." After a beat, Eva turned Earl's face towards her. "Earl, don't give up on Dave."

"I'm not, mate. I think Dave is giving up on me," Earl replied and stared out the window. What he wanted to do was have a good long talk with Dave, but he couldn't have one if the man wouldn't even sit down and discuss it with him.

Eva leaned over and kissed him tenderly on the cheek. "You want some company tonight?"

"Nah, it's okay. Dave might be home."

"Okay. Call me if you need me, okay?"

"Yeah," Earl nodded. Eva kissed him goodbye and, with a deep sigh, he watched her walk away.

Eva watched the car speed away, worried about her friend's state of mind. She hoped he and Dave could talk out their problems. She turned and walked towards her father, who was working on the old motorcycle.

"So, you've met Mabel," she greeted her father as he scraped the remaining paint from the body.

"I used to have a bike like this," Panayiotis enthused. "Brings back memories!"

Eva rolled her eyes; she didn't know what the attraction was with this motorcycle. Her father was in love. "You did?"

"Oh yeah. Just after the Great War ended, I would zip around Larissa in one. Had the sidecar too." He smiled at his daughter. "I would take your mother up to Thessaloniki in it, and we would spend the day. Ah, the memories!"

"You took mutti in that thing?"

Panayiotis laughed. "Yeah, she was a skinny thing; but she was tall, like you, so she scraped her knees a bit when she got in."

Eva shook her head and patted her father on the back. "I see Zoe has won you over."

"Won me over? Eva, this is a classic motorcycle! Wait until I clean off the rust and repaint it. Zoe wanted it hot pink and black, but I've convinced her to restore it to its original colour."

Eva rolled her eyes again. "Yes, Father," she said patronizingly, and left her father to tinker with the machine. She walked up the flight of stairs and entered their flat to find the table had been set beautifully, with two candles on either side.

"Zo, I'm home!"

"In here," Zoe's voice came from the bedroom. She came out wearing a white shirt and black pants. Eva was surprised to find Zoe wearing makeup. She handed her the flowers. "Thank you for today, Zoe. You look great. Elena helped you with the makeup?" Eva asked as she tilted Zoe's face up and touched the tip of her nose.

"Yeah," Zoe replied and made a face. She wanted to look her best when she met Greta. She didn't want to be seen as a kid, even though she was eight years younger than Eva. She was quite sure Greta would be tall and willowy. She wasn't sure why she thought that, since Eva hadn't described her, but that's the mental image she'd formed. "Thank you for the flowers, they are beautiful," Zoe said, wrapping her arms around Eva's neck and bringing her down for a quick kiss.

"You didn't have to get dressed up, love."

"I know," she mumbled as Eva held her. Eva looked down at

the dark-haired woman in her arms and shook her head. "Zoe, I want you to be you, not something you think you should be. Okay?"

"Hmm. You think the makeup is too much?"

"No, it's nice; but it's not you."

Zoe looked up and gave her wife a quirky grin. "Okay," she said and spun around and went back into the bedroom to remove it.

Eva followed her to the bedroom and leaned against the door. "I think Earl is going to need us soon."

"How come?" Zoe asked as she used a tissue to remove the excess makeup from her face. Then she cut off one of the flowers and stuck it behind her ear.

"I think Earl and Dave are going to split."

Zoe turned around and grimaced. "Oh, poor Wiggy. What can we do?"

"Nothing at the moment, love. Just be there for him when he needs us."

"How about we invite him to dinner tomorrow?"

"That sounds good. Speaking of dinner, I'll go and have a bath and then get ready."

"Need any help?" Zoe volunteered and waggled her eyebrows in the mirror at Eva.

"I would love the help, but I don't think I could have a bath and be ready on time if you 'helped' me," Eva grinned.

"It was worth a shot," Zoe muttered to herself as Eva went into the bathroom.

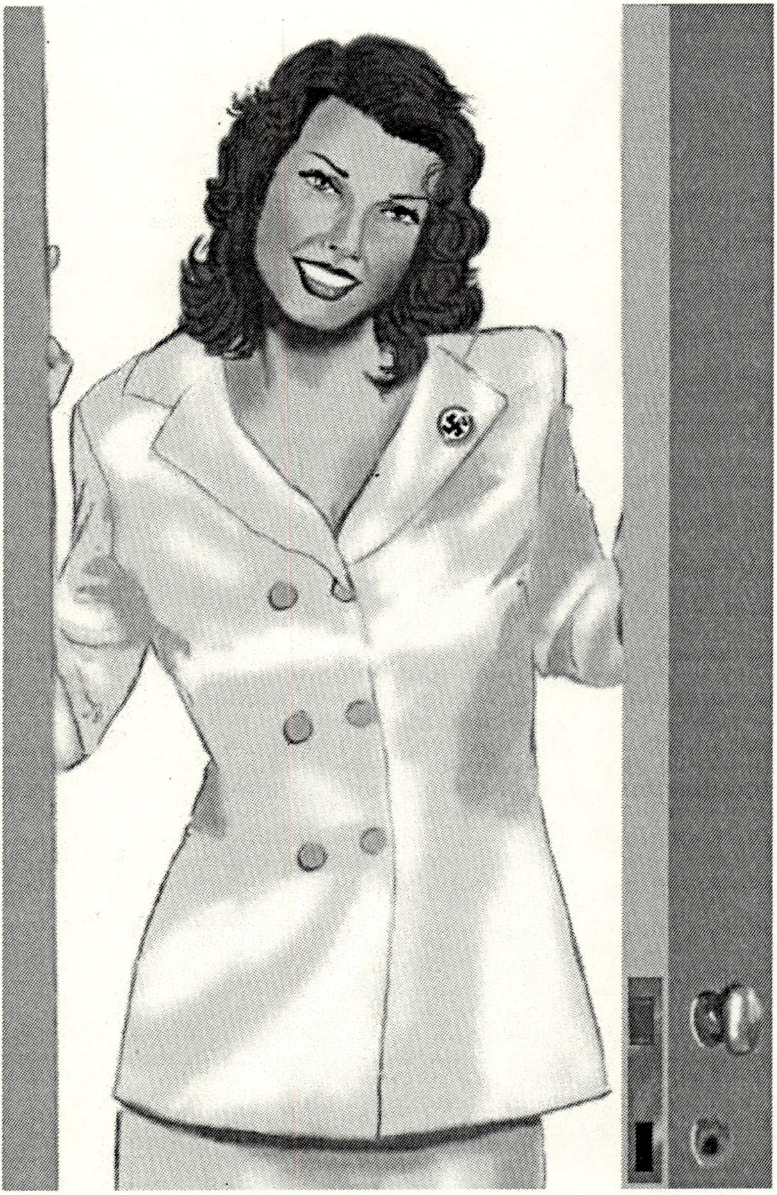

Chapter 8

Zoe put the telephone handset back on the cradle and went to the bedroom where Eva was finishing getting dressed. She sat on the bed, watching her partner comb her hair.

"Dad just called. He asked if you could go down, something about an immigration letter he needs to be taken with you tomorrow?"

"Yeah, he told me this morning," Eva said as she checked herself in the mirror. "I won't be long." She picked up the towel she'd had on when she came out of the bathroom and put it in the laundry basket.

Eva took another look around the flat to make sure everything was neat and tidy, then kissed Zoe and opened the door to leave, startling Elena who was about to knock. She grinned and moved aside to let the younger woman inside before she left.

"Hi, El, what's up?" Zoe asked, seeing her friend's perplexed face.

"I got a letter from Friedrich."

"This is a good thing, isn't it?"

"Um, yeah...I guess. I mean, I don't know," Elena stammered. She handed the letter to Zoe who took it and looked at both sides, only to find them both empty.

"Unless Friedrich is playing at being a spy and writing in invisible ink, I can't see anything."

"Me either."

Zoe chuckled. "Do you think he put the wrong piece of

paper in the envelope?"

Elena nodded. Friedrich had told her he was sending her a letter, but when she got it and found the blank page, she wasn't sure what it meant.

"So are you ready for tonight?" Elena asked her friend.

"Well, yeah, sort of. How often do you meet your partner's first lover?"

"Not often."

Zoe grimaced. "Yeah, not often. Well I hope I don't make a complete ass of myself."

"Don't worry you'll be fine," Elena reassured her.

"So are *you* ready for tonight?" Zoe asked, posing the same question.

"Well, yeah, sort of," Elena replied, mimicking Zoe and causing the two friends to laugh.

❖❖❖❖❖❖❖

Greta was nervous. She didn't know why she was nervous; after all, this was just Eva she was going to see. She held the piece of paper with the address in her hand and looked up at the building, unimpressed with the area. She wondered what had possessed Major Muller to move into a middle class suburb.

She had paid the taxi cab to stop further up the street so she could compose herself, checking her hair and makeup in the hand held mirror and straightening the long white skirt. Greta knew that the strawberry coloured shirt with the tiny gold swastika on the lapel flattered her colouring, but still she had received very strange looks from the taxi driver. "Probably a Jew," she muttered. For reassurance, she fingered her pendant—set with two diamonds and a ruby—and smiled at the memory of the gift Eva had given her all those years ago.

The clouds that threatened a downpour parted and slivers of sunshine peeked through, causing Greta to smile. She walked hand in hand with Eva to their chestnut tree. It had become a joke shared between them.

The previous day they had made love for the first time under the huge branches of the chestnut tree and then spent hours talking and getting to know each other. They talked about their hopes and dreams. It was 1937, and the world was theirs for the taking.

"Greta, um," Eva began, turning to her lover as a blush coloured her cheeks.

Greta was amused. Eva's blue eyes sparkled, and Greta thought she had never seen a more beautiful woman. "Yes, my little squirrel?"

Eva laughed at the nickname she had been given by her lover. "It's not my fault I scared that squirrel."

Greta tried to smother the laugh that was threatening to burst forth, but lost the battle and held on to Eva. Then she put her arms around the dark-haired beauty and they kissed with such passion that Greta found herself going weak at the knees. "You wanted to tell me something?" she asked Eva who was looking at her with those smoldering blue eyes.

Eva fumbled about, took out a tiny box, and opened it. "I want you to have this. Um...the two diamonds are us, and the ruby is...um..." Eva blushed, "it's for our passion," she finished quietly, looking into Greta's eyes. "I want you to wear it and never forget my love for you."

"Oh, darling, I could never forget you. You are the most beautiful creature God put on this earth. I promise to wear it always; and whenever I look at it, I'll close my eyes and see your beautiful face." Greta kissed the young woman and held Eva tight, praying to whatever God wanted to listen that she was going to love this woman until the day she died.

Greta sighed. She swallowed the lump in her throat that particular memory had caused. She checked herself again, but before she could move she noticed a man hurriedly passing her. She checked her watch and realised she was half an hour early. She wondered if she should wait, but dismissed the idea. She had waited too many years.

She walked purposefully to the building and rechecked her paper for the correct flat number. Walking up the flight of stairs and finding the correct flat, she knocked.

The door was opened by a young woman of an obvious ethnic origin. Greta blinked. She hadn't been expecting a Jew to open the door. Maybe she had the wrong flat number after all.

"I'm sorry, I was looking for the Muller residence," Greta apologized.

Elena was surprised to see the woman and was about to answer when her eye caught the swastika pin and she froze.

"Did you hear me, little girl?" Greta asked more forcibly.

"Hey, El, who's at the door?" Zoe's voice drifted out from the kitchen.

"I'm looking for the Muller residence. Do you know where it is?" Greta said very slowly in German. She thought the young girl might be retarded from the way she was looking at her. She then noticed the woman's tattooed inner arm and scowled. A concentration camp inmate. She should have noticed that right off. They were slow and stupid.

Another young woman came to the door and totally ignored her. Greta rolled her eyes and watched as the newcomer talked to the retarded woman. "Hey, El, are you okay?"

Elena nodded and walked back into the flat, leaving Zoe to deal with the woman at the door. Zoe turned her attention away from her distressed friend to the visitor.

"I'm looking for the Muller residence," Greta repeated in English.

Zoe looked at the woman with a scowl. She had just noticed the swastika and realised why Elena had fallen apart. "You are looking for Eva?" Zoe said in German.

"Finally! Someone who can understand what I'm saying," Greta said and smiled. Elena brushed past her and down the corridor.

"Please come in," Zoe said, trying to act the hospitable hostess. "Excuse me for a moment?" she asked, not waiting for a reply before following her friend out the door.

Greta went in and sat on the sofa, looking very bewildered.

Zoe rushed to Elena's flat. Her door was open and she was huddled on the floor, her back to the sofa, crying softly.

"Hey." Zoe held her friend and rubbed her back.

"I'm sorry, Zo. I lost it."

"It's okay," Zoe comforted her friend. She was angry that their visitor was totally clueless about the significance of that flag, and that she chose to wear it in a country that abhorred the Nazis. She found she disliked the woman already.

"I'm okay. Go see to your guest. She probably thinks we are both retarded," Elena said and sniffed.

Zoe wiped the tears away from her friend's face. "No. She can sit there and stew, for all I care."

"Um, hi," Friedrich said through the open door, uncertain if he should enter.

Zoe grinned. "You have perfect timing, Friedrich." She ushered the man inside and told him why Elena was upset.

"Thanks, Zoe."

Zoe went to Elena and gave her a peck on the cheek. "I'll talk to you tomorrow, okay?"

Elena nodded and watched as Zoe left the flat and closed the door. Friedrich dropped down to his knees, and Elena fell into his embrace. They stayed in that position with Friedrich holding her.

"I love you," Friedrich said and smiled. In return, he was rewarded with the brightest smile he had ever seen.

❖❖❖❖❖❖❖

Greta was angry. She was sitting in a flat by herself. That rude child had left her alone, and she had no idea what was going on. She wondered if that dark-haired child worked for Hans and Eva. She would get her sacked if she did.

She looked around the flat and grimaced. It was tiny. She would ask Eva's father why they couldn't find better accommodations, like she and Heinrich had done.

"A little beneath you, Eva," she muttered.

❖❖❖❖❖❖❖

Zoe closed the door to Elena's flat and exhaled. She decided to walk down to her father-in-law's unit and let Eva know that Greta had arrived early. Turning, she was greeted by the welcome sight of her wife coming up the stairs. She hurried over and hugged her.

"Hey, I don't mind a hug, but what's the matter?" Eva asked as she stroked Zoe's cheek.

"Greta's arrived."

"Oh. Where is she?"

"Inside the flat."

"Then why are you out here?"

Zoe sighed. "She has a swastika pin on, Evy. Elena opened the door and saw it and lost it."

Eva was horrified. Greta must surely have known that the image of that flag was viewed with much hatred. She couldn't understand what had possessed her former lover to even put it on. "Is Elena all right?"

"Yeah. Friedrich is with her."

"I'm sorry, Zo. I didn't—"

Zoe looked up in her partner's distressed face. "How could you know, love? It was just a little on the shocking side."

"Are you okay?" Eva asked, holding her wife. She didn't care that they were in the corridor; her main concern was Zoe.

Zoe nodded. "I was a little shaken, but it's okay."

"I'll ask her to remove it. I don't want to see that symbol in our home."

Zoe smiled up and met Eva's eyes. "You know something, Miss Eva? I think I love you. I'll try and behave myself."

Eva responded with a gentle kiss. "Ready?"

Zoe nodded. Eva took Zoe's hand and opened the door to their flat.

❖❖❖❖❖❖❖

Greta stood as the door opened and Eva walked through, together with that annoying child. Greta was not impressed with her.

"Eva!" Greta greeted her long lost lover enthusiastically, crossing to kiss Eva on the cheek.

Zoe scowled. Eva held her hand and squeezed tightly.

"Welcome to our home, Greta."

"Thank you, my dear," Greta replied, scowling at Zoe. "I must say, Eva, your hired help leaves a lot to be desired."

Eva frowned and looked down at Zoe. "I think you've got the wrong idea, Greta."

"Nonsense, Eva. Your maid left me here sitting like a dolt, while that silly Jew was crying her eyes out. All I did was ask her if this was where you lived—"

"Greta, I think we need to tell you—"

"Eva, you don't have to apologize for the hired help."

Zoe had had enough. Greta talked over Eva, which annoyed Zoe a great deal; and she was much too pushy for her tastes. Eva looked down and noticed the chagrined look. She looked back to Greta, who hadn't stopped talking, and knew that Zoe was about to tear into the woman if she didn't do something to shut Greta up and stop Zoe from going on the attack.

"Greta!" Eva raised her voice to quiet the woman down, surprising both Greta and Zoe. Zoe smirked, while Greta had a shocked expression on her face. "Sit down...please."

Greta sat down immediately. She wasn't expecting the once shy and reserved Eva to raise her voice. This was something new. She could see a change in her former lover that she found rather unsettling.

Before anyone could say anything further, they heard a knock on the door. Zoe rolled her eyes and went to answer it. Panayiotis stood there in his grey overalls. He had been enjoying himself so thoroughly with Zoe's motorcycle that he had forgotten to give the keys back.

"Oh...I'm sorry I interrupted you," the former priest apologized, seeing the girls had a visitor. He mentally chastised himself when he realised it was Greta.

"No, Father, perfect timing," Eva said, and taking her father by his hand and tugging him in. Zoe continued to smirk in the background. "Greta, this is my father, Panayiotis Haralambos, Father, this is Greta Strauss."

Panayiotis smiled and offered his hand. "I'm pleased to meet you, Miss Strauss."

Greta looked at the extended appendage with distaste and confusion. She looked between Eva and Panayiotis. "I thought Hans Muller was your father."

"I think I'll leave you to it. Good evening, Miss Strauss. It was a pleasure to meet you," Panayiotis said, handing the keys of the motorcycle to Zoe, who grimaced at him as he left.

"I don't understand, Squirrel, what's going on?"

Eva couldn't help herself, she grinned. She sat down next to Greta, and Zoe sat on the arm of the sofa looking anything but comfortable.

"I haven't heard that nickname in over eight years," Eva said quietly.

"What does that mean?" Zoe asked, earning another scowl from Greta. Zoe answered with a scowl of her own. She was getting very annoyed by the woman's dirty looks.

Eva blushed. Zoe's eyebrows went into her bangs as a smile spread across her face. "Oh, Miss Eva, you have some tales to tell me later," Zoe joked with her partner.

"Eva, what is going on?" Greta demanded, and Zoe turned to her with a frown.

Eva took a deep breath. "Well, it's a long story, but firstly I have to tell you—I'm married."

"You're married?" Greta's voice went an octave higher in total surprise.

"I am."

"Where is he?" Greta asked, looking around the small flat.

"She's right here." Eva took Zoe's hand. "Greta, this is my wife, Zoe."

Greta was shocked. She had never expected this. The woman in front of her was only a child. "Robbing the cradle, aren't we?"

Eva prevented Zoe from doing anything physical by holding her hand tightly, but she could sense Zoe was about to launch a verbal assault. "I don't think I'm robbing the cradle. That is such a crude term," Eva responded.

Greta couldn't believe it. The child now sat on Eva's lap, which totally annoyed her. She finally addressed Zoe. "You're not German?"

"No, I'm Greek," Zoe answered back in Greta's native tongue, "but I've had plenty of practice in speaking German."

"So, Eva, where did you pick her up?"

Eva couldn't hold Zoe back. She tried, but it looked as if Greta wanted a verbal battle and Zoe was going to give it to her. She sat back and shook her head with a wry smile. Greta was in over her head this time.

"She didn't pick me up from anywhere. I picked her up," Zoe responded, eliciting a raised eyebrow from Eva. "Well, I did. Remember when I wanted to kill you? It was my master plan to get close, then whammo!" Zoe said, and planted a kiss on Eva's lips. "Got what I wanted, thank you very much."

"I'm sorry. I don't understand," Greta said, still looking extremely confused.

"Okay, let me help you. But first could you please do us the courtesy of removing that pin?"

Greta looked down at the swastika and then back up at Zoe. "Why? It's gold plated and very valuable."

Eva sighed. "Greta, that image represents something we abhor, and we don't wish to have it in our home," Eva clarified as she squeezed Zoe's hand.

"You abhor what our Fuhrer believed? *You*?" Greta was incredulous. "You were in the Hitler Youth with me. How can you say that? What kind of German are you?"

"I'm not German," Eva replied.

"Eva, I'm back to being confused. You're as German as I am."

"Actually, I'm not. But before I tell you about it, please remove the pin and put it in your bag or pocket."

Greta sighed and took off the pin. She kissed the swastika,

which made Zoe feel ill. Greta opened her handbag and put the pin inside. "Happy now? This certainly isn't what I thought the evening would be like."

"What did you think the evening would be like?" Zoe asked, moving from Eva's lap and bringing a chair over to sit next to her partner.

"I thought I would spend some time getting reacquainted with my lover," Greta said with a smile.

"Ain't gonna happen," Zoe muttered.

Greta made a decision to see how far she could push this child and where it would lead. She needed to salvage the situation. She was the adult here, and Eva's lover; and if someone was going to be with Eva, it would be her. What the child didn't know was that she was declaring war, and the victor got the ultimate prize. Greta smiled. "Afraid of the competition?" she joked.

"I'm sorry, I wasn't under the impression I was in competition for my wife's affections," Zoe replied and then smiled sweetly.

Greta chuckled. "Of course not." She turned to Eva who had a bemused look on her face. "So, Eva, tell me what is going on, apart from you being married to Chloe."

"My name is Zoe."

"I'm sorry, Zoe. I used to have a maid called Chloe," Greta apologised. "How long have you been married?"

"Eight months," Eva replied. "We met in Greece when my stepfather was stationed in Larissa."

"Hans Muller is your stepfather?"

Eva nodded. "I found out the night my mother died," she added quietly.

"Oh, I'm so sorry, Eva. I had no idea. When did this happen?"

"November 8, 1938."

"Oh," Greta said, looking at the woman she had thought she knew. Eva had changed. She was more worldly. "So you were in Greece during the war?"

"Yes. Larissa."

"Never heard of it," Greta replied. She had traveled to Greece before the war. She was an amateur archaeologist and, of course, had to visit Athens and the Acropolis. "Was it a little backwater village?"

Zoe kept her mouth shut, knowing she was being baited.

"Actually it was quite an important village. It's situated between Athens and Thessaloniki, so it was a vital supply line during the war. That's where I found out my father was the local priest."

Zoe knew Eva added the last part for shock value, and it worked. Greta's eyes went round.

"Your father is a priest?"

"Was a priest. He found love, and now he's married to Alberta and they live downstairs," Zoe added quite seriously.

"This is getting weirder. So how did you two get together?"

"I wanted to kill her," Zoe said with a grin, eliciting a horrified look from Greta. "Didn't work out."

"Why? I mean I can see it didn't, but what happened?" Greta was genuinely interested.

"I thought she was a cold blooded Nazi," Zoe explained seriously. "My family was killed by the Nazis, Greta, and I wanted my revenge."

"Oh."

"I found out she wasn't a cold blooded Nazi, which was really good because I fell for her." Zoe gave Eva a grin. "So where were you during the war?"

Greta smiled at the young woman. "I was a cold blooded Nazi," she tried to joke.

Zoe kept the smile pasted on her face. "Well it's a good thing you weren't in Larissa instead of Eva."

Greta chuckled. "You would have killed me?" Greta asked, not quite believing that this child would have been able to do anything of the sort.

"In a heartbeat," Zoe replied.

"I think we are getting a little too serious," Eva interjected, putting her arm around Zoe's waist. "Why don't we have dinner?"

They got up from the lounge room and went to the dining table. Zoe went into the kitchen and brought out the meal, while Eva uncorked a bottle of wine and poured Greta a glass.

❖❖❖❖❖❖❖

Greta sipped her wine and looked over at the two women. They were seated side by side. Occasionally Zoe would push her vegetables to the side, and Eva would push them back. She found it odd behavior.

"I take it you don't like vegetables?" Greta asked with a hint of a smirk.

"No, not much," Zoe said as she looked sideways at Eva, who was grinning.

Greta turned to Eva. "So tell me, Eva, whatever happened to your stepfather?"

"He was arrested for war crimes," Eva replied evenly, wiping her mouth with her serviette.

"What? Why?"

"Because he killed innocent people," Zoe replied.

Greta snorted. "Were they innocent? No one gets killed because they were innocent."

"Is that right?" Zoe asked, cocking her head to the side.

"Of course. People choose which side to support. Only babies are innocent. They don't have the ability to decide. You wanted to kill Germans, didn't you?"

"Yes, but..."

"Of course you did. That's why resistance groups sprang up like mushrooms. No one is an innocent during war. Do you consider Churchill a war hero?"

"Not in the true sense of the word. He rallied his people, and that makes him a hero to them," Zoe replied, sipping her tea.

"I think Churchill is a war criminal rather than a hero. He killed those innocents you referred to in Dresden. I was there, and I saw with my own eyes the death and destruction. Where is he now? He is venerated and worshipped by the masses because of his 'heroic' deeds. The victor writes the history of the battle, Zoe."

Zoe was stunned. She couldn't believe she was having this conversation with this woman, and she couldn't believe this woman's total denial of the atrocities committed by the Germans.

"Hitler bombed London, also killing women and children. Is he a hero to you?" Zoe asked.

"Zoe, you don't understand. Adolph Hitler was the best thing to happen to Germany. He had the solution to Germany's problems."

"The solution was to start a war that killed millions," Zoe muttered.

"Hitler didn't kill millions. That's nonsense," Greta scoffed.

"What about the millions of Jews that died?" Eva asked, taking Greta by surprise. She was certainly not expecting her former lover to even care about Jews.

"Millions? Hardly. Concentration camps were set up so they could work for the Fatherland. They were treated humanely."

Zoe was dumbfounded. "Do you honestly believe that no Jews died in the concentration camps? *None*?"

"Oh, don't be silly, of course they died. The old and sick die every day, and it happened in the camps too."

"So millions died a natural death in those camps?" Eva asked.

"Millions? Where did you get that figure from?"

"The Allies."

"Oh, please. Eva, you of all people should be aware of your history. As I said, the victor writes the history books. Facts have nothing to do with what is written; and in years to come, the truth of what happened in those camps will come to light."

"It already has. The Nazis murdered millions of people, innocent people, because of their race." Zoe was now angry, and she directed her anger toward the smug looking woman across from her.

Greta snorted and shook her head. "Zoe, you are so ill-informed. There is no proof that 'millions' of Jews died."

Eva put a calming hand on Zoe's shoulder, realising her partner was getting upset. "Why don't we get some dessert?" she whispered to Zoe. Zoe nodded and got up and went into the kitchen. Eva watched her go, then turned back to Greta who had a smirk on her face. "Greta, I don't think spouting Nazi propaganda at Zoe is going to make this dinner enjoyable for either of us," Eva said angrily. "Zoe's entire family was killed during the war. I'm not sure what you are trying to do, but knock it off. Excuse me for a moment," Eva said and walked into the kitchen.

Zoe stood, head bowed, near the sink. The cheesecake was forgotten as she was overcome with anger and frustration at this woman's delusion. Eva put her arms around her partner and kissed the top of her head. "Are you okay?"

Zoe shook her head. "She can't believe those lies, can she?" Zoe looked up, the tears tracking down her face. Eva brushed them away and kissed her. "I'm sorry, Evy, I tried."

"I know you did, love. Thank you for making the effort."

"Go back outside. It's rude to keep our guest waiting," Zoe said, wiping away the remaining tears.

"Not until I know you're okay."

"I'm okay. Can we talk about this later?"

Eva nodded and gave her a quick kiss before taking the cheesecake out with her. She placed it on the table. Eva gave Greta a warning look before Zoe brought out the plates.

"I'm sorry I upset you, Zoe," Greta said as Zoe sat down. "I think I should have listened to what my father said many years ago. He told me not to discuss politics or religion at the dinner table."

"Good advice," Zoe mumbled.

"Do you still paint, Eva?" Greta asked, in an effort to move the conversation in another direction.

"Occasionally, but nowadays I tend to get painted," Eva said, grinning at Zoe. "Zoe is a very talented artist."

"So, you did that piece?" Greta and asked, pointing to the portrait of Eva reading a book.

"Yes. Eva sat patiently for me."

"That's a very nice portrait."

"Thank you," Zoe said quietly. "Drawing relaxes me."

"Hmm, much like music. I do enjoy a good opera," Greta said with a smile. "Oh, Eva, do you remember when we went and saw *Romeo and Juliet*?"

"Remember it? I think I won't ever forget it." Eva laughed. She turned to Zoe who had a puzzled look on her face. "It was so bad, half the audience left and the other half stayed to see how bad it would get."

"Which half were you in?"

"We staye.!" Eva said. "Romeo couldn't remember his lines; Juliet fell off her balcony; and it got worse."

Greta wiped away the tears that were streaming down her face from her remembrances of that evening. "We had to stay. We spent good money for it."

"Oh God, don't remind me." Eva said as she recalled the odd jobs she did for her stepfather in order to get the money to go and see the performance.

"Do you like opera, Zoe?" Greta asked.

"I love opera," Zoe said with a smile. "My favourite is *L'Africaine*."

"*You* love opera?"

Zoe looked at Eva and grinned. "One of the many things I've come to love. Since we've been here, we've gone and seen *La Boheme*, *Lucia di Lammermoor*, and *L'Africaine*. I just wish we had a decent opera house to watch them in. In Egypt we saw *Aida*. What an absolutely wonderful production. A little lacking in the costuming, but it made up for it with the pyramids in the background."

"I didn't think you would be an opera fan, Zoe. I thought you would interested in *bebop,*" Greta admitted.

Zoe shrugged. "Well, when I get interested in something, I don't do things in half measures. I fell in love with Eva, I married her." Eva gave her a smirk, but didn't want to interrupt her. She knew that when Zoe got passionate about a topic, she put everything into it. She wasn't going to remind her wife that it was Eva who had done the proposing. "Eva introduced me to opera, and I loved it."

Eva chuckled. "I love jazz."

"*You*? You hated jazz!" Greta said incredulously.

"I didn't hear the right people performing it," Eva replied and squeezed Zoe's hand under the table. "Zoe introduced me to Ella Fitzgerald, Billie Holiday and Jack Teargarden."

"That's amazing. You used to think jazz was for peasants."

"My tastes improved," Eva replied.

Greta looked at her watch and sighed. "I would love to continue chatting with you, but Heinrich is waiting for me. Thank you for the wonderful dinner. Maybe we can do this again some time?"

They all walked to the door, and Zoe handed Greta her coat and gave her a weak smile. "Thank you for coming."

"I think maybe next time we avoid politics at dinner," Greta suggested and ruffled Zoe's hair. Zoe brushed her hair back into place and plastered a smile on her face despite her annoyance.

"It was good seeing you again, Eva." She kissed Eva on the cheek. "I've missed you."

They said their good-byes and Eva closed the door, then turned. "Come here," Eva asked, and Zoe fell into her embrace. "I love you and thank you," Eva whispered to her partner, getting a hug in return.

Chapter 9

Zoe exhaled. She was sitting on the sofa in Eva's embrace. The verbal altercation with Greta had tired her out. She didn't mind an honest debate, but when someone was so dogmatic about their stance it was a waste of time and energy. She closed her eyes and lay in Eva's arms.

"I don't like her," Zoe mumbled.

"I know, love."

"Was she always like this?"

"No, she was very funloving and carefree. I think the war changed her." Eva took Zoe's hand and held it. "I think the war has changed us all."

"How did you change?"

"Do you remember when you asked me about my dreams for after the war?"

"Yeah," Zoe replied. They had been sitting in Eva's office. She believed Eva was a Nazi and was determined to kill her, needing only to get close enough so that she could exact her vengeance. Surprised to find the woman was working for the Resistance, Zoe had wondered what motivated her. "I remember."

"I had no dreams. I doubted very much whether I was going to see the end of the war. I realised that I was alone, and no one was going to want me with my...with my scars and other stuff."

"Other stuff?"

Eva looked down at the dark head rested on her chest and sighed. "I can't have children. Who would want a barren wife?"

Zoe looked up and met Eva's eyes. "I would." She reached

up and caressed Eva's cheek.

Eva smiled, leaned into Zoe, and kissed her. "I didn't know what I was going to do. Then you walked into my life, and for the first time in eight years, I had some hope. I wasn't sure how we would survive, but I had someone to walk with me."

"I've always said I have good timing," Zoe replied, trying to lighten the mood.

Eva chuckled. "You have excellent timing. Do you know when I noticed you?"

"You noticed me?"

"I tend to notice people that hit me with stones, and I definitely noticed you," Eva teased.

Zoe laughed. She had been outside her apartment watching the German patrols and had seen Eva walk by with two guards protecting her. Zoe wasn't sure what possessed her, but she picked up a rock and threw it at Eva, hitting her arm.

"I didn't hurt you, did I?" Zoe asked solicitously, patting her on the arm.

"Well, you did a bit," Eva replied with a mock pout.

Zoe grinned and kissed her arm. "You didn't let your shadows come after me...I've always wondered about that."

"No. Want to know why?"

"Oh please, do tell," Zoe asked, snuggling closer.

"I was in Father's office when you came into the church the day he asked you about coming to work for me. He had already told me you were feisty, and that you wouldn't be too friendly, I didn't see you, but I heard you. I fully expected you to turn him down. Later, when you threw that rock and I saw you, I finally realised who you were."

"Turn down the opportunity of working for the most gorgeous woman in Larissa? No way I was turning that down," Zoe joked. "I'm a friendly sort of gal. Hey, I didn't speak that day, so how did you know it was me?"

"Yeah, very friendly; I had the bruise to prove it." Eva chuckled clutching her shoulder. "How many feisty, unfriendly, green-eyed young women were there in Larissa?"

"I don't know. Did you go in search of green-eyed, feisty women?"

"Didn't have to, you came to me." Eva shook her head and joined in her partner's chuckles over their first meeting. "Come on, I think I've had enough of going down memory lane. Let's go to bed."

"What about the washing up?"

"Tomorrow," Eva said, and taking Zoe's hand, she turned off the lights and they went into the bedroom.

❖ ❖ ❖ ❖ ❖ ❖ ❖

Brushing away her tears, Elena put her head on Friedrich's shoulder. She felt so safe in his arms. At first Friedrich had been shocked at her story about her time in the concentration camp. But he loved Elena and was determined to be supportive, even if that meant waiting for as long as Elena wanted.

"I love you, Elena, and I'll be here for you. Um...I'm not good with words, but—"

Elena hugged him. "Words are overrated."

Friedrich grinned and kissed the top of her head. "You know, you are the first woman who has ever said that to me."

"How many have you talked to?" Elena teased.

"I've had dates before. David would set them up. Great disasters," he chuckled. "I spent so much time trying to write that letter to you. You did get that, didn't you?"

Elena grinned. "I got a letter from you, but the paper inside was blank."

Friedrich was confused. "Huh? I'm sure I put that letter in the right envelope. Oh God!"

"What?"

"Oh God! El, I'm going to die tomorrow."

"Why? Where did you send it?"

"I made some notes for David. Oh damn, I left it on his desk!"

Elena couldn't help herself and laughed. "I'm sorry, that's so funny."

"Are you sure it didn't have anything on it?"

"Quite sure. It was blank."

"David might not go back to the office tonight, and I'll have time to get it off his desk," Friedrich said as he looked at his watch. "I have to get going, Elena. It's late."

"Stay the night," Elena said quietly.

"You...want me to stay?"

"I'm not ready to...you know...um...but if you want, we can snuggle together."

Friedrich smiled. "I'm very good at snuggling, much better than talking."

Elena hesitated for a moment, then put her arms around his neck and pulled him down and kissed him. "I think I love you, Friedrich."

She smiled as Friedrich turned pink. She got up and offered her hand, which he took tenderly, following her with a huge grin.

❖❖❖❖❖❖❖

Eva stirred and opened sleepy eyes. Looking at the clock, she saw it was only 2:00 a.m. and grimaced. She put her head down on her pillow again, and then she heard the banging. It stopped, and then started. Zoe was fast asleep cuddled up next to her. Waking Zoe wasn't something she wanted to do, so Eva slid out of bed quietly, put on her robe and slippers, and turned on the lights to the living room.

She looked through the spy hole in the door and didn't see anyone, but she knew someone was out there. She jumped back in surprise as the banging started again, and then stopped. She went back into the spare bedroom and picked up Zoe's cricket bat, hefting it and took a couple of practice swings. Taking a quick look to see that Zoe was still asleep, she closed the door to the bedroom and walked purposefully to the front door. With a deep breath, she swung it open. She was shocked to see the crumpled figure lying against the wall on the opposite side of the hallway, his long legs stuck out and taking up a good portion of the corridor.

"Matey! Evvaaaaaa! Come and hava...uh...drink!"

Earl sat on the carpet opposite her, very drunk. Two bottles lay at her feet and she realised where the banging had come from. Putting the bat down, she went to Earl and knelt beside her friend.

Eva could smell the alcohol and grimaced. "You're as drunk as a skunk."

"I stink, huh?"

"Yeah, you do. Come on, let's get you inside." Eva tried to get him up, but Earl was unmovable.

"Nah, leave me here. I like it here," Earl slurred, curling up on the carpet. Eva tried to move him, then felt a twinge of pain in her back and stopped. "That was smart, Eva," she said to herself. She straightened and put her hands on her back. "You are a big boy, Earl. I need some help." Eva went back inside to wake Zoe to help her get the big man inside.

She didn't want to wake her wife, but she couldn't move Earl alone; and she knew that if she tried again, she was sure to aggravate her back even more. Kneeling beside the bed, she caressed Zoe's cheek. "Zoe," she whispered.

"Huh?" Zoe grunted and snuggled closer to the pillow.

"Zoe, I need you, love."

"What for?" Zoe mumbled.

"Earl is outside. He's drunk, and we need to move him in out of the hallway," Eva said as she shook her a little.

Sleepy green eyes opened and Zoe frowned. "Did you say Earl is drunk?"

Eva nodded. "Come on, help me get him in."

"You didn't try to move him, did you?" Zoe asked as she struggled to wake up. When Eva didn't reply, she looked up and got a chagrined look. "Eva! He weighs a ton. Did you hurt yourself?"

"I wasn't thinking. I tried to move him and felt a twinge. I think I'm going to need your loving touch later," Eva said.

Zoe shook her head. "What am I going to do with you? Does it hurt?"

"I felt just a tiny twinge. I promise that you can do anything you want later," Eva said as she gave Zoe a conciliatory kiss. "Come on, let's get the drunk inside."

"Remind me about the 'anything you want' bit after," Zoe said and gave her wife a slap on the behind as she followed her out. Her eyes widened when she saw Earl asleep on the carpet.

"Hey, Wiggy, wake up." Zoe shook the big man, who stirred and opened his eyes.

He smiled up at Zoe. "Matey, Zo...Zo...Zoeee."

"Phew, you stink, old boy."

"That's what Eeevvvaaa said."

"Come on, let's get inside."

"Why?"

"Because I said so." Zoe growled in his ear. "Move it."

"Okay," Earl replied and struggled to his feet. Eva's eyebrows rose. Zoe took one arm and Eva the other. They struggled to keep him upright. Zoe felt him lean towards her, which was okay with her since it took a lot of the weight off Eva.

"You okay, love?" Zoe asked as they struggled inside.

"Yeah, but I'm going to suggest he lose some weight," Eva grumbled.

"Hey, Evaaaa...you look...um...nice."

Eva rolled her eyes. They managed to manoeuvre him to the sofa where he collapsed and curled up and fell asleep. They both stood watching him for a few moments.

"Leave him here, I doubt we can get him in to the spare bed," Eva said. She went into the spare bedroom, picked a blanket, put it over Earl and tucked it in.

"What do you think happened?"

"I think Dave may have been home, and I guess they finally talked," Eva said wryly.

"Poor Wiggy," Zoe responded, as she knelt by the sofa. She gave her a friend a kiss on the cheek. "I'll go to his flat tomorrow and get him a change of clothing." Zoe stood and turned to Eva, scowling. "Now, missy, what were you thinking, trying to move him by yourself?"

"I wasn't thinking, Zo."

"You can say that again. How are you feeling?"

"I think it was just a twinge. I'm okay."

"You sure?"

"Yep. Come on let's go to bed," Eva suggested, taking Zoe's hand.

Zoe put her arm around Eva's waist. "When are you going to learn to take care of yourself?"

"Zo, don't yell at me. It's okay. I didn't want to wake you."

Zoe looked at her and frowned. "I think we need to have a chat later."

"Yes, mum," Eva said meekly as she followed her wife to bed.

❖ ❖ ❖ ❖ ❖ ❖ ❖

The morning sun streamed through the window as Eva stirred. She tried to remember what day it was and realised it was Friday, the one day of the month that she was rostered off work. She really wanted to stay in bed and just snuggle up to Zoe, but she knew she had to get up and see to Earl, who would be nursing a hangover. She reluctantly let go of Zoe, put her robe on and quietly closed the door behind her. Earl was sitting up on the sofa and holding his head. Eva stood and watched him for a moment before going over and sitting down next to him and putting her arm over his broad shoulders.

"Do you want something for the headache?"

"Yeah, a gun."

"Don't have one of those, but I have some aspirin."
"Did I cause a fuss last night?"
"You don't remember?"
"Uh...no."
"Well, you went dancing down the corridor stark naked." Eva grinned, but stopped teasing her friend when she saw the look of total horror on his face. "Nah, I'm kidding."
"Oh God, Eva, you have one twisted sense of humour."
Eva went into the kitchen and poured him a glass of water, then took a couple of the painkillers and handed them to him.
"You make a quiet drunk, Earl. You threw a couple of empty bottles against the door to get our attention, and then you fell asleep in the corridor."
"Argh. So how did I end up here?"
"Well..."
"Oh damn, Eva, don't tell me you tried to move me? Please don't tell me that, because if you did I'm going to get an earful from Zoe..."
"Yeah, I did."
"I'm a dead man."
"Nah, I got a tongue lashing instead."
"Are you okay?"
"From Zoe? My behind is a little scorched, but my back is fine. Now, why did you get drunk?"
"Dave finally had that talk with me."
"It didn't go well?"
"You could say that. He said a few things that I didn't want to hear and then walked out; so I decided to drown my sorrows."
"Why didn't you come here?"
"You had your visitor. How would it have looked if I'd turned up?"
"It would have saved us from Greta's racist taunts and kept Zoe from getting upset."
"Argh. That sounds like it was a fun night."
"Oh yeah, thrilling."
The bedroom door opened and a very sleepy Zoe shuffled out, dressed only in a t-shirt and underpants. Her eyes were still half closed as she stumbled towards the bathroom.
Eva grinned as Earl covered his eyes. "Zoe," she called.
Zoe looked up and saw Earl and yelped. She ran back into the bedroom and slammed the door.
"Not so loud, Stretch." Earl yelled after her and then regret-

ted it. "Ow." He held his head until the earthquake in it stopped. "Hey, she's cute when she's just woken up."

Eva chuckled. "Yeah, she is."

A few moments later, the bedroom door opened again and Zoe came out wearing jeans and a red spotted white shirt that she had tied at the waist. "I forgot you were here." She went over and sat by Earl's side. "So, big guy, you got a little sloshed last night."

"Sloshed is a good word."

"Yeah, so is stinky," Zoe said as she sniffed. Earl stuck out his tongue. "Where're your keys?"

"You're not driving the beast."

"I have wheels."

"Oh, I forgot about Mabel." Earl searched his pockets until he found his keys. "Where are you going?"

"To your place to pick you up a change of clothes."

"Oh." he handed the keys to Zoe, who got up and patted him on the shoulder. Eva held the door open for her. "Drive safely," she admonished her wife, who rewarded her concern with a quick kiss.

Zoe tossed the keys in the air and caught them again as the door closed. As she started up the hallway, Elena's door opened and Friedrich walked out. Zoe stopped and her eyebrows went up in total surprise at seeing the young man there so early in the morning.

"Good morning, Friedrich."

"Um...morning, Zoe," Friedrich stammered, blushing. Zoe smirked and stood there watching him.

"I'll see you tonight?" he said to Elena, and got a quick nod and a small kiss in response. He hurriedly bid farewell to Zoe and ran down the stairs.

Zoe went over to her friend and put an arm around her shoulders. "Anything you want to tell your best friend?"

Elena grinned. "You tell me about the Nazi bitch, and I'll tell you about Friedy."

"Friedy? Ohh do tell. Put some clothes on first. You can tell me while we go over to Earl's and pick up some clothes."

"Why are we going there?"

"Earl got drunk last night, and he stinks to high heaven."

Zoe waited until Elena had dressed, and the two friends walked down the stairs to Zoe's motorcycle in animated conversation about the previous night's events.

Chapter 10

David pushed open the door to his office, dropped his briefcase next to his desk and took off his jacket. He took a sip from the mug of water he had brought with him from the tiny office kitchen. He had a long day ahead of him. They had received word that the Latvian they were after had escaped and was probably already halfway to Brazil. They had been close to catching him, but someone had tipped him off. He sat looking through the file for a few moments before his eye was caught by a letter addressed to him. He picked up the letter opener and slid it through the envelope.

The door opened and a very frazzled looking Friedrich came in, his suit a little crumpled and his hair messed up. Not the usual way David saw his friend early in the morning.

"Good morning, sunshine, you look like you slept in your car again."

"David, please tell me you haven't opened the letter I sent you?"

David remained quiet and only smiled.

"Well, did you?"

"You told me not to tell you," David quipped and got a nasty look from his friend. He held up the envelope. "Is this the one?"

"Can I have it back?"

"Why?"

"It's personal," Friedrich replied, hoping David was going to just give in. Just once he wanted to win an argument with his friend.

"You sent it to me. See it has my name on it...David Peterson."

"I put it in the wrong envelope, okay?" Friedrich removed his jacket and loosened his tie, which got a surprised look from David.

"Ah. So was this supposed to go to Miss Elena Mannheim? Hmm?" He held the letter in his hands and took a sniff, hoping it was perfumed. He was most disappointed that it wasn't.

"If you must know, yes it was."

"About bloody time," David muttered and handed the letter back to a relieved Friedrich who shoved it in his pocket. "Did you sleep in the car again?"

"No," Friedrich replied and smiled broadly.

"Why are you so chirpy?"

"I told her," Friedrich replied, putting both of his hands in his pockets and rocking back and forth, which made David laugh.

"You told her? You mean you actually said the 'L' word?"

"Yep," Friedrich replied, feeling very proud of himself. "Sure did."

"Good boy. And did she run screaming off into the night?" David joked.

"No, you heathen, she didn't. She loves me back."

"Really? Were you sure it was Elena?"

Friedrich threw an eraser at him in mock outrage and grinned. "I stayed the night at her place."

"Whoohoo! He scores. There is hope for you yet."

"Oh, calm down. We didn't...you know..."

"The word is S-E-X. Say it with me. You know you can."

"I don't know why I like you, David."

"I'm charming, and I give you great advice about your love life. I'm actually very good for your love life." David winked at Friedrich who was shaking his head. "Okay, so you didn't have...you know. What did you do?"

"We talked and we cuddled."

"Cuddling is good, leads to 'you know.'"

Friedrich gave him a look and shook his head. "Elena went through a tough time in the concentration camps, and I think we need to take things a little slow," Friedrich said as he sat down.

David frowned. "Elena was in a concentration camp?"

"Yeah, Bergen."

"I was there when the Americans liberated Dachau," David

replied quietly, looking down at the desk. He had been with the British army which landed at Normandy, but was seconded to the 7th Army because of his language skills. Their German speaking officers had been killed, so David found himself working with the Americans.

Friedrich leaned against his own desk and waited for David to continue.

"The first thing I noticed was the stench. It smelled of death; we could smell it just going towards it." David stopped and took a sip of water. "You've seen the pictures. I saw it with my own eyes. The people who weren't dead looked like they had been starved. They looked so defeated, Friedrich. There was this one face I remember above all else. I don't know how old she was, but she looked young. We...we were putting the bodies on a truck to go and bury them, and I made the mistake of looking into this woman's face. Her eyes were open, and her brown eyes stared back at me, Friedrich."

David stopped and took a deep breath. "She must have seen such horrors before she died. I don't know who she was, just another murdered soul. Her eyes just looked at me. She weighed absolutely nothing, Friedrich. Nothing."

"How many?" Friedrich quietly asked.

David remained silent. The sound of cars passing and the clock ticking were the only sounds in the office as the two men sat in silence.

"I don't know, too many. I was sick from seeing all those bodies. Then I snapped. I couldn't take it any more and I turned, took the gun off my shoulder, and shot two of the camp guards. It was the first time in my life I'd killed another human being, Friedrich. It still didn't make me feel like these people got any justice."

"Is that why you started working here?"

David nodded. "I vowed to that young woman I would try and make them pay for what they had done. I'm doing my little bit, but it's not going to bring them back. Nothing will bring them back."

"My family was killed at Auschwitz," Friedrich said quietly as David raised his head and met Friedrich's eyes. "So...I am doing it for them. I vowed to fight for their justice too. I couldn't do anything to stop them from dying, but I can do something to bring their murderers to justice."

David wiped away the tears from his eyes with his handkerchief, then blew his nose. "There are times, Friedrich, when I wonder if what we are doing is enough. They will be tried in a court and given a fair trial. Doesn't seem like enough."

"One tiny drop of water can lead to a torrent," Friedrich replied. "It takes just one drop and then another and another. Eventually all those drops form a huge body of water."

David smiled. "So we're drops of water?"

"I believe so. If I work alone, I am but one single drop; but when I work with others with the same goals, we become a body of water. We can achieve a great deal."

"I like that analogy."

"Yeah, so do I. It was words of advice from an old man I spoke to recently. He told me that what we are doing is going to change mankind's attitude and bring to light what was kept hidden."

"Wise old geezer."

"Yeah, he is."

"So tell me, fellow drop of water, where's my letter then? Did Elena get it?"

"Elena said she got a blank piece of paper."

"What? Friedrich, you were in real la la land. Why did you send Elena a blank sheet of paper?"

"I didn't send her a blank piece of paper, I sent her the love letter I was writing. I sent you my findings on the immigrant list." He put his hand in his pocket and retrieved the letter he took from David, opening it up he found that it also was blank.

"This is a blank piece of paper," Friedrich said as he sat and smoothed out the letter on his desk. He looked up at David with a frown. He examined the envelope and found that it wasn't the envelope he had put the letter in the previous night. "This isn't my envelope."

"Oh goddammit, not another one! Jesus, I hate those bastards!" David swore. "Did you make a copy of the notes?"

"Of course I did." Friedrich picked up his briefcase and pulled out a file. He removed the carbon copy of his letter and gave it to David. "I think we have about six on that list that we need to bring in for some serious questioning."

David read off the list and came to the last name. "This list could be useless by now."

"Why?"

"Well, they had the original, right? They would have been tipped off. They could be anywhere by now."

❖❖❖❖❖❖❖

Earl was feeling much better after having a warm shower. He toweled his hair and walked out into the living room. Noticing that neither Eva nor Zoe was there, he went to the spare bedroom which doubled as the room for their art. Zoe was fixing up the spare single bed and moving some of the artwork off the bed.

"What are you doing?"

"Fixing the bed."

"I can see that. Did you and Eva have a blue?"

"Nup. This is for you."

"Zoe, I live only five minutes away."

"We don't want you to be by yourself," Zoe replied as she looked up at Earl and gave him a big grin. "You're staying with us for a few days."

"But, Zoe—"

"Eva said so, and when Eva says so, you listen."

"You don't listen when Eva says so."

"Sure I do."

Earl snorted and sat on the bed. "I don't want to hear squeaking coming from your room."

"Huh?"

"I woke up last night, and there was a massive squeak coming from your room."

"Squeaking? What are you talking about?"

Earl rolled his eyes. "Zoe, do I have to say it out loud?"

"Yes, I'm not very bright," Zoe joked.

"You and Eva were...you know..."

"Having sex? Horizontal dancing, making love...?"

"Zoe!" Earl cried out. He was taken aback by Zoe's descriptions. He wasn't a prudish man, but he'd never talked about sex with Zoe. Eva was usually on the receiving end of his jokes. He always treated Zoe like his little sister.

"Earl!" Zoe mimicked him and gave him a smirk.

"Stop it. You know what I mean."

"Our bed doesn't squeak."

"How do you know?"

"What do you mean, how do I know? It doesn't squeak. It was Mr and Mrs Timmins. Their bedroom adjoins this spare room. They have the squeaky bed."

"So why did you let me think it was you two?"

"You are so cute when you blush."

Earl shook his head and watched as Zoe put a pillowcase on the spare pillow. The room had been christened as the "art" room. It held Zoe's paint palettes and half finished pieces that were leaning against the wall. There was a sign on the wardrobe which caused Earl to grin. A crayon coloured sign that read "Enter Eva's Little Dark Corner" hung on the door to Eva's dark room. He turned the sign over and chuckled as he read aloud, "Enter at Your Own Risk." The signs were decorated with little characters that Zoe had drawn. Eva's photos were framed and hung on the wall all over the flat, as was Zoe's artwork. He especially liked the photograph of Zoe, standing alone with her back half turned to the camera, watching the sea at sunset.

Eva came into the bedroom wearing a light undershirt, which got Earl's eyebrows raised into his hairline. Eva gave him a grin. "Zoe, where is my green shirt?"

"I ironed it, yesterday," Zoe replied, and walked out to where she had half finished ironing their clothes and plucked the shirt from the hanger. Holding it out to Eva, she pulled it back when Eva went to get it. "A kiss will get you a shirt."

Eva grinned. "Is that right?"

"Yep." Zoe nodded her head and puckered up.

Eva leaned down and kissed her on the top of her head. Zoe gave her a mock scowl, but still handed the shirt over.

"Thanks, love," Eva said, starting to button it up. "A kissed head is still a kiss. You didn't say where." Eva chuckled at Zoe's expression. She turned to Earl who was looking fondly at them. "Whose bed is squeaking?"

He groaned loudly and fell onto the bed and covered his eyes.

"Earl thinks we were making passionate love, last night," Zoe replied. Sidling up to Eva and buttoning the shirt up, she tucked it into her skirt, getting a quick kiss for her efforts.

Eva grinned. "You heard Mr and Mrs Timmins. This bedroom and their bedroom have a very thin wall between them. That's why we took the other bedroom. Our bed doesn't squeak. I oiled it last week," Eva added knowing she was going to get Earl to blush, which he did.

"See, I told you it doesn't squeak."

"Hey, I have to get going. I'll see you tonight," Eva said to Earl who just remained on the bed and waved good-bye to his friend. Much to her dismay, Eva had received a call earlier asking her to come in to work that day. Two of the interpreters were off sick and they needed all the help they could get. Eva didn't want to go in on her day off, but she didn't have much of a choice.

Eva and Zoe walked to the door. Eva straightened her skirt and put on a light jacket, while Zoe picked up her briefcase and handed it to her.

"I'm really glad you're here today, I didn't want to leave him alone. I'm sorry."

"Don't worry, I'll give you a call later. You'll have another day off, and we can sleep in then," Zoe promised, giving her wife a kiss as she walked her out.

Chapter 11

The oppressive heat had caused the flat to become stuffy, so the door to the balcony was opened, allowing a slight breeze; and an electric fan whirled nosily in the background. Earl sat sprawled on the sofa, his long legs stretched out in front of him. His face was turned up to the ceiling with his eyes closed, and smoke from his cigarette drifted up from the ashtray which was perched precariously on his thigh.

Zoe had been watching him from the kitchen as she was making some tea. She wanted to say something to comfort her friend, but she didn't know what to say to him. Earl had been there for them when they needed him with the whole Muller fiasco. Zoe snorted at the thought of how it might have ended, had it not been for Earl.

She picked up the mugs and went into the living room, placing them on the low table and then picked up the ashtray from Earl's thigh and put it on the table as well.

"Hey, Earl, I brought you a cuppa." She patted him on the leg to get his attention.

Earl opened his eyes and gazed at his friend. "Thanks, Stretch." Taking the offered cup with both hands, he took a sip and looked back up to the ceiling.

"You want to talk about it?" Zoe asked, as she settled down on the carpet, sitting cross-legged and sipping her tea.

Earl twirled the cup, watching the tea for a moment. "Dave was jealous."

"Of what?"

"I wasn't spending enough time with him, and I was spending too much time with you two," Earl said. He picked up his cigarette and took a drag.

Zoe was surprised. "I'm sorry, Earl."

Earl shrugged his shoulders. "He told me that if I wanted to spend so much time with women, then I might as well go date them."

"That was nasty."

"That's a nice word for it, Zoe. Did you get jealous of Eva when she worked with me?"

"No, should I? I spend a lot of time with Elena. Eva doesn't make me choose between her and my friends. That's petty and childish."

"Petty and childish...yeah, that just about sums it up. When he told me how he felt, it was like he gutted me."

"Gutted?" Zoe asked, not familiar with the expression. Her English was good and she thought she understood what Earl meant, but she wasn't entirely sure.

Earl grinned. "Sorry. I mean that it totally devastated me, you know what I mean?"

Zoe took a deep breath. "Yeah, I do. When my mother was killed, all I wanted to do was crawl under a rock and hide."

"I'm sorry, Stretch, I didn't mean...I forgot."

"How were you to know?" Zoe asked, placing a comforting hand on his knee.

"Eva told me your family died. I should have remembered."

"Yeah, my two brothers died defending Greece in 1941 when the Italians invaded; and then Mihali, he was my older brother, died fighting the Germans," Zoe replied.

Her three brothers had been her best friends, and they had spent summers going down to the river to fish, or racing around the village in their go-carts with Zoe in the driver's seat and the three of them racing the other kids. It was an innocent time. Mihali was her hero. He was ten years older, and she followed him everywhere. She could still remember the day he left to face the German invasion.

It was quite a warm spring day. Zoe wanted to finish her chores and head for the river to cool off, but before she could do that she had to finish milking the goat, which gave her all sorts of problems. She hated feta cheese, and the poor goat was prob-

ably sick of giving its milk, but her papa wanted feta so Zoe had to milk the goat. The goat was the only animal that Zoe hadn't named. She hated the goat, and she was quite certain the goat hated her, so it went nameless.

Her last job before being allowed to go to the river was gathering the chicken eggs. She had been in the chicken coop trying to get her favourite hen, Aliki, to move so she could collect the last remaining eggs. She wasn't having any luck moving the old hen, short of resorting to picking her up and moving her; but when she had tried that before, the hen had pecked her hands.

She was scolding the hen when a shadow fell across the chicken coop. Zoe looked up and saw her older brother Mihali standing there, laughing at her antics.

"Zoe, Zoe, Zoe. I'm going to tell you, the only way that hen is going to give you her eggs is if you cook her and make a nice chicken soup." Mihali laughed and moved past Zoe to pick up the hen, despite its squawking.

"I'm not going to eat Aliki. That's cruel!" Zoe cried, grabbing the hen to her.

Mihali shook his head and chuckled. "I would love some chicken soup right about now." He made a smacking noise with his lips as Zoe scowled at him. She then noticed he was wearing a Greek army uniform, his black army boots polished to a shine.

"Where are you going?"

"I'm going to fight the Germans, little one. They have invaded."

"Oh no! I don't want you to go." Zoe cried out, dropping the eggs, putting her arms around his waist and squeezing tightly. She buried her head against his chest and began to cry.

Mihali held his young sister for a few moments, wiping at his own tears which he quickly brushed away before Zoe could see them. "Zoe, Greece needs me," he told her softly and kissed the top of her head.

"I don't care, I don't want you to die. I need you," Zoe replied and held on to him. "You're going to die."

"No, I'm not. I'll be back."

"No, you won't. You're going to go away like Elias and Petros and never come back."

Mihali closed his eyes and took a deep breath. Opening his eyes and pulling away from his sister's embrace, he held her at arm's length, going down on one knee. Lifting her chin with his finger and looking at the emerald eyes that reminded him of the forest, he kissed her on the cheek.

"Zoe, I'm not going to die. I'll be back, I promise I will. We will defeat the Germans like we did with the Italians, you'll see."

"What if you don't defeat them?"

"We have God on our side, little one. He will help us. Remember what Father Haralambos said to us last Sunday? He said, 'Who can stand against Greece when God is fighting on your side?' Do you believe that?"

Zoe nodded. She wanted to believe that God was on Greece's side, wanted to believe so much.

"*God* is *on our side*. I will come back, and when I do, I'll teach you how to swim in the river and then we can go and catch some fish. How does that sound?"

"Promise me you'll come back?"

"I promise you that, with God's help, I will do my best to come back."

"I'm sorry, Zo," Earl apologised again as he watched his friend, her eyes glistening with unshed tears rising from her memories.

Zoe wiped her eyes and cleared her throat. "It's been a while since I let myself remember them. Mihali was the last to leave."

"Do you try and forget?"

"No, it's just that when I do remember, I get upset; and I don't want to do that."

"What about your Mum and Dad?"

"Papa died from a heart attack when we found out Mihali was killed. Mihali was his pride and joy." Zoe stopped and took a breath. "He loved us all, but Mihali was his first born and Greeks have a soft spot for their first born. Mama was killed soon after Muller arrived."

"Eva's stepfather."

"Yeah," Zoe replied and took a sip of her own tea, trying to get her emotions under control. "Actually, one good thing came out of the war—I met Eva."

Earl put the cup down, picked up his cigarette and took a long drag from it. Zoe made a face as some of the smoke drifted towards her. She didn't smoke cigarettes, and though Eva occasionally had a cigarette in the flat, she would eventually take it outside since Zoe didn't like it.

"Can I ask you something?" Earl asked as he watched the smoke drift upwards.

"Sure."

"Do you and Eva argue?"

"Sure we do. Doesn't everyone? But we have a rule."

Earl turned to his friend and gave her a curious look. "A rule about arguing?"

"Oh yeah," Zoe chuckled. "We don't allow the sun to set with us still being angry with each other."

"That's the rule?"

"Yep. We don't argue a lot, but there are times when we might get cranky with each other."

"I've never heard of rules about arguing. All I know is that I'll yell, he'll yell, then we don't speak to each other for days."

"That doesn't solve any problems."

"No, I guess it doesn't. I never thought to have rules for arguing. I guess it makes sense."

"Sure it does," Zoe said, and memories of her first big argument with Eva surfaced.

The sun glared down from the sky as Zoe sweltered in her long white pants and loose shirt, the beads of sweat trickling down the sides of her face. This scorching African weather brought back fond memories of the lazy summer days that had been spent in Larissa with her family, a place she knew she would never return to.

Zoe's eyes lit up as she entered Cairo's marketplace, the bustling center of this huge city. Traders from all over Africa and the Middle East brought their goods here to trade. The rich colours of the exotic woven carpets, the rhythmic drum beats of the Arabian music that flowed out of the shops, and the sweet smell of the burning incense blended with the strong aroma of freshly made Arabian coffee—they left Zoe in awe of this amazing land.

As Zoe walked through the souk, she found herself surrounded mostly by men who were busy attempting to attract customers to their shops. Zoe was almost overwhelmed by the variety of languages that she could hear. The crude English of the Australian soldiers around her provided a stark contrast to the melodic Arabic spoken by the shop keepers. The few women that Zoe did manage to spot amongst the crowd in the market were dressed from head to toe in what appeared to be a black kaftan that only left their eyes showing. She was curious as to why on earth they would wear black in the blistering heat.

She had heard all sorts of stories about the markets in Cairo from the soldiers, and Zoe was eager to experience them for herself. Zoe found herself strolling from store to store, stunned by the ornate jewelry and handicrafts. She had never seen anything like it before. She couldn't wait to get back home and tell Eva.

She met up with an Australian solder, Barry, who had befriended them when they first arrived in Egypt and had ended up becoming a good friend to them both. The afternoon dragged on, and Zoe lost track of the time until Barry told her that he had to go on guard duty, and asked if he could walk her home.

Approaching her home and rounding the last corner, they caught sight of Eva talking to Mohammed, their landlord.

Zoe knew she was going to have some explaining to do, because she had told Mohammed that she was only going for a couple of hours, and Eva looked extremely upset. Barry waved goodbye to them and rushed off, so that he wouldn't be late getting back to the camp.

Eva turned when Mohammed said something to her. She looked extremely tired. She was wearing a loose-fitting white shirt and Bedouin pants, which Zoe had bought for her from a travelling merchant. Her shirt was plastered to her back, which made Zoe wince since her partner hated the hot weather, and from the looks of her it didn't look like Eva was comfortable.

Eva thanked Mohammed and walked purposefully towards her. She grabbed Zoe by the arm and roughly dragged her inside their house.

"Hey!" Zoe protested and pulled back her arm.

"Where have you been?" Eva demanded, brushing the hair away from her eyes.

"I went to the marketplace. Didn't Mohammed tell you?"

Eva was beyond angry. She had been pacing for hours, wondering where Zoe had gone and why she wasn't at home like she had said she would be.

Zoe was sure she heard several curses in Greek and German, and a few in Italian. It wasn't until Eva approached her and was standing only a few inches away from her that Zoe realised Eva's eyes had turned an icy blue with rage. When Zoe attempted to touch her, she pulled away.

"Didn't I tell you not to go out by yourself?" Eva raised her voice, her hands balled at her sides.

"Why? Why can't I go anywhere without you?" Zoe was getting angry herself. She wanted to share her new experiences with Eva, but she was bitterly disappointed that Eva wasn't interested. And to add to the indifference, she was angry. "Do I have to only go out with you?"

"Zoe, you don't understand!"

"What is it that I don't understand, Eva? That I'm a young kid? What are you? My mother? I thought you were my lover."

"I do love you, that's why I didn't want you out there," Eva said, running her hands through her long hair and letting out a frustrated sigh. "You don't understand, Zoe. Cairo is not Larissa. It's dangerous."

"How much more dangerous than Larissa? Don't you think I can take care of myself?"

"Zoe—"

She was so angry that Eva was treating her like a kid. "Don't! Don't tell me what to do." She pushed Eva away, opened the door, and slammed it shut behind with so much force it shook the frame.

She didn't go far, just to a semi private area surrounded by bushes. The sun had set and the evening was getting cool, but she didn't want to go back inside. It hurt her that her lover didn't trust her. She kicked the nearest palm tree out of frustration and sat down, bringing her knees up to her chest, and started to cry. She sat there for hours, alone and angry with Eva.

She fell asleep, and woke only when she felt herself being lifted. Opening her eyes, she saw Eva's sunburned face in the moonlight. Eva carried her inside their home and closed the door without saying a word. Zoe was put to bed in silence, and the bedroom door closed, leaving her there alone.

In the morning, Zoe was still angry with her partner and was determined to have it out with her. She angrily got up and went into the living room, finding Eva asleep on a sofa that was far too short for her tall partner.

Eva had looked so uncomfortable that Zoe's anger dissipated. Even asleep, Eva looked tired and her eyes were red. Zoe knelt by the sofa and gently woke Eva. Sleepy, bloodshot, azure eyes opened, and Eva winced at her cramped position. Zoe helped her partner to sit up, and they sat together, Zoe trying to find the words to express her anger.

"Why don't you trust me?"

Eva had closed her eyes and sighed. "Zoe, I do trust you." *Eva turned towards her and went to her knees in front of Zoe, holding both her hands in her own larger ones.* "I love you, Zoe, and I don't want anything to happen to you."

"What could happen to me? Barry and the other boys were there."

"Cairo is notorious for kidnappings, Zoe. The marketplace is one of the most dangerous places in Cairo. It's not uncommon for young women to be snatched from the streets and disappear."

"Why didn't you tell me that?"

"I didn't want to scare you. I know now that was stupid of me, but Zoe, I never want to lose you."

Zoe was astounded. They had had their first argument, and it was over something they could have easily resolved. "I'm sorry I walked out."

"I'm sorry I got angry. I should have stayed calm, but I was worried; and the more I worried, the angrier I got." *Eva looked sheepish.* "Zoe, I don't want to argue with you, but if we ever do I'd like to resolve matters quickly."

"If you had told me why, I would have listened," *Zoe said, and cupped her lover's face and looked into her eyes.* "You wouldn't have had to sleep on this sofa. But, I want you to stop treating me like a kid."

"I'm not—"

"Eva, you do. You are overprotective sometimes, and as much as I love you, I want to be your equal. I'm your lover, not your kid sister."

"Okay, but Zoe, I am older than you and I've been here before, so I would like you to listen to what I have to say."

"Now that I understand *why* you didn't want me to go, I won't."

"Deal," *Eva said and gave her a huge grin.* "Can we make up now?"

"Oh yeah," *Zoe answered, and fell into Eva's arms. They both fell backwards to the floor, with Zoe straddling Eva's long body.*

"I don't ever want to fight, but if we do, I want us to resolve it before the sun sets. I don't want to sleep alone and angry," *Eva told her, as she held Zoe against her chest.*

"Hello, Zoe!" Earl snapped his fingers in front of Zoe's face. "Where did you go?"

"Cairo," Zoe said with a grin. "What were you saying?"

"I said that I couldn't imagine Eva angry."

"Eva doesn't like to argue, but that doesn't mean she doesn't. She's gorgeous when she's angry. Her eyes go all icy blue, very sexy."

Earl shook his head. "Is that because of her stepfather?"

"What? Her eyes looking sexy?" Zoe joked and got a grin from her friend. "Eva is a very calm person normally. I've only seen her all out angry when I didn't listen to her in Cairo and went out on my own. The things Muller did to her...I used to think the fight was taken out of her by him," Zoe replied, not knowing how much Earl knew about Eva's stepfather, or the circumstances surrounding him. "She just doesn't like to argue. She gets cranky, but no full out dummy spits."

"Eva told me about her stepfather...I mean, I made a crude remark when I saw her back."

"She told you about Muller and the beatings?" Zoe asked. She was surprised at that since Eva never talked about it with anyone other than family.

"Yeah, well, we were both hot and sweaty..." Earl looked up and saw Zoe's lopsided grin. "You have a one track mind. You know what I mean?"

"Eva all hot and sweaty...nice image...thanks, Earl." Zoe joked and playfully punched him on the shoulder.

Earl shook his head. "And they say men are horny."

"Hey now. That's my wife, and I can daydream about her being all hot and sweaty."

"Do you want me to finish the story, or do I leave you to your daydream?"

"Oh no, please go ahead." Zoe waved him on and grinned when Earl rolled his eyes.

"We were hot and sweaty on one of the machines, and Eva wasn't wearing the cotton undershirt she normally wears under her uniform, that's why I saw them."

"What did you say to her?"

Earl blushed and took a deep breath. "I said that I didn't know you and she were into kinky sex."

"You didn't." Zoe exclaimed. "Tell me you didn't really say that to her."

"I did. I know I was crude. She gave me one of those looks she does so well."

"Which one? The eyebrow look, or the scowl that could kill

at ten paces?"

"The scowl. She just went all quiet—well, quieter than normal—and just continued working. I was sure I had lost her as a friend that day. I was trying to figure out a way to apologise, when she came up to me and told me that her stepfather had beaten her. My dad never laid a finger on me growing up, so I just couldn't figure out why any parent would do that."

"Because he was an animal," Zoe replied. "When I met her, she was the loneliest person I had ever seen."

"I think the worst thing my father did to me was to prevent me from going to see Don Bradman playing at the Sydney Cricket Ground. I had saved up to go, and he knew I was just counting the days until I went."

Zoe had met Mr Wiggins, and he was the most loving man towards his son. He was a tall man with thick white hair and a beard, and reminded her of Santa Claus. She had spent a good deal of time discussing cricket with the older man. She made the mistake of asking who Don Bradman was, which elicited a very shocked expression from the older Wiggins. A full-scale explanation of the game and the cricketers ensued. "You didn't go and see Bradman play?" Zoe asked.

"He grounded me because I didn't do my chores and I answered back to Mum. No Bradman. I could argue with him 'til I had gone blue in the face. Dad decided it, and that was that."

"That's how normal fathers react, Earl. Muller was a deranged Nazi. Hey, I'm supposed to be cheering you up. Come on, let's do something that will take your mind off your hangover. How do you feel about cataloging Eva's pictures?"

"Yeah, why not?"

"Earl," Zoe put her hand on his shoulder and smiled at him. "When you find someone to love you, and all that mushy stuff you don't like to talk about, you will find that making rules about arguing is good."

❖❖❖❖❖❖❖

The hot weather brought Eva and Debbie out of the office and into Hyde Park, which was only a few minutes walk. With its beautiful walkways, and a fountain in the center, the park was truly an oasis in the middle of the central business district of Sydney. Eva stopped and gazed at the stone structure for a moment as the water showered down. The beautiful day brought out many office workers, and they were sprawled all over the grass, eating their lunch and talking.

Eva hadn't been aware of the park until one day Debbie stuck her head in the door and shooed her out of the office and into bright sunlight. The park was one of Debbie's favourite spots, mainly when the usually busy people traffic had subsided. Eva was most surprised to see the chained-to-the-desk receptionist go out for lunch, until Debbie revealed that usually between 12:00 and 1:00 p.m., the entire office was closed for lunch.

Eva sat with her back against a tree and perched her lunchbox on her thighs. The smell of cut grass reminded Eva of home, a smell she associated with carefree summers.

"So, what do you think?" Debbie asked as she took a bite of her lunch. She watched as the ever-present pigeons devoured a piece of bread she had thrown to them.

"It's really nice, I didn't know it was here."

"Yeah, it's a well kept secret." Debbie laughed at her own joke, since the park was of considerable size.

Eva grinned. "Zoe and I went to the Botanical Gardens a few weeks ago. Beautiful place."

"Yeah, I enjoy it there myself. Hey, I've been meaning to ask you, those photos in your office, did you take them?"

"Yep they're mine," Eva replied and opened her lunch box to reveal a huge piece of mousaka, which was one of Eva's favourite dishes.

"What's that?" Debbie pointed to her lunch.

"Mousaka. It's Greek. It has eggplant, potato, mincemeat and pasta."

"Looks very rich."

Eva grinned. "Yeah, Greek food is very rich."

"I hope you don't mind me asking, but how do you stay so slim?"

"I walk most mornings when I have the time, and on weekends Zoe and I rent bicycles and ride around Centennial Park," Eva replied as she took a bite from her lunch.

They had found the park quite by accident one Sunday, and spent the day just relaxing. Zoe had watched people passing by on bicycles and wondered where they could rent a couple. They were soon given directions, rented the bikes, and spent quite a relaxing Sunday cycling around the park, which was one of the most serene places in the city.

"Oh," Debbie said, and went back to her lunch. She wanted

to ask her new friend about Zoe, but wasn't sure how she could go about it. "Have you been a photographer long?"

"A few years."

"Does Zoe take photos?"

"No, Zoe is an artist. She paints. I have a nice photo of her painting me taking a photo of her," Eva said as she smiled at the memory.

It had been a rainy day, and they had spent Sunday inside. Eva wanted to take photos of Zoe painting. It wasn't until later that Zoe showed her what she was working on. It was a painting of Eva with her camera taking photos of Zoe.

Debbie laughed, scaring some of the pigeons that had decided to come closer in search of food. "How old is Zoe?"

Eva gave her a smirk. "Is this another interrogation?"

"I'm sorry, Eva, that was out of line," Debbie apologised. She hadn't meant to blurt it out but she couldn't help it. Eva was an interesting woman.

"No, that's all right. I'm sure when Zoe comes up this afternoon, you can ask her."

"Thanks, I will. Does she drive a car...?" Debbie realised she was asking another question and clamped her hand over her mouth. Eva laughed at the expression on the receptionist's face.

"No, she rides a motorcycle called Mabel."

"Mabel?" Debbie chuckled. She looked down at her watch and tapped it for Eva to see. "I think we'd better be heading back."

They picked up the rubbish, made a final check to see that they hadn't forgotten anything, and walked away, unaware that a pair of blue eyes watched them leave.

❖❖❖❖❖❖❖

Friedrich was hot and frustrated. He took off his jacket and rolled up the sleeves of his white shirt as he worked on trying to find the right combination to the safe.

The large grey safe was old; the paint was peeling off and rust was taking its place. It had been in the office for a very long time and was seldom used.

Friedrich wanted to ask David why they had never used it before, and frowned at the lock that refused to open no matter how many times he attempted a different combination of numbers on the sheet of paper that he held. He let out a frustrated sigh as David walked through the open door with two cold bottles of Coca-Cola.

"You won't ever make a good burglar, Freddy."

Friedrich scowled at him as he went back to the safe. "And you can't copy numbers correctly."

"I'm a lover, not an accountant," David replied and got another scowl from Friedrich.

"I won't even try and understand that joke."

"I know, I'm a true comic genius; George and Gracie get their material from me."

Friedrich snorted as yet another combination was tried and failed. "What's in this safe?"

"Nothing at the moment."

Friedrich sighed and scrunched the paper in his hand, throwing it in the bin. "Well, the numbers don't work."

"Really?" David teased his friend and patted him on the back. "Here, have a Coke, it will cool you down."

"Did you have a chance to go over that list I gave you this morning?" Friedrich asked as he took a long swig of the soft drink.

"Yeah, I did. I've requested passport photos from the Immigration Department, and they should arrive some time on Monday. Then we can try and match them with the photographs we have."

"And where are we going to store them?"

"In the safe," David replied, hiding a grin as Friedrich rolled his eyes.

"You are a funny man."

"I told you, I'm a comic genius. Come on, Freddy, smile. You'll have the weekend to court the lovely Elena. I'll have to get another safe; but until then you can take the photos home with you, and I'll take the list."

"I'll order the new safe," Friedrich muttered as he picked up the telephone.

"Don't forget to keep the numbers in a safe place," David chuckled and got hit in the head by a folded newspaper.

Chapter 12

Zoe manoeuvred her motorcycle into the office building's basement carpark and looked around for a suitable spot in the crowded facility. She found a small space in a corner and turned off the ignition just as a large Ford was parking, its owner giving Zoe a dirty look as he parked next to her. Zoe pulled off her helmet and gloves and put them in the sidecar, then grinned at the driver. She patted the bike and strolled the short distance to the steps leading up to Eva's workplace.

Debbie looked up at the whirring fans and sighed. It had been a very long and tiring day, and the heat had made everyone a little more cranky and irritable. She looked at the clock again and realised that she would soon be able to shut the door, much to everyone's relief.

Debbie heard the stairway door open and hoped it was either Alexander or Dierdre coming back from appointments and not another client. She was very relieved to see Zoe push the doors open.

"Hi, Zoe."

"Hey, Deb. Wow, it's hot in here." Zoe picked up a magazine that was lying on the low tables and fanned herself.

"The Federal Government Sauna. We're open for business," Debbie joked.

"Is Eva still seeing clients?"

"No, she's gone down to the file room; and if you think it's hot up here, you should be subjected to our filing room. We call it hell."

"Hell?"

"Boiling hot all the time, even in winter," Debbie explained. Their filing room was situated below the basement carpark. It had no ventilation, and it was stuffy with all the old files from the various departments in the building. Debbie had the misfortune of spending a considerable amount of time down there filing away. She hated the cockroaches that survived in the heat, and she hated the mice that scurried around and left their calling cards in between filing bays. She gratefully accepted any offer by the interpreters to take files down there.

"Eva hates the heat," Zoe said. Her partner suffered a great deal in the summer and cold baths were always a treat. Zoe had found a unique way to cool Eva down during the very warm nights by taking a towel and wetting it, then placing it over Eva's feet. It cooled her down and made it easier for her to sleep. They had tried sleeping out on the balcony, but the mosquitoes made a meal out of them—so it was either the cold bath or the wet towel. Zoe loved the heat, so it didn't bother her as much. She often wondered why they didn't move to a colder climate than Sydney's.

"Does she?"

"Oh yeah. She's a winter bunny that one. Give her a cold day and she's happy," Zoe replied. "So how long do you think she'll be?"

"I'm not sure. She was going to pick up some files for herself, and she said she would get a few that I needed. All depends if she can find the others before passing out from the heat."

Zoe frowned. She wasn't sure that Debbie was joking about the lack of ventilation. "Is she okay down there?"

Debbie looked up and met Zoe's concerned look. "Oh, I'm sorry, Zoe. It's a joke around here, about hell. It's not that bad."

"Oh, okay. I wouldn't want to find that my partner had passed out or anything," Zoe muttered, not fully understanding the Australian sense of humour. "I'll just wait here." She picked up a magazine that was lying around and thumbed through it, not really interested in the articles. She would look up occasionally to check if Eva had returned.

She finally found an interesting article, but stopped reading when she heard the door open. She put the magazine down, thinking that Eva had returned. Getting up to greet her partner,

Zoe got a shock as she watched Greta walk in. "Wow," Zoe muttered to herself. Greta was dressed impeccably. She wore a cream coloured silk shirt with a burgundy coloured tight skirt, and matching shoes that gave her an extra two inches in height. Her auburn hair was unrestrained and cascaded down her back. *Wow, she's gorgeous,* Zoe thought, running a hand over her short haircut and glancing down at the casual shirt and pants she wore.

Greta walked up to the reception desk and stood there looking very impatient as Debbie got off the phone.

"I want to see Miss Haralambos," Greta demanded in a very thick German accent. "My name is Greta Wagner."

"Have you got an appointment?" Debbie asked, trying to understand what the woman was saying. She hoped that Eva hadn't made a late appointment, but looked in her appointment book.

"No. Is she free? I won't be long."

"I'm sorry, Mrs Wagner, Miss Haralambos isn't here at the moment," Debbie patiently explained.

"Oh?" Greta frowned.

Zoe looked back at the entrance, praying that Eva wouldn't come through it. She turned her attention back to Greta, who was far from happy.

"Give her my number." Greta pushed a piece of paper over to Debbie and turned, catching sight of Zoe. With a smile on her face, she went over to the younger woman and extended her hand, which Zoe took. "We meet again. It's Zoe, isn't it?"

Zoe refrained from making a nasty remark and smiled. "Yes, Zoe Lambros."

"Of course. I'm sorry, Zoe, I get very forgetful with names. The older one gets, the more one forgets."

"I wouldn't know about that," Zoe muttered.

"No, of course not; you're still a teenager," Greta chuckled. "Are you waiting for Eva?"

Zoe nodded.

"How sweet. I bet Eva loves that," Greta said as she put her gloves back on.

Zoe wondered why anyone would wear gloves just for the sake of it in the heat of the day. "What are you doing here?"

"I was hoping to speak to Eva."

"Why?"

Greta cocked her head a little and regarded Zoe with a smile. "My, you are the jealous type, aren't you? What are you worried about, Zoe? Are you worried I'm going to steal her away from you?"

"I'm just curious as to why you are here. I'm not worried about my wife being stolen away."

"Of course you're not. Although I know if an old lover turned up, I would be very worried. You know—comparing notes and all of that. I'm sure you have nothing to worry about." Greta regarded the youngster with mirth. She did enjoy taunting little Zoe. The child was obviously not used to sparring with someone of Greta's intelligence, and on some level the older woman felt sorry for her. She was sure Eva had used the young woman to get out of Greece. She didn't blame her former lover. She thought it was an ingenious way to escape—disguising herself as a collaborator with the Greek cause.

"Well, I'm happy for you. You are fortunate to be married to Eva. She is one of the sexiest women I've known."

"She is," Zoe agreed, wondering where this conversation was going.

"Tell me, Zoe, does Eva still close her eyes and hum when she's been—?"

"I don't discuss my personal life with people I hardly know, Greta," Zoe interrupted. The last thing she wanted to do was talk about her sex life with this woman, especially since she knew Eva so well.

Greta laughed. "I meant nothing by that. You are an amusing young woman."

"I don't think you know Eva as well as you think you do," Zoe replied, not believing what she had just said.

"Zoe, sweetie, I was Eva's first lover, so I know all there is to know about her. How she looks after she's satisfied, how she knows how to pleasure me, and I know how to satisfy her. I'm sure you are doing your best." Greta sighed exaggeratedly and looked at her watch. "I would love to continue chatting with you, but I have to go. Give my regards to Eva, won't you? Thank you, sweetie." She patted Zoe's cheek, then spun around and walked off, leaving a humiliated young woman in her wake.

Zoe let out a frustrated cry as she sank down into the nearest chair and put her head in her hands, rocking back and forth. "Oh, gee whiz, Zoe, that was the dumbest thing you have ever done," she scolded herself. "How to make yourself look more stupid in one easy lesson."

Debbie looked over and was concerned to see a distressed

Zoe. She approached the young woman and put her hand on her shoulder. "Zoe, are you all right?"

Zoe brushed away the tears and took a deep breath. "Yeah, fine," she muttered.

"Do you know Mrs Wagner?"

"Yeah, I do, sort of." Zoe took a deep breath to calm herself. "Did Mrs Wagner give you a phone number?"

"She wanted me to give it to Eva."

"Can you destroy that number?" Zoe asked, hoping Debbie would just throw the number in the nearest bin.

"I can't do that, Zoe, I'd get into trouble if Mrs Wagner made a formal complaint that I didn't give it to Eva."

"Oh. You can give it me, and I'll give it to Eva."

Debbie smiled and shook her head. "Can't do that either."

"Okay, thanks anyway," Zoe muttered.

"Would you like a cup of cold water or something? You look a little flushed."

"No, I'm fine."

Debbie didn't think Zoe was fine, but she didn't want to push her so she went back to her desk to finish cleaning up.

The glass doors swung open a little while later, and Eva walked in with several large folders under her arm. She spotted Zoe absently flipping through a magazine and walked over.

"Hi, Zo. I won't be too long. Just have to drop these off and get my bag. Have you been waiting long?"

"Hi. Um...no, not long," Zoe replied quietly. "I'll wait here until you finish."

Eva looked surprised at her wife's quiet response and turned to Debbie who was picking up leaflets and brochures from the information roundabout. Debbie crooked her finger for Eva to come over.

"What's wrong with Zoe?" Eva asked the receptionist. "Did something happen while I was away?"

"Mrs Wagner came in looking for you a few minutes ago, and I got the impression Zoe knew her."

"Did they talk?"

"Yeah. I'm not sure what they said because they were speaking in German, but Zoe was upset afterwards."

"Oh. What did Mrs Wagner want?"

"She asked me to give you this." Debbie leaned over to her desk and picked up the piece of paper with Greta's phone number and passed it to her. Eva looked at the paper for a few seconds, then stuck it in her pocket.

"Thanks, Debbie."

"Is everything all right?"

"I don't know," Eva said with a frown. She walked to her office and picked up her bag, closing the door behind her and giving the key to Debbie.

Eva took Zoe's hand and they walked down the stairs in silence. Unable to wait any longer, Eva stopped at the bottom of the stairs and turned to her partner. "Zoe, are you all right?"

"I'm fine," Zoe mumbled.

"Everything all right with Earl?"

"Hmm. He said he was going to spend the night at his place in case Dave called."

"Do you think he will?" Eva asked, trying to get Zoe to open up to her.

Zoe shrugged and walked over to the motorcycle, climbing into the sidecar, allowing Eva to drive. Eva was perplexed about her wife's behaviour. She wondered what Greta had said to her partner to make her this subdued.

❖❖❖❖❖❖❖

The flat was quiet as Eva walked out of the bathroom, one towel around her and one towel wrapped around her head. The cool bath had relaxed her a great deal and she felt invigorated. Wandering into the kitchen, she noticed it was empty. She padded back out and looked outside at the balcony, which was also empty.

"Zoe?" Eva called out and a faint "here" came from the bedroom. Eva strode to the bedroom and opened the door. Zoe was curled up on the bed. "Are you feeling all right, love?"

Zoe nodded, which did nothing to alleviate Eva's anxiety about her partner's health. Eva lay beside her and gently turned Zoe towards her. She was very surprised to find the young woman had been crying.

"What's wrong, Zo? Why were you crying? Was it something I said?"

"No. Um...did Debbie tell you about Greta coming to see you?"

Eva nodded. "Debbie mentioned that Greta came by. She also said you talked with her, and you looked upset. Did Greta do anything to upset you?"

Zoe nodded and sniffed.

"Do you want to talk about it?"

"You're going to think it's stupid."

"No, I won't. Would I be wrong if I said you don't want me to see Greta?"

"You can see her, I can't stop you," Zoe said defensively. What she really wanted was for Greta to go back to Germany and disappear, but she didn't want to upset Eva by revealing that particular wish.

"But you don't like it?" Eva continued her questioning. Since the moment that Greta had come back into her life, she knew that she needed to have this conversation with Zoe at some point. She also needed to find out what Greta had said to Zoe to get her so upset.

"No, I don't like it...but...I know you want to see her because she's a friend of yours, and I don't think I have the right to tell you not to see her."

"Yes, she is a friend of mine; but that doesn't mean I'm not going to take your feelings into consideration." She kissed the top of Zoe's head, scooping her close. "What are you worried about?"

"I'm not worried," Zoe lied. She was very worried about Greta attempting to get Eva back, but she didn't want to voice the thought that had been running around her head since Greta's arrival.

"Zoe, don't lie to me," Eva gently scolded, lifting Zoe's chin and looking into her eyes. "We have always been honest with each other. Greta bothers you, you can tell me that. I'm sure if I were in your shoes, it would bother me as well."

Zoe looked up sheepishly at her wife. She hadn't been able to lie to Eva and didn't want to. "I don't like her."

"You don't like her or her politics?" Eva prodded gently.

"Both. I'm afraid that you might want...um...I'm afraid you might fall in love with her," Zoe replied and looked down, ashamed that it looked like her trust in her partner had evaporated and ashamed at herself for hurting Eva.

"What did she say to you?"

Zoe took a deep breath. "That she knows how to satisfy you, among other things."

Eva was taken aback. "You satisfy me in every way, Zoe."

"Do I?" Zoe asked hesitantly. She wanted to believe that she was able to make Eva happy and content, but she knew she was inexperienced, something Greta had made painfully obvious to her.

"Oh, Zoe!" Eva exclaimed. Zoe's insecurities were laid bare, and all Eva wanted was to reassure her wife. "It's true Greta is more experienced, she's older. Yes, she did know how to satisfy me and she did know what made me happy, but that's in the past."

"What if she wanted to win you back?"

Eva frowned. Greta was playing mind games with her wife, and she hated the way Zoe was being abused. "Your touch is the only one I want. I want to wake up with you, go to sleep with you, share my bed with you." Eva caressed her wife's cheek and brushed away the tears that had begun to silently track down Zoe's cheeks. "She can't win me back. You are the only one that owns my heart. Do you believe me?"

Zoe nodded, closed her eyes, and snuggled against Eva.

"Zoe, the vows we made before God—I truly believed in what I was promising. I didn't say those words because they sounded nice. I've committed myself to you, and that's the end of that. Do you remember what I said to you 11 months ago?"

"That there are three people in our marriage—you, me and God, and that makes us stronger," Zoe replied, remembering the night so clearly. Eva's vows to her were engraved in her heart.

"And with God in our marriage, nothing on earth can break us apart. God is still in our marriage, love. Just because a woman I knew so many years ago wants to steal my heart, doesn't mean she's going to. I can't give it away; you have it."

"I'm sorry, Evy, it's just that Greta makes me feel like a kid, out of my depth."

"Out of your depth? I don't understand."

"She's more sophisticated, a woman of the world, and I'm a peasant from some backward Greek village."

Eva shook her head and took Zoe's hand and placed it on her chest near her heart. "Zoe, you own my heart, my body and my soul. And you aren't a peasant from some backward Greek village, and I don't ever want to hear you say that again. You are a beautiful Greek woman with all the qualities I love. You are kind, gentle, loving, talented; and you make me feel like I'm the luckiest woman alive. I look forward to each day because I know I'm going to be with you. Don't you know that? Every night I thank God you are with me."

Eva cupped Zoe's face in her hands and very slowly leaned

down, pressing her lips to Zoe's. With her kiss she wanted to leave her wife no doubts about her love. She deepened the kiss and was rewarded with a quiet moan as she slipped her hands under Zoe's cotton shirt, running her hands over her partner's back.

"Oh God. Stop," Zoe managed to say before she lost coherent thought and let Eva make love to her.

"Stop?"

"Yeah. I want to apologise and ask you something, I don't think I can do that if I'm not able to think straight."

Eva grinned. "Well, we don't want that."

"Eva, I'm sorry. It's just that Greta hit me for a six and I felt so stupid. She said some things that I just couldn't get out of my mind."

"It's all right, love, I understand," Eva replied and kissed her gently. "Greta doesn't know what we share. I want you to remember what I said to you, okay?"

Zoe nodded. "I've been thinking about something for a long time. Um...would you mind if I changed my last name to Haralambos?"

Eva smiled. "Why would I mind? I thought you wanted to keep Lambros in memory of your family."

"You are my family, Evy. I won't ever forget my parents or my brothers, but I want to do this because I want us to have the same surname."

Eva was deeply touched and replied by kissing her wife ever so gently. "It would be an honour if you took my last name."

"Okay," Zoe grinned. She had been thinking about changing her surname for some time. Not until her chat with Earl did it crystalise in her mind that she could never forget her family, and it didn't matter that her surname would be different.

"Can I continue where I left off?" Eva asked with a smirk.

"On one condition."

"Oh?"

"You lose the towel," Zoe replied as she removed the towel from Eva's body and flung it out the bedroom door.

Chapter 13

The room was cast in shadows as the light from the street lamp filtered through the open window. It was another warm evening, and the sound of the cicadas reached Eva as she lay in bed, quite content to stay curled up with her wife. She looked down at the woman who lay asleep tucked under her chin, her dark bangs falling over her eyes. She grinned when she noticed a small hickey on Zoe's neck, which she was sure would be noticed and joked about. Zoe was an outgoing woman in general, but tended to be rather shy when it came to sex.

Eva found the contradiction in her partner's personality quite endearing. Where Zoe was outgoing, chatty and quietly aggressive outside the bedroom, inside she let Eva take the lead. Over the last couple of months, Eva was pleasantly surprised to find Zoe's natural boisterous personality was coming through in their lovemaking.

When she had been talking to Zoe earlier, Eva realised that eleven months had passed since they'd exchanged vows on the *Patris*. Soon their one-year anniversary was going to roll around, and Eva wanted it to be memorable.

Zoe's hand was resting on Eva's belly. Eva placed her own hand over the smaller one, lifted it to her lips, and kissed the palm. She had experienced so much, and had gone through her own private hell—which she'd never thought she would live through. On more than one occasion she had thought about suicide; it would have been preferable to the abuse she'd had to endure.

Eva looked down and grinned as she remembered what Zoe had told her back in Larissa about falling in love. She'd called it "falling in heavy like" and firmly believed that love came after. Eva wasn't sure if she believed in love at first sight, but she liked Zoe's idea about "heavy like."

Eva was devastated to learn that her father was going to be sent on a train scheduled to be blown up by the Resistance. Zoe was angry over what promised to be another senseless death of someone she loved, and she ran off—which increased Eva's anxiety. Her feelings for the young woman were growing, despite her fear that her stepfather would find out. She didn't want to put Zoe in danger from him.

When Zoe did eventually come back to the house, she was wet, tired, and emotionally spent. Eva took charge, ordering that a bath be drawn by Despina, their housekeeper. She ushered the young woman into the bedroom, gently scolding her as she removed her skirt. She was unaware of the effect she was having on Zoe.

Zoe started to unbutton her blouse with shaking fingers. Eva thought the shaking was due to the cold. She helped Zoe remove the blouse and put a blanket around her shoulders to warm her up. Eva tried to avoid looking into Zoe's eyes, afraid that if she did she would reveal her feelings for the young woman.

Zoe covered Eva's hands with her own and then looked up into her impossibly blue eyes and made contact. She told Eva she had thought that their first time together was going to be more romantic than standing in the bedroom feeling cold and being scolded for being wet and muddy.

"You were thinking about it...about me?" Eva asked, placing the blanket around her friend's shoulders to stop Zoe's shaking.

She'd resisted her feelings for so long, not wanting to get involved with anyone. She had cut herself off and maintained that icy exterior, built walls around her heart to prevent anyone from hurting her again, managing to stay remote and aloof until she met this young woman. Zoe had gone in and begun to disassemble the wall she had worked so hard to build.

Zoe embraced her, quite content to stay where she was; and it felt so right.

"I've never fallen in love with a woman before...I've never been in love before," Zoe had revealed.

"Well that's... What did you say?" Eva asked with a start as she realised what Zoe had just admitted.

"I've fallen in love with you," Zoe repeated, giving her a shy smile.

Eva wanted to believe what Zoe was telling her. Wanted so much to feel that finally she could love again. "Maybe we..." Eva said hesitantly.

"When I said you weren't going to be alone, I meant it, Eva Muller. I just said I was new at this and, well, you are just going to have to show me."

"You surprise me, Zoe," Eva said quietly as she gazed at the blanket-covered woman. Her long chestnut coloured hair was matted with mud, but her eyes shone brightly and looked up at Eva with emotions that Eva thought she would never see directed at her again.

"Oh? How so?" She cocked her head sideways and watched the now fidgeting woman that held her.

"When I told you about Greta..." Eva said haltingly, looking down at Zoe.

"I didn't freak out, is that it?"

Eva nodded. She hadn't been sure what would happen when she revealed her love for another woman to Zoe. She couldn't believe it had only been a little over a week since she had confided in the younger woman. She remembered how Zoe held her as she told of her pain and the beatings—the regular beatings her father inflicted on her to drive her "perversion" out of her, the beatings she endured at the hands of her uncle on orders from her father. The shame of being berated by her aunt. The rapes by her uncle's friends as he tried to find her the "right man for the job."

They spent the night talking. It felt good to be able to tell someone the whole truth. She had revealed a little of what she'd gone through to Father Haralambos, but not the full story. She didn't think she could voice her deep pain. Until Zoe came into her life. She had to make certain that Zoe knew where they were headed.

"Why should I freak out? You were hurting, and you needed a friend so badly."

"You are special, very special, to me," Eva said tenderly and, cupping Zoe's face in her hands, she slowly leaned over, pressing her lips to Zoe's. Gently at first, so as to explore the sweetness of this young woman, Eva slowly became more aggres-

sive until she could feel the excited response from Zoe and sought to quench her desire.

    Zoe's first kiss was special to both of them. For Eva it was the beginning of learning how to love again and not being afraid. For Zoe it was learning how to deal with her feelings and the love she had for the tall woman.

    Eva tried to warn her about what could happen, but Zoe was not deterred and as it turned out, Zoe saved her life after Reinhardt shot her.

    And much later, on the *Patris*, when they were emigrating at last, Eva had been sick with the flu. The bug was spreading through the passengers. The ship was going through a storm, which didn't help when her stomach was already doing flip flops. In between trying not to think about her aching head or the cramped bunk that was causing her back to ache, she thought about the young woman that had captured her heart. Zoe was nursing her through. She had been patient when Eva couldn't sleep because of the coughing fits. Zoe would climb up behind her and hold her until she went to sleep.

    "Ah, Zoe, my love, you are one of a kind," Eva whispered to the sleeping woman, who mumbled something and burrowed even closer. She lifted Zoe's hand and looked down at the ring on her finger. Zoe always wore the ring, a cheap, tin plated ring that Eva had found in one of the ports that the ship docked in. She could still picture the look of total surprise on Zoe's face when she'd blurted out, "Will you marry me?"

    Eva didn't know where she drew the strength from, but she'd managed to get out of the bunk. Though she felt horrible, she wanted to do this the right way. She went down on her knees in front of Zoe and was quite surprised and pleased when Zoe also got down on her knees.

    They would have made quite a sight if anyone had walked in. Zoe gave her a huge smile.

    "Zoe, I never thought I would do this, but God knows I've been wanting to since Egypt. I've always believed in marriage..." She stopped and coughed, Zoe patting her on the back and giving her a quick kiss. "I love you and I want to spend the rest of my life with you."

    Zoe didn't say a word as tears ran down her cheeks. She brushed them away. "I love you, as well," she choked out.

"I promise before God to take care of you, to love you with everything that I am, to protect you and to be there for you when you need me."

Zoe looked down shyly, took Eva's larger hands in her smaller ones. "Eva, I want to spend the rest of my life with you, to take care of you when you don't take care of yourself, to comfort you when you need me, and to love you with all my heart, my soul, and my body."

"Zoe I want you to remember that there are three in this marriage—you, me and God. It's like a bound cord—when you have three strands, nothing can snap it. No power on earth can break our marriage if we remember that."

Eva had fumbled until she got the tin plated ring out of her pocket and placed it on Zoe's finger. "I know it's not much, but when we get to Sydney I'll buy you a real band."

"I don't want another ring," Zoe insisted, gazing down at the ring on her finger.

"It's only tin plated—"

"I don't want another ring," Zoe repeated and looked up into Eva's eyes. "I love you, Eva, and I thank God every day for you being in my life." She closed the space between them and kissed her new wife and held her.

Eva had starting coughing again, which wasn't at all like she wanted this moment to be like; but she had said what she'd wanted to say.

Zoe helped her back onto the bunk and tucked her in. "As much as I would love to show you how much I love you, you're sick and I don't want you getting sicker."

"I'm sorry I didn't have—"

"I love the ring. My mama had one like it, and I never heard her complain."

"You know what that means now?" Eva asked her new wife.

"That I can love you morning, noon, and night?"

Eva grinned. "Hmm. No that wasn't what I was thinking."

"What were you thinking?"

"You own my heart, my soul, and my body...and I trust you completely," Eva replied quietly. "The body is a little dented, my soul a little beaten, but my heart has your name engraved on it."

Zoe gasped slightly at Eva's words. "Oh Eva." That's all she said and leaned down and kissed her partner, hoping that through her kiss she could convey her emotions.

Eva sighed contently. Nearly a year had passed since then, and they had settled into the new country and gained a greater understanding of each other and their little quirks, which made her love Zoe all the more.

Eva got out of bed quietly, not wanting to disturb her wife who was sleeping soundly. She picked up her robe and threw it over her shoulder, put her slippers on, and went to the wardrobe and took out a towel.

As she left the bedroom she caught sight of the bath towel that had been flung out the door earlier. Grinning, she picked up the towel, detoured to the laundry and put it in the basket. What she wanted was a nice cold bath. The hot evenings were tiresome for her, and she found that by having a cool bath she was less tired and cranky in the morning.

She stood by and watched as the bath filled, then poured some perfume into the water. They had scoured the department stores looking for a bathtub that would be big enough to accommodate her long frame. The bath that was in the flat when they arrived was so small that even Zoe had problems stretching out in it. The one they settled on was long and wide, big enough to hold both of them at the same time.

Eva stretched out and let the water come up to her chest and sighed. She closed her eyes and rested her head on the rim, letting the cool water relax her.

Zoe leaned against the bathroom door and grinned. She enjoyed watching Eva when she thought she wasn't looking. Her wife was lying in the tub, her breasts peeking out of the water; and Zoe grinned as an idea came to her. She padded back out and into Eva's dark room and picked up her camera. Quietly she made her way back to the bathroom where Eva was still lying with her eyes closed. Zoe smiled, brought the camera up and focused, and took the photo.

Eva heard the click and her blue eyes flew open in alarm to find a grinning Zoe holding the camera. "Zoe!"

"Eva!"

"Oh, Zoe, that wasn't fair!" Eva said sitting up slightly out of the water.

"Oh, nice view there, Mrs H," Zoe replied and took another photo. "You looked so peaceful that I want to paint you, and I can't do that if I didn't have a picture. You don't want to pose for hours in the water, you'll go all pruny and stuff."

"You have painted me many times," Eva responded and sank

back in the water.

"Yeah, but you're my inspiration," Zoe said as she put the camera on the chair and dropped her robe to the floor and climbed into the tub.

"Oh, nice view, Mrs H," Eva mimicked Zoe's previous comment.

"Hmm," Zoe hummed as she sat back between Eva's long legs and leaned back onto Eva's chest. Eva put her arms around her. "This is nice, but the water is a little cool."

"Want to heat it up a bit?" Eva whispered suggestively, nibbling Zoe's ear, and letting her hands roam her wife's body, the action eliciting a low moan.

"I think I feel warmer already," Zoe admitted, tilting her head to one side as the woman behind her used her lips and her tongue to weave a sensual path of pleasure along her wife's neck.

A small whimper escaped from between Zoe's lips as she reached up to entangle her fingers in Eva's soft dark hair. "Mmm...that feels so, so good," the young woman murmured.

"You're right, love, it does," Eva's lips whispered against the silky skin.

The tall woman leaned back, her hands sliding up to Zoe's shoulders to pull her wife's small body back against her reclining figure. Eva kissed the girl's ear, lightly running the tip of her tongue along the edge. The cool water surrounding them, the feel of the beautiful young woman in her arms, Eva closed her eyes at the pleasure that ran through her body in response to the sensations. She wanted to lay this way forever. Knowing that could never be, she decided to take her time and explore her wife's body, choosing a slow seduction to drive the beauty leaning against her to the very brink.

"Relax, my love," she whispered, feeling Zoe's muscles twitch in anticipation of her touch.

"Are you crazy? Evy, you want me to relax right now? With you touching me this way?" Zoe responded impatiently.

"Good things come to those who wait, love," Eva replied with a hoarse whisper, her breath warm against Zoe's ear, doing much more to the young woman than Zoe anticipated.

The throaty chuckle that followed the dark-haired woman's comments caused goose flesh to surface along Zoe's skin, even the parts of her that were covered with the cool water. She could feel an intense feeling of warmth circling out from her belly, settling in the area between her legs. Her nipples hardened at the mere sound of her wife's voice, and Zoe couldn't hold back a small moan of desire.

"Oh, yes," Eva sighed, as she viewed her wife's body responding to her. She suddenly felt the same passionate desire rise within her own body.

Spreading her own legs wider, Eva stretched her long arms out to run her hands along the tops of Zoe's thighs, pressing gently outward, until the younger woman's pose mimicked Eva's. She ran her hands back up the same smooth skin, this time on the inside of her wife's thighs. Zoe released another tiny whimper, which turned into a full throated groan as Eva continued to let her hands slide up further, stopping to let the palms of both hands cover two perfect breasts.

Eva could feel the hard points of flesh pressing into her palms and was nearly undone by the electric jolt that clenched hard at her abdomen, running down to her center. Her own breathing was becoming ragged now as she watched her young wife bring her own hands up to cover Eva's. Zoe pressed the hands against her chest, reveling in the sparks of pleasure the action caused.

"So nice," Eva groaned, watching her normally shy wife's forward behavior. Zoe turned her head to look at her lover, reaching up and letting her fingertips stroke the face that was leaning in toward her. The young woman ran her index finger along her wife's soft lips, letting the digit trail down across a proud chin, stopping to tease the small indentation in Eva's chin. Zoe unconsciously smiled, a lazy seductive smile, almost as if she were enjoying a private moment.

"What are you grinning so devilishly about?" Eva asked with almost a whisper.

"This," Zoe replied, once again letting just the tip of her finger tease the pronounced dimple in her wife's chin. "It's very...very..." Zoe tried to think, as the dark-haired woman continued to caress her skin. "Sexy," she finally answered, breathlessly, almost shyly.

Eva graced the young woman with a tender, lopsided smile and reached in to place a gentle kiss on those sweet lips. Opening her mouth slightly, she ran the tip of her tongue along the edge of her wife's upper lip before capturing the mouth in a slow, sensual kiss. Her mouth swallowed up Zoe's moans as the young woman reacted, not only to the kiss, but her wife's hands that continually teased her body. They continued this way for a long while, Eva's hands seemingly caressing everywhere at once.

Eva felt their kisses become more insistent, more passionate as the moments passed. One long arm snaked around the smaller woman's waist, pulling her back until she could feel Zoe's backside pressing tightly against the dark curls between her legs. The intensity of the kisses grew, Eva's tongue exploring the sweetness of her lover's mouth. When at last the two women reluctantly pulled apart, they were each flushed and breathing in short gasps.

Eva reached down and tenderly kissed her wife once more, her hand sliding along the flat abdomen, her fingers swirling past the curls to feel warm silky flesh. She stroked the smooth flesh lightly.

"Oh, Evy," Zoe murmured against her wife's lips. "Please don't tease me any longer, I can't stand it. I feel like I'm going to die if I don't feel your touch."

Eva couldn't help the easy smile that spread across her normally reticent features. Her young wife had a flair for melodrama and now was no exception. The dark-haired woman felt the same breathless anticipation, however. Capturing the young woman's lips once more, Eva stroked the warm flesh beneath her fingers, pressing them slowly deeper. To Zoe, the pace was achingly slow.

"Please," Zoe pleaded, her legs spreading wider in silent invitation.

Unable to prevent the groan that escaped from her own lips, Eva accepted the soundless invitation and entered her wife, immediately feeling the inescapable rush of her own impending release. It took only moments for Zoe's body, which had indeed been teased to the brink, to tense and arch against the woman who held her. Both women cried out as they rushed headlong into the arms of their climax, their bodies jumping and quivering against one another.

"Oh God," Zoe murmured, letting out a contented sigh and resting her head on Eva's breast as Eva's arms wound tightly around her. "Thank you." Zoe slid up Eva's body and gave her a gentle kiss.

Zoe was rewarded with one of Eva's most dazzling smiles, which made her heart race. She closed her eyes and settled against her partner. They sat in the cool water for a few moments, Zoe drawing figure eights on Eva's belly. "Evy."

"Hmm?"

"I'm getting cold," Zoe murmured.

Eva responded by pulling the plug with her toe, which got Zoe giggling as the water drained away. Zoe stole a quick kiss, got out of the bathtub and picked up a towel and wrapped it around herself.

"Don't go away," Zoe ordered her partner as she raced out of the bathroom and into the bedroom and picked up another towel.

Eva watched with a bemused smile as Zoe padded back into the bathroom with the towel, and opened it up in invitation as Eva's tall frame came out of the bathtub. Zoe wrapped the towel around her and hugged her.

They walked back into the bedroom arm in arm, Eva removed her towel and Zoe's, leaving them at the foot of the bed as they snuggled up in bed, and Eva began to hum Zoe's favourite song.

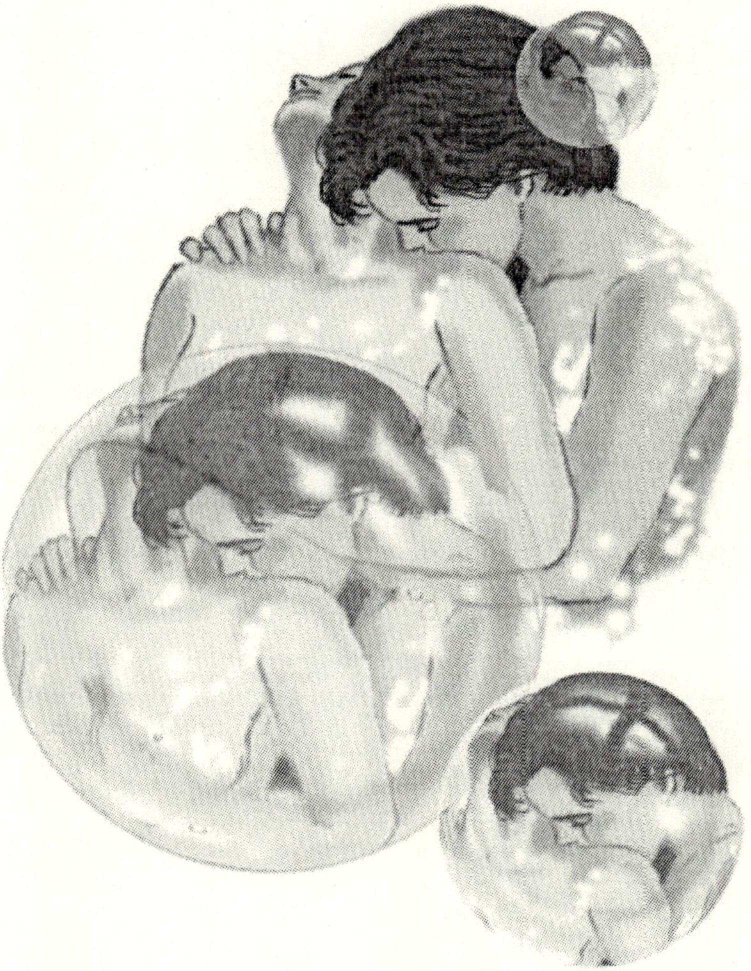

Chapter 14

Friedrich smiled as he put the flowers down next to the chocolates and sat down to write a note to Elena. He wanted this just right. Putting the tip of his pen in his mouth to think, he smiled as he scrawled some of his thoughts in the card. He would have liked for the letter he had written to Elena a few days ago before to have reached her, but whoever broke into their office didn't have a romantic streak in their body. Friedrich wondered if they even read the letter. He chuckled to himself, thinking that if they did they would have had the decency to send it.

The door opened and David walked in with files under his arm, stopping when he saw the flowers.

"Oh, Freddy, for me? I'm touched." David planted a kiss on the top of Friedrich's head, which got him a slap on the leg for his troubles. "Hey that's no way to court me."

"You are a heathen, go away."

"But, Freddy, don't you love me anymore?" David planted his elbows on the desk in front of his friend, batted his blond eyelashes and smiled.

He was rewarded with a groan. "I wouldn't go out with you if you dressed up in a frock and heels. You make an ugly woman," Friedrich replied and grinned.

"You mean I'm not a good looking sheila?"

"You're an ugly sheila."

"Oh, I dunno, Freddy. I made a pretty good Juliet in high school."

"You played Juliet?"

"Sure did. I was told I was the best Juliet ever. All boys high school. We didn't include the kissing, but the dying was fun." David struck a pose as if he was on a balcony and opened his arms in search for Romeo. "Romeo, Romeo, wherefore art thou Romeo?"

"Probably ran far away from you since you're so ugly." Friedrich grinned and got cuffed across the head.

"Drama critics!" David huffed dramatically.

"What are those files in your hands, Juliet?"

"The Immigration Department sent the passport photos, so it looks like we're working tomorrow," David said happily and watched as Friedrich, groaning, realised his weekend off was going to be spoilt once again.

"I was planning on spending the weekend with Elena," Friedrich whined. That got a chuckle from his friend.

"I feel for you my friend; my heart goes out to you." He picked up the box of chocolates. "Hey, chocolates too. Not bad. You actually listened to all my pep talks. Good boy."

"Yeah, pep talks on how to get a woman to fall for me in one easy lesson. I think I did okay without your help."

"Excuse me? Let me remind you, old boy, that if it wasn't for me you would still be standing there 'umming' and 'uhhring' all over the place. When you marry the lovely Elena, I want you to name your firstborn after me." David shook the box and got a dirty look directed his way by Friedrich, who continued to write. "Naming your firstborn after me will ease my pain at losing the future Mrs Peterson. You remember that gorgeous redhead a few weeks ago?"

Friedrich remembered that particular incident all too well. They had been trying to find a Polish general who'd collaborated with the Germans, and they got word he was in Sydney. Much to David's disgust, Friedrich called and David had to apologise to his new girlfriend about leaving halfway through dinner. The man they found wasn't the Polish general, and by the time David got back, his date had left. David had taken every opportunity to remind his friend about him losing the future Mrs Peterson.

"How was I to know that Polish guy had the same name?"

"Let's not get into another debate about it. I could have had Mrs Peterson to dinner that night."

Friedrich snorted. "Sure, and I'm a regular Casanova," Friedrich replied and accepted the folders, sticking them in his bag. "I ordered the safe. They will be bringing it on Monday."

"Hopefully that will keep our secret files secret."

Friedrich sealed the letter and put it in his shirt pocket before putting on his jacket and his hat from the hat rack.

"So, Casanova, are you going to snuggle and cuddle with Elena?"

"Why?"

"Well snuggling and cuddling lead to 'you know,' or so they tell me." David chuckled. "I could learn a few things from you." David slapped his friend on the back as they left the office.

❖❖❖❖❖❖❖❖

The full moon lit up the pavement as Friedrich walked towards the block of flats, muttering to himself. He held the flowers in one hand, his briefcase in the other, and the box of chocolates under his arm. He hoped he wasn't going to drop the chocolates.

Panayiotis was walking back from church, his black robes making a gentle swish every time he walked. He smiled as he saw Friedrich stop and look up to the heavens. He wondered if he was praying and stopped a few feet away so as not to interrupt him.

Friedrich sighed and took a good grasp on the flowers. He was nervous. He probably didn't need to be, but he'd never asked anyone to marry him before. He was sweating a bit, and he took out his handkerchief and dabbed his brow.

"Good evening, Friedrich," Panayiotis greeted him and put his arm around his shoulders. "How are you tonight? Sit down for a moment."

"Oh, Mr Haralambos, I'm...I'm...good," Friedrich stammered.

"You don't look good to me. Come over here and have a sit down before you fall down." Panayiotis led him to a small park bench just outside the grounds of the apartment block.

"Ah...thank you."

"Are those for Elena?" the former priest asked, and grinned as the suitor nodded. He liked the young man. They had been introduced by Elena just after Friedrich came out of hospital. He doubted Friedrich remembered that meeting, since he was concussed at the time, but Panayiotis was impressed by the young man. "So."

"So," Friedrich sighed. "Oh God, I am such a wimp."

"What are you talking about?"

"Um...Elena likes you. She told me she talks to you and stuff."

"And stuff," Panayiotis said. Only recently had Elena sat down with him and talked to him about her experiences in the concentration cam., He suspected Zoe had a hand in that since Elena was a shy young woman.

Panayiotis had finished polishing the gold crucifix and put it back on the wall and stood admiring it for a few moments. He had heard a knock on the door and opened it to find Elena standing there looking very awkward.

He ushered the young woman inside, and she sat down on the edge of the sofa. Zoe had told him that Elena wanted to speak to him, but that was all he knew.

"Um...did Zoe tell you why I'm here?" Elena quietly asked, hoping Zoe had broken some of the ice.

"No, she only told me you wanted to speak to me."

"Um...Mr Haralambos...I know you're a Greek Orthodox priest...I mean former priest and, well, I'm Jewish but...can I talk to you about a personal matter?"

"It doesn't matter if you are Jewish or I'm Greek Orthodox, Elena. There is only one God and He doesn't discriminate," Panayiotis had said, having an inkling of where the conversation was going.

He was aware that the young woman had been in a concentration camp, the number tattooed on the inside of her arm revealed that. He and Father Eleftheriou had counselled a few Greek Jews who were liberated from the camps. They went down to the docks to help out Rabbi Jacobson when he needed their help with the Greek immigrants. His former role as a priest in Greece during the Occupation was useful. The tales he heard made him want to cry, and he poured out his soul to Ally who listened patiently as he related the tragic events. He was very fortunate to have his wife to speak to. He wondered who Father Eleftheriou had to discuss things with, apart from God.

In between bouts of crying on his shoulder, Elena had related her experiences. He did the best he could and, despite being Greek Orthodox, he used the Old Testament and the scriptures the Rabbi had used to comfort the people they had met. He had hoped it would help the young woman, and since then she had visited him often and they talked.

"Mr Haralambos, I want to ask Elena to marry me," Friedrich said shyly and looked up over his glasses, brushing away a mosquito that was buzzing him.

Panayiotis put his arm around his shoulders and squeezed. "That's excellent news."

"Huh...yeah, but I don't know if she wants to."

"Hmm. So how would you know, if you don't ask her?"

"I wrote a letter, but it got lost."

"You were going to propose marriage to her by letter?" Panayiotis' bushy eyebrows went up, and he resisted the urge to chuckle.

"Yeah," Friedrich replied. "But this time, I got her some flowers, chocolates and I've written what I want to say..."

"Throw it away."

"The card?"

Panayiotis nodded and put his hand on Friedrich's chest. "Say what's in your heart."

"But..."

"Elena deserves it, my boy. Be yourself. Now go and propose to her." Panayiotis got up, pulled Friedrich up with him, and pushed him towards the flats.

Friedrich looked towards Elena's building and grinned, then turned back and gave the older man the card from his shirt pocket before he started up the walkway to the entrance.

"Another happy customer," Panayiotis said to himself, put the card in his pocket, and followed Friedrich to the flat.

❖❖❖❖❖❖❖

Friedrich stood at the door and closed his eyes, saying a quick prayer before knocking. He waited a few moments until the door opened. He couldn't stop the smile that spread across his face at the sight of the woman he wanted to marry. Elena ushered him in and closed the door.

"Oh, flowers!" Elena gushed. "And chocolates!"

Friedrich grinned. He made a mental note to himself to thank David. Elena gave him a chaste kiss on the cheek as they held hands in the middle of the living room. Friedrich looked around and noticed the candles on the decorated table.

"I'm sorry I was so late...um," Friedrich stammered, realising it was getting late and he had promised to be here earlier.

"That's okay. I figured you might have been delayed," Elena replied as she went to the kitchen and found a vase. She spent a few moments admiring the flowers and enjoying their perfume. She brought the vase out and placed it on the table.

Friedrich fidgeted. *I should have asked David how to do this*, he thought to himself, regretting having given the card to the former priest. "Elena, I...um...I need to talk to you."

"Is something wrong?" Elena asked as she sat down, watching Friedrich who turned his back on her for a moment. Elena frowned at his odd behaviour. When he finally turned around, he gave her a half-hearted smile and sat down on the sofa. "Friedrich, what's wrong?"

"Well, you know I sent you a letter, and the Nazis got it, and it would have said everything I wanted to say. Then I wrote a card, but when I came over here, Mr Haralambos took it from me and said to say things from my heart, but now I can't find the words to ask whether you want to marry me or not." He took a breath and continued. "And it would have been nice."

"Yes," Elena said and smiled broadly.

"It would have been really nice if I did it the old fashioned way, you know, and–"

"Friedrich," Elena interrupted, "I said yes."

"It was so romantic and everything, and now I don't know how to say it." Friedrich stopped when he realised what Elena had just said. "Huh?"

Elena shook her head and grinned. "I said, yes, I'll marry you."

Friedrich's eyes went wide, and he dropped to his knees in front of the young woman who would soon become Mrs Friedrich Jacobs. "You mean, you want to marry me?"

"I don't see anyone else asking me," Elena joked.

"You mean you want to marry *me*?" Friedrich pointed to himself in total disbelief.

"*Yes*, I want to marry *you*." Elena pointed at him and got scooped up in his arms and whirled around the room.

"Whoohoo!" he yelled as he twirled the laughing young woman. He put her down, and Elena watched as he fished around in his pocket. "Um, I hope you like this. It was my mother's." He smiled broadly as he placed a diamond ring on her finger.

Elena looked down at the single diamond sparkling in the light and put her arms around his neck. "Oh, Friedrich, this is so beautiful!" she cried as she kissed him tenderly.

They sat down on the sofa together as Elena admired the ring. "I'm sure my mother would be proud to see you wear that ring—a beautiful ring for a beautiful woman," Friedrich said shyly and gave her a quick kiss.

Chapter 15

The thunder clapped as rain splattered onto the window, and Eva woke with a start as the thunder once again sounded overhead. She looked down at her wife who was sleeping through the noise and marvelled at how she could do it. Zoe wore a very happy smile on her face, which made Eva grin in reaction.

Eva snuggled down and scooped her still sleeping partner closer to her. She could feel Zoe's breath on her chest, and it tickled a little. She ran her hand lightly through Zoe's dark locks as she remembered their lovemaking in the bathtub and later as they cuddled and talked. *I will have to do something to stop my wife from painting me naked,* she chuckled. She did threaten revenge, but she didn't think Zoe took her seriously as the conversation descended into a ticklefest.

Talking to Zoe was like a soothing massage: it relaxed her. She shook her head at the analogy that she'd conjured up, but that's how she felt.

Zoe loved to talk to her—little things like the day's events, quirky things that came to her partner, and terrible jokes—something Greta never did during their brief time together. Just one of the many differences between the two women. There was one thing Zoe didn't tell her last night, and that was what Greta had said to her to get her upset, so upset that she didn't want to talk.

Eva frowned as she thought about Greta. She didn't want Greta to upset Zoe, and her former lover had somehow managed to find Zoe's weakness and exploit it. Eva was sure that was the reason Zoe had been quiet and didn't want to talk about what had happened at the office. *I'm not going to let my wife suffer because of a former lover,* Eva thought to herself as she looked down at Zoe who began to stir and opened blurry emerald eyes.

"You're frowning. You're going to get worry lines," Zoe gently scolded as she traced the worry lines on Eva's brow. "What were you thinking about?"

"I've made a decision," Eva said quietly.

"Hmm?"

"I'm not going to see Greta again."

Zoe hitched herself up on her elbow and let her hand rest on Eva's belly. "Not that I don't like that idea, but why not?"

"She hurt you, and I don't like it when you hurt," Eva replied, stroking Zoe's cheek with the back of her hand. "You're too precious to me."

Zoe tried to swallow the lump that had formed in her throat as Eva continued to caress her cheek. "I love you," she said quietly and let her head rest on Eva's chest. Eva leaned down and kissed her gently.

The sound of the rain and the now distant thunder made Zoe close her eyes and smile. She didn't want to force Eva to choose, it wasn't fair of her. She lay there enjoying the feel of Eva's fingers playing with her hair.

Eva looked up at the rain splattered window and sighed. "I don't think we can go riding, today."

"Oh, I don't know." Zoe murmured and rolled on top of Eva, causing Eva to chuckle and then reverse their positions.

"You are insatiable, you know that?" Eva stared into her wife's mischievous emerald eyes. "You are so addictive."

"I have one addiction, Miss Eva," Zoe replied a little breathlessly as she was back to lying on Eva's breasts.

"Oh?"

Zoe nodded. "One very tall, blue eyed, dark haired, absolutely captivating, drop dead gorgeous wife."

"Really?" Eva teased.

"Oh yeah. My favourite sport is climbing," Zoe ran her hand down her wife's hip, "over valleys and gullies," and inside her thigh, which drew a little gasp from her wife and made Zoe grin; and then she brought her hand up Eva's flat belly. She cupped her wife's breast as she continued the tour, "and over peaks." Zoe grinned impishly "Climbing up your body is one of my favourite sports." She leaned over and blew a raspberry in between Eva's breasts causing her spouse to chuckle.

"Do you plan on going climbing today?"

"Oh yeah!" Zoe said enthusiastically. As she was about to launch an assault, they heard a knock on the door, which made Zoe groan loudly and collapse on top of her wife. "I'm going to kill whoever is on the other side of that door," she muttered. "Don't move, I'll be right back."

"I'm not moving a muscle," Eva responded, watching as her wife grumpily got out of bed and put on a robe.

Zoe stood there admiring Eva for a few seconds and waggled her eyebrows at her. "You will remember where we were?"

"Over valleys and gullies," Eva replied and got an evil chuckle from Zoe as she left the bedroom.

Zoe ran her hands through her hair as she closed the bedroom door, and did a little happy skip as she went to the front door. She opened it to find Elena with a mile long grin on her face.

"Elena, it's 8:00 a.m., and it's Saturday. Please tell me we don't have any classes today." Zoe ushered her friend inside, hoping it wasn't that she had forgotten any classes or else she was going to be extremely upset.

"Look." Elena stuck out her hand under Zoe's nose.

Zoe looked down and saw the ring. They looked at each other, and they both screamed at the same time. Zoe embraced her friend and danced around the room hollering and yelping. All the hollering brought Eva out to check on the cause of the commotion, and she leaned against the bedroom door watching the two women dancing about.

Zoe caught sight of her and ran towards her, stopped and stood on the tips of her toes and kissed her. "Elena is getting married!"

"To who?" Eva asked mischievously.

Elena gave her a grin. "He asked me last night!"

"Why didn't you tell me!" Zoe cried out and then remembered what she was doing last night and gave Eva a quirky little grin.

"Well, it was late, so I didn't think you would be up. He was so cute last night, not all what I expected."

"You didn't..."

Elena looked blankly at Zoe and then it registered what Zoe was trying to ask. "No. We're going to wait until we're married."

"I'm happy for you, Elena." Eva came over and gave her

friend a hug. The shorter woman grinned at the bear hug from Eva, who normally wasn't a demonstrative affectionate person. She often wondered how that could be, since she knew Eva couldn't keep her hands off Zoe, but she probably was very shy about expressing her feelings to those she didn't know. "I'll just go and put on some clothes."

Zoe gave her a playful slap on the behind as she passed and grinned when Eva waggled her eyebrows at her.

Knowing that they needed to talk, Eva left the two friends alone as she went to dress. While Elena was her friend as well, it was Zoe their neighbour felt closer to, because of their ages being so close.

"So, how did he do it? Was he romantic and everything?" Zoe asked, having another look at the ring.

"How did Eva propose?"

"Oh, God, Eva is the most romantic woman. Sick with the flu and nearly ready to pass out, she still went down on her knees," Zoe replied, swooning with the remembrance, causing Elena to chuckle at her antics.

"Oh, she beats Friedrich in the romance stakes. Do you remember that letter he sent that wasn't a letter?"

"The secret spy one, yeah."

"Well that was supposed to be his proposal."

"NO! Oh God, that's funny."

"Yeah, but last night he brought flowers and chocolates. He was so sweet," Elena sighed and got chuckle from her friend. "I want to thank you."

"What for?"

"For agreeing to go to the dance with David. Friedrich is so shy, he wouldn't have asked me in a million years. Would you do me a favour?"

"If I can."

"Would you be my bridesmaid? And I want to ask Eva if she would be my witness. You're about the only family I have, so—" Elena didn't finish as Zoe wrapped her arms around her and gave her a tremendous hug.

❖❖❖❖❖❖❖

Friedrich walked down the corridor of his office building with a huge smile on his face and humming. He had placed a carnation in his lapel. He stopped and smelt the flower as Joe, the new janitor, stopped what he was doing to watch him.

Friedrich greeted the man with a nod and continued to hum as he entered his office. Joe watched him for a few minutes and shook his head, taking his mop and bucket to another office.

"Good morning, David," Friedrich greeted his friend who was sitting with his feet propped up on the desk.

"*Good* morning?" David swung around and looked outside to the miserable weather, then turned to his friend with a mock scowl. "Okay, who are you, and what have you done with Freddy?"

"The Nazis got me and have replaced me with a spy," Friedrich joked as he took off his jacket.

"That's pathetic, Freddy. They would have replaced you with someone who told better jokes. So, you got some 'you know' finally, huh?" David grinned and returned to reading his file.

"Better than that, Mr Peterson, much much better."

"Nothing is better than 'you know,' Freddy," David muttered and took a peek over his file as Friedrich took off his hat and with a flourish sent it sailing towards the hat rack. It missed and fell in the rubbish bin. David burst out laughing and shook his head.

"You're going to a wedding, David."

"Did Edna finally settle on a date this time?" David asked referring to their mail clerk, who had invited them to her wedding only to have it postponed due to the groom's nerves.

"Not that I know of." Friedrich went over and retrieved his hat and put his hand over David's file with a huge grin on his face. "She said yes."

"Who said yes?" David asked, knowing full well his friend was talking about Elena but wanting to string it along. He was happy for his friend who he had spent hours with, trying to teach him how to talk to women.

"Miss Elena Mannheim, soon to be Mrs Friedrich Jacobs, a gorgeous, intelligent woman."

David grinned as he got up and put his arm around Friedrich's shoulders. "So you finally asked her. Good one, old boy!"

"She said yes, do you believe that?"

"No, but then I don't understand women," David replied as he swerved to avoid Friedrich's playful punch. "So when is the big day?"

Friedrich settled in his chair and sitting back, smiling. "We haven't discussed it, but I hope it's soon."

"Me, too. You're too happy." David looked up, only to get hit on the head by a balled up piece of paper. "Are we going to do some work today, or daydream about the lovely Elena?"

"We have to work?"

"Yes, that's what they pay us to do." David shook his head and wondered if his friend was going to do anything productive today. "Here, you go through this lot, and I'll go through this lot. We got another shipload yesterday."

David handed him the files and the photographs from the Immigration Department, and they settled down to go through the thousands of names, cross checking them with their wanted lists.

Friedrich stopped for a moment and looked over at David. "David, would you be my best man?"

"Only if you pay me." David grinned up at his friend and got another rolled up paper on the head. "Yes, of course I'll be your best man. Who else would organise your bucks night?"

They settled once again and spent the next two hours looking at their respective lists. Friedrich scowled at the photo in his hand and checked it against the photograph the Immigration Department had given them. The woman looking back at him had blond hair and the one in the photograph from Immigration had dark. *But that wouldn't be hard to change,* he thought to himself.

"I think I may have something," Friedrich said. David got up from his desk and stood behind his partner as he was handed the information sheet on the woman in the photo. Friedrich read the reports and was sickened. He had read many reports that made him sick to his stomach, but even he was shocked by what he was reading.

"She worked at Dachau," David said quietly and thought back to the brown eyed woman that haunted his dreams.

"And Auschwitz. My God," Friedrich whispered as his mind registered that the names of two of the most wanted war criminals were connected with the woman. "Dr Bruno Weber and Dr Josef Mengele...she assisted both of them."

"The Angel of Death." David pulled out the chair and sat down next to Friedrich. His hatred for the man known as the Angel of Death, Dr Josef Mengele, was well known in the department. David had spent time in Germany searching for the man who was responsible for the deaths of thousands of Jews sent to Auschwitz. The doctor's horrendous genetic experiments made him sick. He had spoken to survivors of that horror camp and listened to countless tales about the man who had decided who lived and who died.

He recalled the interview he had with one survivor, Hani Schick, a mother of twins who, together with her children, was subjected to experiments by Mengele. She told him of Mengele's tortures and how her two children had died.

Friedrich took a deep breath and put the file down. His good humour of the earlier hours had evaporated. "Where is Mengele?"

"Probably halfway to Argentina," David replied, still reading the file. "Weber has been arrested and is awaiting trial." He picked up the photograph and stared at the smiling, happy woman. "These men are animals, but you would think that a woman would have had more compassion," he whispered to himself. "What does the Immigration file say?"

Friedrich picked up the paper, his hand shaking a little at the realisation that a member of the "medical" team from Auschwitz, the monsters that took the Hippocratic oath and then butchered thousands, was here. "According to the transportation papers, her name is Erika Wagner. Her photograph matches that of Greta Inga Strauss, assistant to Drs Mengele and Weber. Mrs Wagner is married to Heinrich Wagner and arrived here 10 January. I don't have any information on him."

David held the two photographs in his hand. "I want to find this bitch, Friedrich."

Chapter 16

Friedrich sat back in his chair and let out a discontented sigh. It had been a frustrating day, although neither of them was at all surprised that the address on the immigration papers was wrong. He didn't think that Strauss would put down her correct details. Some of the criminals they were seeking had "kangaroos in the top paddock," as David described them, meaning they weren't very bright. This woman, though, was very smart, and from the eyewitness accounts, also very dangerous.

They had spent the afternoon looking for the address they had listed for her, which turned out to be nothing but a hole in the ground at a new building site. Neither man was very happy about this, as it was still raining. The very warm, muggy weather, the rain, and the wild goose chase resulted in two rather cranky investigators.

Back at the office, the whirring fan overhead did nothing to alleviate Friedrich's discomfort as the humidity sapped his energy.

"Freddy, go home," David said as he came in carrying another lot of files, letting them drop on his already messy desk.

"Do you think she's still here?"

"I don't know, mate. I hope she is," David sighed as he picked up the photograph of the Strauss woman and put it up on his noticeboard, then took two steps back to look at it. "If she is, I want to make sure we don't have any cock-ups or spying janitors to fuck things up."

Friedrich looked up sharply at David's swearing, and chose not to say anything about it since they were both tired and irritable. "Why are you putting her picture up if we don't want to alert the 'grapevine' that we know that she's here?"

David looked back at him sheepishly and took the photo down. "I'm getting old, Freddy."

"Aren't we all," Friedrich muttered as he took the photographs from David and put them in the file, which he placed in his briefcase. "I'm going home. I suggest you do, too. Good night, David."

"Night, mate," David replied as the door closed quietly. "Wish I had a nice lady to go home to."

❖❖❖❖❖❖❖

Friedrich shut the car door and ran up the path to the block of flats, putting his briefcase on top of his head as cover as the rain continued to pelt down. He opened the foyer door and bumped into Panayiotis, nearly causing the older man to fall over. Friedrich's quick reflexes prevented him from hitting the hard ground.

"Oh, I'm sorry, Mr Haralambos!" Friedrich apologised as he held the man by the arm and steadied him.

"Quite all right, Friedrich," Panayiotis replied.

Friedrich bent over and retrieved the former priest's cane and handed it back to him. "How is Mrs Haralambos tonight?"

"Oh, she's fine, has a little headache. You know how it is, the older you get the more aches you get."

"Yes, sir," Friedrich agreed. "I mean, I don't know about that, but..."

Panayiotis chuckled and clasped the young man's shoulder. "I know what you meant. So, young man, did you propose?"

Friedrich beamed. "Yes, sir. It wasn't all that romantic, but she said yes."

"It's not the delivery that counts, it's what's in your heart." Panayiotis patted Friedrich's chest. "Elena is a good girl."

"Yeah, I know."

"Good boy. Now go up and see your fiancée, since I'm sure she is looking forward to seeing you."

"Yes, sir, good night." Friedrich replied and picked up his briefcase, then bounded up the stairs. Panayiotis watched him for a few moments.

"Ah, to leap about like that again." He grimaced as he turned. The pain in his leg had made it difficult for the older man to get out, and he limped back to his flat and closed the door.

❖❖❖❖❖❖❖

Friedrich stopped at the landing and combed his hair, then took off his tie and shoved it into his briefcase. He checked himself again before going to Elena's flat and knocking. He frowned when he didn't get a reply.

Zoe's door opened and her head popped out, grinning when she saw the young man. "Hey, Friedrich, she's over here." She pulled the door open wide and held it for him as he entered the flat.

As soon as he stepped through the doorway, he was greeted by Eva and Earl, who were seated at the table and playing chess. Elena came out of the kitchen with a smile, going over and giving him a hug and a chaste kiss.

"Congratulations, Friedrich!" Eva and Earl both said, as Earl moved one of his pawns on the board.

"Thank you," Friedrich said shyly. He was even more surprised when Zoe hugged him and gave him a peck on the cheek.

"I'm very happy for both of you," Zoe whispered to him, and turned to give Elena another hug.

"Are you guys free tomorrow for dinner?" Eva asked.

Elena looked at Friedrich, who shrugged. "Yep, we're free. We'll see you tomorrow!"

They bade farewell to their friends, and Zoe closed the door behind them. She went back into the kitchen and brought three cups, giving Earl and Eva a cup of tea before taking hers over to her workspace.

She placed both hands on the cup, looked at her work and grinned.

"She's not painting you again, is she?" Earl asked as he took a sip, glancing up at the grinning Zoe.

"I hope not," Eva replied. "Zo, what are you painting?"

"Something for the bedroom," Zoe replied, still grinning as she met Eva's twinkling blue eyes.

"A nice landscape?" Earl asked. He looked at the board, then back up at Eva with a scowl.

"Yeah, a mountain-with valleys, gullies...and peaks," Zoe replied as Eva snorted her tea all over the chessboard, causing

Zoe to look down at her painting and giggle out of Earl's sight.

"Hey, are you all right?" Earl patted Eva on the back as she gave a couple of coughs, then rose to get a towel from the kitchen to dry the chessboard and pieces.

"Oh, yeah," Eva said, passing Zoe on her way to the kitchen and giving her a slap on the behind. She came back out, and before heading to Earl, she put her arms around Zoe's shoulders and Zoe leaned back into her. Eva pulled Zoe's dark hair back from her face and whispered in her ear.

Earl watched Zoe's hands go very still as she listened to what Eva was whispering to her. A bright blush started creeping up Zoe's neck and face as Eva gave her a peck on the cheek before rejoining him.

Earl continued to watch Zoe as Eva wiped down the chessboard. Zoe headed for the balcony door, opened it, and stepped outside into the cool evening air, leaning on the wet railing and letting the light rain fall on her for a few moments.

"Is Zoe okay?" Earl asked, concerned for the young woman. "She looks a bit flushed."

"Yep," Eva replied, glancing out at the balcony and her cheeky partner, giving Zoe a wink when her wife turned around to come back inside, still a little flushed despite the cool shower she had just subjected herself to.

❖❖❖❖❖❖❖

Elena closed the door to her flat and turned to find Friedrich smiling. She wrapped her arms around his waist and looked up into honey coloured eyes.

"I have been floating all day today," Elena said as she hugged him. She leaned up and gave him a kiss. "Did you tell David?"

"Yep, sure did. I asked him to be my best man."

"Oh, that's nice! Eva and Zoe are going to be there for me." Elena took his jacket and his briefcase and laid them down on the low table. Taking his hand, she led him to the sofa and they sat down. "Did you have a good day?"

Friedrich smiled ruefully. "I'm not sure what a good day is supposed to be like at our office. We lose someone, and it's a bad day; we find someone, and it's still a bad day."

"Catching them to face justice is good, isn't it?"

Friedrich nodded. "Yes, it's good; but for every one of these people we catch, more escape and go free."

"Like rats," Elena said quietly.

"Yeah. Today, I think we may have caught one in our net...an assistant to Dr Josef Mengele."

"Who is Dr Mengele?"

Friedrich sighed. He was glad that Elena never met the butcher. It was a small consolation that she had been at Bergen-Belsen and not at Auschwitz like his family. He turned to her and held her smaller hand in his. "He performed medical experiments on Jews at Auschwitz. He would decide people's fate as they came in on those trains. I've read one report that said he put up a chalk mark on a bunk, and any child not reaching that mark was sent to the gas chambers." He took a deep breath and held Elena tightly.

Elena put her head on Friedrich's shoulder. She shook her head sadly at yet another brutality against the Jews and shuddered at the thought of children being killed on one man's whim. "Have they caught him?"

"No," Friedrich said quietly. "He's probably off to Argentina or Brazil. That's where they end up."

"Your family died in Auschwitz. You don't think..." Elena didn't even want to say the words aloud because it pained her to think of Friedrich's family in that butcher's hands.

Friedrich nodded. "My sisters died at Auschwitz. I wish you could have met them, Elena. You would have liked them. They were fun. They were very beautiful girls, dark hair and grey eyes. I got my mother's brown eyes, but they looked like papa. Heidi was a little older than Viveka." Friedrich smiled as he remembered the many playful arguments his sisters would have about who was the oldest of the twins.

"Heidi and Viveka–they are beautiful names. How old were they?"

"Fifteen," Friedrich said quietly.

Elena gasped at the realisation that Friedrich's sisters may have been part of Mengele's experiments and turned to her fiancé to see silent tears trailing down his cheeks. She brushed away his tears with her hand and cupped his face. "I'm so sorry, Friedrich," Elena said as she kissed him gently and held on to him. "Do you know where this assistant is? Are you going to catch him?"

"It's a woman, a cold blooded Nazi butcher," Friedrich said bitterly.

"I'm sure you and David will catch this monster...won't you?"

Friedrich turned to his fiancée. "At lunch time I went down to the synagogue and prayed. I made a promise to them that I would do everything I can to catch her and send her to Nuremburg."

"I know you'll catch her," Elena said with conviction. She wanted to believe that good people did win out at the end, and that was how things worked. "Do you know where she lives?"

"Nope, she gave a false address. We wasted a couple of hours looking down a hole in the ground. Maybe something will turn up on Monday."

"You never know how these things turn out, sweetheart."

"Hmm. Do you want to snuggle a bit?" Friedrich asked. He got his answer as Elena put her head on his shoulder.

❖ ❖ ❖ ❖ ❖ ❖ ❖

Greta had found the small house soon after arriving and had paid in cash for it, much to the amazement of the previous owner who gladly took the money. It wasn't what she was used to, but it was better than the squalid conditions of the immigrant hostel. Heinrich, her husband, decided he wanted to stay elsewhere, which suited her quite nicely. The shrubbery in the front of the house afforded her quite a bit of privacy and protection from the street, which Greta liked a great deal.

Dieter Wierner was a tall, broad shouldered, young man with blond hair and the bluest eyes she had ever seen. *A true Aryan*, Greta had thought when she met him. He had been her contact as soon as she'd left the ship, and he helped her with the necessary papers and purchasing the house.

She knew him as Dieter, but suspected that wasn't his real name. She really didn't care one way or the other as long as he kept her true identity a secret. The encounter with Eva was a mixed blessing. She wasn't sure why she went to the interpreter service. Dieter had told her it was a stupid move, but she was sure there had been divine intervention.

Greta turned to the liaison, who stood in the lounge room of her new house. "Do they know I'm here?"

"No. I've gone through their files and your name does appear, but it's in the finalised section. They think you're dead."

Greta chuckled. "I think this is where I say, the news of my death is greatly appreciated." She continued to chuckle at the idiocy of the War Crimes Tribunal's investigator's office. "I thought you said they were thorough."

"They usually are. They caught Muller and Rhimes."

Greta rolled her eyes at the mention of the men. She had been briefed as to what had happened and wondered how a man like Rhimes, she thought of him as intelligent, could allow Muller, who must have been out of his mind, to even entertain the thought of going after Eva all because she was a lesbian. *Stupid man.*

"Muller was affected by the explosion, although I don't understand why Rhimes did it."

Dieter shrugged. "I don't know."

"So what do you know about Peterson and Jacobs?"

"Nothing, really. They work for the unit, they capture the idiots that put their real names on their immigration papers and just plod along. They are insignificant, really."

Greta pursed her lips in thought. She didn't like to leave things to chance, but on the basis of what she'd heard, it wasn't likely that the two investigators were going to find anything. She turned back and watched the rain for a moment. "Jacobs...that's a Jewish name?"

"*Ja.*"

Greta rolled her eyes and let out a frustrated sigh. "They are everywhere, aren't they?"

Dieter snorted. "Just about everywhere you go, there is a Jew."

"It's too bad we didn't have time to finish the Fuhrer's plans," Greta said disappointedly. "I met him a couple of times, you know."

"You did?" Dieter was impressed. He had wanted to meet the great man, but was hindered on every occasion. "What was he like?"

Greta grinned. "Oh, he was such a charismatic man, so full of energy and ideas for Germany. His eyes were so full of life," Greta said as she thought back to when Josef introduced her to the great man. She found herself tongue tied for the first time in her life, which amused their leader a great deal. He had made a joke, which relaxed her, and they discussed the work that was being done at Auschwitz and what Josef was accomplishing. She sighed as she thought about her mentor, Josef Mengele, a truly brilliant man whose work was never going to be fully appreciated. She could still remember how the Fuhrer had praised the whole team at Auschwitz, and how proud she was to be a part of it.

"A little hero worship?" Dieter commented with a smile.

Greta chuckled. "A huge case of hero worship. I met him in 1936; he was everything a leader should be. I wish you could have met him, Dieter. He was truly a giant among men. The world owes a great deal to him and men like DrDrs Josef Mengele. Have you any news about Josef?"

"Sadly, no."

"I hope he was able to escape those rabid American dogs. What about Bruno?"

"He was arrested and is due to face trial."

"Bruno was also a good doctor, but Josef was truly a marvel to watch. I feel privileged to have worked with him."

Dieter watched her as she sat on the sofa, pulling her feet under her. He liked the tall woman; she had something about her that just made her stand out. He was rather excited when he'd found out who she was. He had met her husband, an insignificant man, and wondered if he had a chance with her. "Would you like to go out tonight?" he asked.

Greta gave him a lopsided grin. "I'm a married woman, Dieter."

"Oh, well, I thought..."

"Heinrich is a good man, a drunk, but a good man. For now, I play the dutiful wife. I'm sure there are other young women to wine and dine?"

Dieter nodded and looked up into smiling blue eyes which totally captivated him. "I'd best be going."

"Have a nice evening, Dieter, and keep me updated."

The young man nodded and was seen to the door. Greta watched him leave and closed the door quietly behind him.

Chapter 17

Friedrich smiled, opened sleepy brown eyes, and gazed down at the dark head resting on his chest. He sighed contently, holding his fiancée in his arms. *My fiancée*, he thought and lightly pinched himself to see if he was dreaming. And if he was, he didn't want this dream to end. He had found the woman he wanted to spend the rest of his life with. He looked around the room, so different from his own one bedroom flat. His flat was very drab, and Friedrich used it just to sleep in, since he had no one to go home to and seldom ate at home. It was going to be different now. Elena's room was airy; it had lace pink curtains on the window. Several stuffed toys that usually sat on the bed were on the dresser. Friedrich loved the bed. It was an antique, steel framed bed with the most comfortable mattress. He had seen one in an antique shop and thought it would be great to own and share it with someone he loved.

He looked up at the ceiling and grinned. They had decided not to consummate their love for each other until they got married, but he did enjoy cuddling and lying next to this woman who kissed him with so much love that his heart was ready to burst.

"What's the goofy grin for?" Elena asked as she gazed up at him. She had been awake for half an hour just lying in Friedrich's embrace and savouring the moment.

"Good morning." Friedrich kissed the top of her head as Elena cuddled and put her arm around his waist. "I was thinking this was a dream, and I would wake up any minute."

"Do you want to wake up?" Elena asked.

"No. I want to keep dreaming like this for the rest of my life," Friedrich replied.

"That's so romantic," Elena sighed.

"Does it make up for the proposal?"

"No." Elena gave him a mock glare and then chuckled. "We'll work on your romantic streak."

Friedrich chuckled.

"So, fiancé, what are we doing today?" Elena asked.

"I have an appointment at 9:30 to see Rabbi Mordecai."

"For the wedding? Isn't that a bit soon?"

"I wish it were for the wedding. Rabbi Mordecai met my father in Auschwitz, and I've been putting off talking to him."

"Why?"

Friedrich sighed. He wasn't sure why he had put it off and wasn't sure if the reason would make any sense. He wanted to believe his family would be back from the concentration camps and held out hope that if no one told him that they were indeed dead, then maybe if he wished hard enough they wouldn't be. It was nonsense, and he told himself so, but having someone who was there tell him that they were dead would make it real. He shook his head.

"I believed that if I didn't hear it from someone who saw them at the concentration camp...that somehow it wasn't real. That I would find that it was possible for them to have survived."

Elena closed her eyes and tightened her hold on her fiancé. She didn't know what to say and chose to let Friedrich continue.

"We interviewed the Rabbi just after he came to Sydney, and one thing led to another, and we talked about my family. I didn't want to hear what he had to say, and told him that I would discuss it another day."

"How long ago was that?"

"Six months," Friedrich replied. "He called me at the office yesterday and said that we really needed to talk."

"Do you want me to come with you?"

Friedrich smiled. "I would love for you to come, but I don't want it to cause you pain."

"It won't cause me any pain, and I want to be there for you." Elena cupped his stubbled cheek as Friedrich leaned down and kissed her gently. "I'd better get up and have a bath," he mumbled as he continued to hold his fiancée.

"I've washed the clothes you left behind last week. Do you have a tie?"

"It's in my briefcase."

"Well, Mr Jacobs, do you want to get up?"

"Hmm...well, Miss Mannheim, I like it here but I do have to get up," Friedrich reluctantly agreed and pulled the covers off. He wore only a pair of boxer shorts and, much to Elena's amusement, they were coloured pink.

When she saw them she couldn't stop laughing, and laughed even more when Friedrich explained how he'd put his white boxer shorts and a red shirt in the same wash, and they came out pink. She hitched herself up on her elbow and watched him walk out. "Hmm...this is nice," she said to herself and grinned.

She got out of bed herself and padded out to the kitchen to make some coffee for Friedrich and tea for herself.

"Elena, do you have any razors?" Friedrich asked from the bathroom.

"Top shelf," Elena replied, and giggled at the idea that entered her head. She wanted to go in and show him, but she decided against it. She sipped her tea, then set the cup on the table as she went into the laundry to find the boxers and shirt she had washed for him.

Finding what she was looking for, Elena knocked on the bathroom door before opening it slightly and putting a towel and his boxer shorts on the chair next to the door. She closed the door and grinned.

Elena took out the ironing board to iron his trousers from the previous day. Once that was done, she hung them on the hanger and went in search of his briefcase to look for the tie that was probably crinkled.

The briefcase lay on the floor next to the sofa. She bent down and picked up the case, but lost hold of it. It hit the floor, spilling the files and the tie out onto the carpet. The picture of Greta lay prominently next to the tie. Elena dropped to her knees and was picking up the files when she spotted the picture.

Friedrich walked out of the bathroom with the towel wrapped around his waist and frowned when he saw the contents of his bag on the floor. "Elena, what happened?"

"I dropped the bag," Elena said quietly as she continued to stare at the photograph.

Friedrich took off his towel, put on his trousers and walked to where Elena was kneeling on the floor. He put his hand on her shoulder and went down on his knees to help her collect the files.

"I know that woman," Elena said softly.

Friedrich was shocked. He stopped putting the files back in order and turned to her. "You know this woman?"

Elena nodded.

"From the camp?"

"No, she was here last week."

Friedrich sat down on the carpet with a thud. "She was here? In this flat?"

"No, she was a dinner guest at Eva and Zoe's." Friedrich swore and got a startled look from Elena. "What's the matter, who is this woman?"

"What do you know about her?" Friedrich asked, chastising himself for his swearing.

"Well, Zoe told me that Greta was Eva's first lover and..."

Friedrich groaned. This was going from bad to worse. He wondered if Eva was aware of the woman's war activities. If so, he really didn't know what to do next. Eva would alert her former lover, and they would never catch her. He would have to ask Elena not to reveal anything about the photograph. On the other hand, maybe Eva didn't know about her activities, in which case they had an excellent chance of capturing her.

"Friedrich, what is going on?" Elena asked as her fiancé sat there with a scowl on his face.

"I need to call David," Friedrich said, and got up and went to the phone.

Elena scowled and picked up the file. Leaning against the sofa, she began to read. She let out a gasp as the details in front of her painted Greta as a monster. She could hear Friedrich talking to David, then looked up as Friedrich knelt beside her. He took the file from her hands and put it in the briefcase.

"Did that really happen?" she asked quietly, her mind not wanting to accept what she had read.

Friedrich nodded. "Yes. It happened in other camps, as well, but Auschwitz was where this woman was."

"I don't think Eva knows." Elena thought about her friend who had one of the most gentle of personalities.

"David is coming over, and we're going to question her," Friedrich replied, running his hands through his wet hair.

"Friedrich! I know Eva, and she doesn't know." Elena was upset that Friedrich or David would think that Eva knew anything about this woman's activities. "You make it out to sound like an interrogation!"

"Sweetheart, David and I are just going to ask Eva a few questions, that's all." Friedrich tried to calm his fiancée down, as she was becoming rather angry. "I hope they are still in."

"They go to church on Sunday morning," Elena mumbled. "You really can't believe Eva would know about her, do you?"

"I don't know what to believe, Ele," Friedrich replied and sighed.

❖❖❖❖❖❖❖

Panayiotis and Ally walked along holding hands as they joined Eva and Zoe on the walk home from church. Zoe kept a step ahead of Eva and occasionally looked back at her in-laws and pursed her lips. She shook her head, deciding that she had had enough of not being able to hold hands with her wife in church or outside. She took Eva's hand and squeezed it.

Eva looked down at the joined hands and gave her a grin. "I was wondering how long it would take," she said with a wink.

They had spent the morning in church, and then some time talking to Father Eleftheriou after the service. He wasn't aware of their marriage, and Eva thought one day she should tell the priest before he tried to get her involved in church dances for singles.

"I don't like it either, love, but—"

"But nothing, Evy." Zoe nodded. "I think he's going to get quite a shock when he finds out. I hope he doesn't bar us from the church."

"Don't worry, love," Eva said as she kissed her wife on the top of her head.

"I'm not worried. I just don't want to go to another congregation. I like it there."

"Yeah, so do I, although I much preferred the congregation in Larissa."

Zoe looked up and grinned. "Even Mrs Elimbos?" Zoe asked, referring to the old woman that hit Eva with her cane when Eva had visited the church.

Eva gave her a lopsided grin. "Yeah, even Mrs Elimbos."

"Who is Mrs Elimbos?" Ally asked as she held on to her husband's arm.

"An old woman who lost 5 sons to the Germans," Panayiotis

explained. "She took exception to Eva coming to church and hit her with her cane."

"Oh dear. That must have been a very trying time for you," Ally said, directing her statement to her tall step-daughter.

"It was difficult," Eva agreed quietly. "See you for dinner, okay?"

"I'll bring up the lemon meringue pie," Ally promised. She and Panayiotis watched as Zoe wrapped her arm around Eva's waist and walked up the stairs to their own flat.

They found David and Friedrich waiting for them outside their door. Zoe looked at Eva in question, then shrugged. "So, what's up?" Eva asked, then folded her arms over her chest and waited. She had an uneasy feeling this had to do with her past since David was present.

"Friedrich and I are here on business—"

"I figured that out, David," Eva said icily. Eva disliked the man, even though he had tried to save their lives during the whole Muller fiasco. She had discovered that it had been his bright idea to use her as bait in the first place. The fact that nothing happened to Zoe was the only thing that made Eva tolerate him. Zoe turned to her wife, took her by the hand, and led her to the sofa where they sat down. Zoe's hand went to Eva's knee and gave it a little squeeze. "What's this about?"

"Has Muller escaped or something?" Zoe asked.

"No." David pulled out Greta's photograph. "Do you know this person?"

Eva took the photograph and immediately recognized her former lover. She frowned when she saw that the woman was wearing the uniform of the SS, the feared secret police. "Yes, that's Greta Strauss." She handed the photograph to Zoe who looked at it, then looked up in shock at Elena and then her wife. Eva had a composed look on her face, but Zoe knew the turmoil going on underneath.

"That's an SS uniform," Zoe stated quietly, and Eva turned to her and nodded.

"How do you know Miss Strauss?" David asked.

Eva exhaled. "I knew her in Germany, before the war."

"What was your relationship with her?"

Zoe scowled. "What business is it of yours?"

"Zoe," Eva quietly reproved her wife.

Zoe turned to Eva with a scowl and cupped her wife's cheek. "No, Eva. I've had enough of this stupidity. When are they going to learn that you are not a Nazi and never have been? Does every fucking Nazi have to be traced back to you?" Zoe lost her temper completely, which didn't surprise Eva but shocked David and Friedrich, who looked at each other in surprise.

Eva turned to the two men and sighed. She wasn't going to apologise for Zoe's outburst, because it was what she wanted to do as well.

"Look, Eva, I'm not trying—" David tried to get back to the questioning and not be distracted by the fiery young woman.

"Of course you are! You are trying to link Eva to this," Zoe angrily interjected.

"No, I'm not. I'm trying to find out her relationship to the Strauss woman," David patiently tried to explain.

"She was my lover," Eva said quietly. "I lost contact with her November 8, 1938."

"It's interesting you remember the date."

"It was Kristalnacht. I'm sure you would remember it too," Eva said and watched Friedrich's eyes close. "My mother died that night as well, so you could say it's a date that I can't forget."

David sighed. He looked at Zoe, who was shooting daggers at him, and hoped his next question wasn't going to be his last. "What happened that night that you lost contact with Miss Strauss?"

"What the hell does that have to do with everything?" Zoe asked, knowing David was picking on one of Eva's open wounds, and she wasn't going to let him hurt her wife.

"She's right, Mr Peterson. What does my past have to do with it?" Eva asked.

"Look, Eva, I am here in an official capacity as an officer of the War Crimes Tribunal. You can either answer my questions here, or I can call you into the office for a more formal setting. Now I realise you are both upset, but I need answers and for you not to obstruct me in any way."

"Did you practice that little spiel while you were waiting for us?" Zoe shot back at him causing David to glare at her.

"Okay, can we all cool down a moment, please?" Friedrich spoke for the first time since they entered the flat. "Eva, Greta Strauss is wanted for crimes against humanity under the War Crimes Act. We want to find out everything we can so we can do our jobs."

Eva nodded as David loosened his tie.

"Okay, let me ask this again—what happened that night?"

Zoe sat back down and took Eva's hand. "Greta and I were in the Hitler Youth, and a group of us went out. We were urged by the brown shirts to join in the destruction of Jewish property."

"You took part in Kristalnacht?" David asked. He knew that the majority of the Hitler Youth took part that night, so he wasn't really surprised by that revelation.

"Yes. I participated in burning down a synagogue," Eva admitted quietly, looking down at her hands.

"Then what happened?"

"I fled and went home, while the rest of the group continued."

"Why?"

"It was wrong. I didn't want to be a part of it."

"Was Greta Strauss involved?"

"Yes."

"You said you lost contact with Miss Strauss after that night. What happened that brought that about?"

Eva met David's blue eyes and didn't answer for a few seconds. "My stepfather found out I was a lesbian and was in a relationship with Greta, and he beat me."

Zoe closed her eyes. She held back the tears knowing Eva was going to need her, and she wasn't going to fall apart when she needed to be there for her wife.

David stopped writing in his notebook and looked up. "Muller beat you because you were a lesbian?"

"Yes. That's also the night my mother died."

"So, you got a spanking from your stepfather, and you stopped seeing Greta?"

Zoe's stormy green eyes bored holes in the man, but she was held in place by Eva's strong arm. "No, Mr Peterson, I was beaten to within an inch of my life. The only thing that stopped him from killing me was that it wouldn't look good for a German officer to kill his own child," Eva angrily responded.

"I'm sorry, Eva." David tried to apologise. His anger was getting the better of him, and he took a few moments to compose himself. Getting angry with the tall woman wasn't going to get him any closer to catching Strauss.

Eva ignored his apology. "Mr Peterson, continue your questions, and I will answer them as best I can."

"What happened after that?"

"I was sent to live with my uncle, and I lost contact with Greta."

"That was the last time you saw her?"

"Yes, until recently, when she came to the interpreter section of the Immigration Department."

David and Friedrich looked at each other. "She came to your office and saw you?"

"Yes."

"How did she know you were there if you had lost contact with her?"

"I don't think she knew I was there. I just happened to be the German interpreter on duty at the time."

"A big coincidence."

"One of life's little mysteries," Eva responded sarcastically.

"Quite. What did she want?"

"Information about family law."

"Why?"

"I don't know, we didn't get to discuss it. I was in shock from seeing her again."

"So you invited her to dinner?"

"That's what old friends do, Mr Peterson, invite people they like to dinner."

"What happened when she arrived?"

"We ate, we talked about old times, and she left."

"And that was the last time you talked to her?"

"Yes. Zoe saw her at the office when she came to pick me up." Eva smiled at her wife for the first time since the questioning had started and wrapped her arm around Zoe's shoulders.

David turned to Zoe. "You were alone with Miss Strauss?"

"No. Debbie the receptionist was there when she came in looking for Eva," Zoe responded.

"What did she want?"

"To take me to lunch and make passionate love to me. What do you think she was there for?" Zoe responded as Eva coughed to hide the chuckle at her wife's temper.

David ignored the last comment as he wrote in his notebook. "She came to see Eva?"

"Yeeessss," Zoe said, drawing out the word in frustration.

"And?"

"And what? Eva wasn't in the office; she had gone down to hell."

"Hell?"

"Their filing room."

"Okay, so Eva wasn't there, and Miss Strauss saw you."

"Yes."

"You're not being very forthcoming, are you, Miss Lambros?" David said as he tried to put a lid on his own temper once again.

"That's Mrs Haralambos to you, Mr Peterson. Your questioning is hurting my wife, and frankly I couldn't give a rat's ass about your investigation," Zoe retorted.

Friedrich decided to take over the questioning, quite sure that otherwise they would come to blows if he knew anything about his new friend. Elena had told him about Zoe's protective streak towards Eva. "Zoe, did Greta say anything to you?"

Zoe turned to Friedrich and grimaced. "She wanted to speak to Eva. Since she wasn't there, she gave a phone number to the receptionist to get Eva to call her."

"She gave you a phone number?" David piped up and got a glare from Zoe.

"Yes, I got a phone number."

"Do you still have it?" David asked Eva, hoping she did. It was the breakthrough they had been hoping for—any bit of information that might lead them to their target.

"Yes," Eva replied. She patted Zoe's thigh as she got up and went into the bedroom to find the jacket she had been wearing. She retrieved the piece of paper and held it out to David, who took it and jotted down the number in his notebook. He indicated the phone and Eva nodded.

He dialed the number and waited for a few seconds and then hung up. "That's the German Community Club," he said in frustration.

"I guess I would have had to leave a message for her to contact me," Eva replied. "Can you answer some of my questions? Why are you after Greta?"

"Do you know Dr Josef Mengele?"

"Not personally, no. I have heard of him. My stepfather met him before the war and talked about him on occasions."

"Dr Mengele was called the Angel of Death in Auschwitz." David handed Eva a sheet of paper and she began to read. She scowled as she read and the blood drained from her face. Zoe looked at her with concern as Eva handed her the sheet.

"Oh God," Zoe whispered as she read about Mengele and

the experiments. "God."

"Greta Strauss assisted in those experiments," Friedrich said as Zoe's hands trembled.

Eva took her wife's hands and held them tightly and then brushed away the tears as they silently tracked down Zoe's cheeks. She leaned in and whispered to her distraught wife. The two men felt out of place, witnessing a very tender moment between the two. David cleared his throat.

"What do you want from us?" Eva asked.

"Help in catching her," David responded and waited for the explosion to come. He was quite surprised when all he got was a nod from Eva. "She is extremely dangerous. Can you call her and get her to come over here?"

"Why not get her to meet me at the office?"

"It's too crowded. I've seen that office; it's packed to the rafters. Can you tell her you're interested in restarting the relationship?"

"A bit hard to do when I've told her I am married, and quite happily at that," Eva said, squeezing Zoe's hand.

David was stumped. He turned to Friedrich with a questioning look.

"What if you told her that you changed your mind? Women do that, don't they?" Friedrich asked and got a glare from Zoe.

"I'm not a woman who changes my mind about the woman I love and promised to spend the rest of my life with, Friedrich," Eva responded. She liked the young man, but he did have a tendency to put his foot in his mouth.

Zoe gave her wife a quick kiss and then settled back down next to her and held hands.

"Greta doesn't know that. You could say that Zoe was cheating on you, and you had decided that you want to be with Greta instead. You can invite her to the office, have Zoe there, have a mock argument so she can see you are really are fighting."

"Isn't that rather melodramatic?" Eva asked.

"What about if you invited Greta to your office, allowed her to kiss you, and Zoe accidentally walked in?"

"And then I kill her," Zoe piped up and grinned.

Eva smirked at Zoe's enthusiastic idea. "I don't think they want her dead, love."

"So, do you think that would work?"

"It could. Then what?"

"You bring her back here, and we'll be waiting," David said

as he tapped the pen on the notebook.

"Oh yeah, we know how you are really good at getting in place to capture Nazis," Zoe snorted, referring to David and Friedrich's botched attempt at capturing Muller and Rhimes. "The only thing that saved you from being killed was Earl."

"How so?" David asked.

"Had anything happened to Zoe, I would have killed you both," Eva replied simply. "Earl captured those two while you were sitting on your bums in an empty flat."

"How were we supposed to know that Mrs Jenkins had told them to come up here and let them in?"

"It was a stupid idea to begin with!" Zoe interjected. "You will remember what flat number it is, won't you?"

David sighed. "We will be here waiting."

"Okay," Eva agreed and watched as the two men got up.

"We'll come by tomorrow to finalise the plans, and then you can ring Greta and set it up."

They agreed on that arrangement, and Eva saw them out. She closed the door quietly and leaned against it, letting her head drop down. Zoe's arms wrapped around her waist and hugged her, her cheek against Eva's back.

Eva was disgusted by what she had read about her former lover, a woman she thought she knew but quite obviously didn't. The horrific experiments that Greta assisted with were making her sick to her stomach. She wasn't sure how she could even pretend to show affection to her former lover and not think of the poor unfortunates who had perished. Somehow she needed to focus on the job ahead. She felt Zoe's arms around her and swallowed. Eva turned in her wife's embrace. "I'm sorry," Eva said, stroking the younger woman's cheek.

"What for?"

"For what I'm about to do to you," Eva replied, and let her tears fall. She didn't want to hurt her wife, but it was the only way they would get Greta back to the flat. "I don't want to do it, but it seems like the only way."

Zoe looked up into clear blue eyes and she put her hand on Eva's chest. "I know I own your heart," she said softly. "Just don't let her kiss you too much," Zoe tried to joke as her voice broke.

"I promise," Eva responded and leaned down. She cupped her wife's face in her hands and kissed her passionately, causing Zoe to moan as the kiss deepened.

"And not like that," Zoe said a little breathlessly as they parted.

"I reserve those for only you," Eva reassured as she hugged her wife. It was going to be difficult to fool Greta, and she wasn't an actress, but she would have to do it. She had to for all those who hadn't stood a chance when they were sentenced to their deaths.

Chapter 18

"You're going to do what?" Panayiotis asked incredulously. He was sure he hadn't heard his daughter correctly. Eva sat on the sofa with her hands folded in her lap, with Zoe nearby looking extremely uncomfortable. "All right, tell me again why you are going to help these two try and arrest this Greta person."

"They can't arrest her because they don't know where she is," Eva explained once again to her father. She looked at Ally and grimaced. The older woman was sitting next to her husband with a perplexed look on her face.

"I see. So once again you become the bait?"

"Something like that," Eva muttered.

"I think those two boofheads need their heads read," Earl muttered. He had been fixing a door at her father's flat when Eva had called them all up to let them know what they were about to do, so none of them would get any nasty surprises.

"Uh huh." The former priest scratched his head. "And Zoe is okay with you being the live bait?"

"Hell no," Zoe muttered and put her hand over her mouth when she realized she'd cursed. "Sorry, Dad."

"We don't have a lot of options open to us, Father," Eva responded.

"Really? Why don't they use the resources of the government to track this woman down? Surely the police can find her."

"I don't know."

"Eva, my child, it's not that I don't want you to help them, but..."

"Father, I know, but this is the only way. She has to be caught."

Ally looked between father and daughter and frowned. "What's so important about this Greta person?"

Eva paused for a moment. "Greta assisted in medical experiments at Auschwitz."

"I don't understand. I ran experiments during the war..."

"On human beings?" Eva asked, knowing her stepmother experimented on animals and not on living, breathing human beings.

A collective gasp went around the room at the revelation with Earl's "bloody hell" and "my God" coming from both Ally and Panayiotis.

"She worked with Dr Josef Mengele, experimenting on twins and other prisoners. The figures don't really tell the full story and I don't think we will ever know it, but she assisted this Dr Mengele."

"She was your lover?" Earl asked and shot a quick glance at Zoe, who continued to scowl.

"Yes."

"And Peterson and Friedrich want you to bring her to your flat." Earl repeated what Eva had told them, and the more he thought about it, the worse it got. "I have a feeling I'm going to need your cricket bat again, Stretch."

Zoe gave him a half smile at the reference to the last time Earl had dealt with one of David and Friedrich's stellar ideas—the capture of Muller and Rhimes. "It's in the spare bedroom."

"They want me to ring her and tell her that I'm taking her up on her offer—"

"What offer?"

Eva grimaced. She didn't like to even think about what she had to do, let alone say it out loud. "That I've decided to leave Zoe."

"This is going from bad to worse. Who came up with this brilliant idea?" Earl asked, not believing it could be either Eva or Zoe who dreamt this up. It was a stupid idea. Any fool with eyes could see that those two were so much in love with each other it would be like cutting off a part of themselves if they parted.

"David," Zoe mumbled.

"Figures. The man is a major boofhead," Earl replied. He had no time for the investigator, and he made no secret of the fact to Friedrich, who he liked a great deal.

"So, what's the plan?" Panayiotis asked, trying to understand the latest upheaval in his daughter's life. One, he thought, she could do without.

"Well, I call her and give her my spiel, then she meets me at the office. Zoe interrupts...um...when I'm kissing..."

"Jesus wept on the cross!" Earl raised his voice and got a mortified look from the former priest as the swearing was getting a little too much for the older man. "Sorry, Father H, but that is *the* most idiotic, absolutely hairbrained idea I've ever heard! *You* are going to kiss *her*?"

"Yes," Eva replied.

Earl scowled and got up from his perch on the couch to go to his friend. He put his arm around her shoulders, "Eva, my dear friend, you are a lousy liar, and there is no way you are going to convince this killer that you are fair dinkum about her and dumping Zoe."

"You can say that again," Zoe piped up and got a playful slap on the thigh.

"I don't want to do it, but that's the only solution." Eva protested defensively. "It's not as if I'm looking forward to kissing another woman, let alone having her hands all over me."

"All right, so we have you trying to convince this killer that you are in love with her." Earl went over the scenario, and Eva nodded. "Zoe comes in when you are playing tongue hockey."

"Tongue hockey?" the former priest asked and shook his head.

"Okay, Zoe comes in when you are getting this woman all steamed up about getting back together. What is Zoe going to do?"

"Get my flame thrower and cook her into a crispy critter," Zoe muttered.

"Zoe!" her father-in-law scolded. "As much as we don't like this person, I don't believe that thinking about killing her will make Eva's job any easier."

"I know, but the idea of Eva in Greta's arms makes me sick," Zoe answered, looking up into worried blue eyes. "I know she has to do it, but I'm going to wash her mouth out with peppermint mouthwash afterwards."

"So, what is Zoe going to do?" Earl persisted, wanting to

have the plan laid out.

"Zoe is going to come in, see me kissing Greta, and then we'll exchange some nasty words. I'll ask Greta to take me home to pick up some clothes. Greta and I will go home, and then David and Friedrich take over."

"That's if they can find the right flat," Earl mumbled and got a hiked eyebrow from Eva. "Well, I'll be camped in Elena's flat, in case my batting prowess is needed. Where is Zoe going to be?"

Eva looked at her wife and grimaced. She would have to try to get Zoe to stay with Earl in Elena's flat, away from the danger. "With you."

"*No way*!" Zoe yelled and shot up from the sofa. "I am not going to leave you."

"Zoe, it's going to be dangerous for you if you are there." Eva tried to reason with her mate, knowing it was a lost cause; but this was one argument she was going to nip in the bud. She would not let Zoe be put in a dangerous position. "I don't want you there."

"No," Zoe scowled.

Panayiotis looked at his two daughters: one of them was ready to let her temper get a full showing, while Eva sat there quietly trying to stay calm. "I think now would be a good time, Earl, for me to show you the kitchen and let these two talk it out privately." The older man got up from his favorite chair and ushered his wife and Earl out of the room.

Zoe turned her back and looked out at the city skyline from the window. She wasn't going to leave her wife to face the danger by herself. Not this time. Not like the last time where her beloved had faced her own private hell while she was drunk and out sleeping. Not this time.

"Zoe," Eva whispered in her ear as she went over and put her arm around her small partner's shoulders, "you can't be in our flat."

"I don't want you to do this by yourself," Zoe replied, leaning back and closing her eyes. She wanted this whole nightmare to end and wished she never heard of this Greta Strauss. "Greta isn't as stupid as Muller and Rhimes. We may not be as lucky this time around."

"I know, love, but I don't want you to get hurt."

"What about you?" Zoe turned and faced her wife, placing both hands on Eva's belly. "What about you, Evy? Who is going to protect you?" she asked, looking into her eyes and shaking her head. "You are going to get hurt again."

"I wasn't hurt."

"You are a lousy liar, Evy," Zoe retorted, knowing her partner was heartsick every time she thought about Muller and Rhimes in the same room. They had discussed it, and Eva admitted she was terrified of what Muller would have done if Zoe had woken. "Being hurt doesn't always mean physical harm, and you know that."

Eva looked down into concerned emerald eyes and knew the truth of that statement. "If you got hurt, Zoe, I don't know what I'd do."

"I won't get hurt," Zoe replied, thinking she was going to get to be with her wife after all.

"No. You're staying with Earl." Eva was determined that Zoe's safety would come first; and although a part of her wished she could have her wife with her, she knew that her head would overrule her heart on this occasion.

"Arghhh!" Zoe let out a frustrated yell. "You're not going to be safe."

"I'll have David and Friedrich..."

"Oh yeah, those two inspire confidence," Zoe said sarcastically.

"Zoe, I'm not going to let you be in that flat."

"I don't like it."

"I know you don't," Eva replied. She sighed as Zoe put her arms around her waist, burying her head in Eva's chest and began to weep. "I don't want to see you hurt, love. It would kill me if anything happened to you." She kissed the dark head resting on her chest and sighed.

❖❖❖❖❖❖❖

Elena stuck her head around the door, trying to find her friend. She spotted Zoe talking to her father-in-law and entered the flat. Friedrich was in her flat and, given the recent events, was unsure if he would be welcome at dinner.

Zoe turned and saw her friend and called her over.

"Hi," Elena greeted Zoe and gave her a hug. "I'm sorry."

"Not your fault, El. Where's Friedrich?"

"He doesn't want to come. He thinks you don't want him."

"What a load of rubbish," Zoe muttered and walked out of

the flat, leaving Elena standing alone for a few moments.

Zoe reached Elena's flat and knocked as Elena caught up with her. The door opened to reveal Friedrich with slightly rumpled hair and no glasses, which made him look much younger. Zoe brushed past him, much to Elena's amusement.

"Okay, what's this about you not wanting to come to dinner?" Zoe asked, folding her arms across her chest.

"Uh, Zoe...I don't think Eva would want me to be there," Friedrich stammered. "I'm sorry. I don't want anything to hurt Eva or you."

"Friedrich, I don't blame you for wanting to catch Greta. God knows I want to rid her from our lives. I just didn't like the way David was questioning Eva," Zoe said, as she sat on the edge of the sofa.

"I know, and I'm sorry." Friedrich combed back his hair and picked up his glasses, which lay on the table in the lounge room. "I promise we won't let anything happen to Eva."

"You'd better not." Zoe gave him a mock glare, but there was no mistaking that it was meant as a warning. She took him by the arm. "Come on, let's eat."

The smoke drifted sideways as a light breeze blew the BBQ smoke inside the flat along with the aroma of the sausages and steaks. Earl stood in front of the BBQ wearing one of Zoe's aprons, which was much too small for him, and wielding a pair of tongs, turning the meat. Clad in shorts and a cotton shirt, Eva grinned at him as she came out to join him on the balcony. She sat on the wicker chair and stretched out her long legs as Earl cooked.

"Zoe likes hers well done."

"I know, burnt sacrifice style," Earl replied and got a chuckle from his friend. "You remember that first time we had a BBQ at Cremorne's point? She came back with her steak, looked me up and down, and said, 'I want to sacrifice this cow to the BBQ gods.'"

Eva laughed and emitted a sigh at her own memories of that day. They were finally settled into their flat after spending the morning cleaning and setting it up. Earl arrived with a picnic hamper, a BBQ and some wine, and promptly took them to Cremorne Point, a beautiful part of the north shore of Sydney overlooking the harbour, where they spent the evening eating and talking.

Earl turned another sausage and smiled at his friend. "I'll be waiting, Eva."

"I know you will, Earl. No matter what happens, keep Zoe away."

"I don't think I can guarantee that, my friend. I will try, but if Zoe wants to do something, Zoe is going to do it unless I knock her out."

"Try," Eva replied, snagging a little piece of the cooked meat and popping it in her mouth.

"Did Greta really do that stuff?"

Eva nodded. "I've read the witness reports and the notes that David and Friedrich had. I don't know this Greta; she isn't the woman I fell in love with."

"People change..."

"Not so drastically, Earl. I guess I never took notice before, but she idolized Hitler."

"Were you ever a member of the Party?"

"No. I didn't believe as fervently in the cause as some of my friends did; many elements of it sickened me. Hitler was good for Germany in the beginning, but my mind was made up when I read *Mein Kampf*."

"What does *Mein Kampf* mean?"

"My Struggle. It was about his ideals and his beliefs. Did you know he was an artist?" Eva turned as Zoe stepped out onto the balcony. She patted her lap and grinned as Zoe took up the invitation and sat down.

Zoe leaned in and gave her wife a quick kiss. "Who was an artist?"

"You would hear that bit, wouldn't you?" Eva teased with a lopsided grin. "Hitler was an artist."

"Oh. He should have stuck to art," Zoe muttered. "So why are you discussing Hitler?"

"I was telling Earl I read *Mein Kampf*, and it made me decide that I didn't want to join the Party and be a part of it."

"I would have joined the Communist Party if I was old enough." Zoe took the hot bread roll Earl offered her off the BBQ.

"You? A Communist?" Eva was surprised, as Zoe never mentioned she leaned towards socialist policies.

"No, I loved their colors." Zoe grinned. "It was a change from the blue and white flags, and I found them different."

Earl and Eva chuckled as the last of the steaks and sausages were cooked and put on the large platter. Earl covered the BBQ and left the two women alone outside for a few moments.

"Friedrich and Elena here?" Eva whispered and got a nod from her partner. "I guess we'd better get inside."

"Hmm," Zoe replied and snuggled against Eva's chest.

"Come on, love," Eva whispered and kissed her. Zoe got up reluctantly and watched as Eva's tall frame got out of the chair. She took her hand, and they walked back inside to dinner with their friends.

Friedrich was standing admiring Zoe's artwork and fidgeting awkwardly. He wasn't sure if Eva wanted him there, despite Zoe's reassurance. He began to study the photographs that were on the wall next to the artwork. One photograph in particular intrigued him, and he went to have a closer look. He loved waterfalls; they had a magic about them that had fascinated him since he was a young boy.

"You like that?" Eva came up from behind and stood there watching him.

Friedrich jumped when he heard her voice, turned slightly, and looked up. He gave her a half smile. "Uh, yeah...I like waterfalls," Friedrich stammered. He was quite intimidated by Eva; she towered over him and always seemed so aloof and quiet. She was standing so close to him that Friedrich could smell her perfume. He didn't know anything about fragrances, but it had a hint of jasmine, which he liked. He looked up and met her clear blue eyes, and they both smiled.

"Hmm, so do I. The photo was taken in the Blue Mountains when we went bush walking about a month ago. Very nice spot."

"Y—Yes, it is," Friedrich agreed.

"Friedrich, I don't bite."

"Not unless I ask her to." Zoe came up, putting her arm around Eva's waist, giving a little squeeze. "Are you going to stand here yakking or come to dinner?"

"We're being summoned," Eva responded and took Zoe's hand as they led Friedrich to where everyone was seated.

The large dining table was Eva's idea; she'd enjoyed having dinner parties before the war, enjoying the company of friends. Eva's father was seated at the head of the table, and Ally was next to him. Elena and Friedrich sat together, Earl was seated opposite them, and Eva took the seat opposite her father, with Zoe next to her. It was a nice arrangement that would make for a light evening.

Panayiotis said a prayer before they started eating, and then it was a free-for-all as the chatter rose.

"This is nice," Zoe leaned in and whispered.

"Hmm," Eva agreed.

"Congratulations are in order for you both I hear," Panayiotis grinned at the two young people. "So, have you decided when you will get married?"

"Not yet. Probably later this year," Friedrich replied, taking Elena's hand and giving it a little squeeze.

"In my younger days, I made wedding gowns; so if you like, we could sit down and design one for you, Elena." Ally reached over and touched the young woman's hand, giving her a huge smile. Elena returned her smile and looked over at Zoe who had a huge grin on her face.

"Do you need a photographer?" Eva asked.

Friedrich looked at Elena in surprise and nodded. "We hadn't thought about photographs."

"I'll let you know if I find a good one for you," Eva teased. That got a chuckle from everyone, her sense of humour catching Friedrich by surprise. "I would love to take your wedding photos."

"Thank you." Friedrich accepted her offer, his nervousness in her presence easing slightly. "When did you take up photography?"

"Ah, a long, long time ago. Back in Germany, I toyed with the idea of becoming a photographer before going to university. It's a relaxing hobby," Eva replied, taking a bite from her salad.

"Do you have a darkroom?" Friedrich asked and Eva nodded.

"Are you a photographer, Friedrich?" Zoe leaned in and gave the young man a smile.

"No...my sisters were. I built one for them before leaving Germany."

"We converted the walk-in closet in the spare bedroom as our darkroom, which is good."

"It's great for snuggling and cuddling too," Zoe added as everyone laughed.

"For that as well," Eva agreed and got a quick kiss from Zoe. "Are your sisters here?"

Friedrich stopped for a moment and shook his head. "They died at Auschwitz."

"Oh, I'm sorry," Eva said and looked down at her dinner.

"And that's why you catch the bad guys, right?" Earl piped

up as he met Eva's eyes. "Unless, of course, you get the wrong flat number." Everyone laughed, which broke the tension slightly.

"Hey, that wasn't my fault, you know," Friedrich pointed his finger at Earl who was still laughing. "How did we know Mrs Jenkins would send them here? I would have rather been with Elena than sitting in a dark room trying to think up ways to kill David."

"It didn't help that Mrs J got a 'lets-be-nice' attack," Zoe piped up. She glanced at Eva, who had a half smile on her face. She bumped Eva a little and gave her a wink before resting her hand on her bare knee and giving a little squeeze.

"It also didn't help that a certain someone, who shall remain nameless, got drunk that night," Earl teased as Zoe gave him a lopsided grin. "Who knew you were so amorous when drunk?"

"She doesn't need to be drunk," Eva said and got a slap on the thigh from Zoe before getting a quick kiss.

"See?"

The evening wore on as they ate and enjoyed themselves. Eva sat back, enjoying the evening, knowing that the next day they would deal with Greta and everything that came their way, but the night was for fun and the company of good friends.

Chapter 19

Eva lay awake in bed in the dark. The sound of the grandfather clock in the lounge room could be heard, as well as the distant sound of cars through the open window. It was another warm evening. The rain from the previous day disappeared, only to be replaced with warm and muggy conditions. Zoe was curled up next to her, her arm draped around Eva's waist. They had spent an enjoyable evening with her parents and friends, which she found soothing.

She was scared of what would happen with Greta, and hoped it wasn't going to turn into a disaster. Her father took both her and Zoe aside, and in his own style put them at ease, telling them they would have to go through a little more hardship before they could get on with their lives. She marveled at how he always knew the right words to say.

"You're thinking too much," Zoe mumbled and looked up into Eva's worried face.

"I thought you were asleep," Eva replied, brushing aside her wife's errant dark locks and running her fingers through Zoe's hair, scratching the back of her neck a little as Zoe sighed. Eva smiled, and it occurred to her that if Zoe were a cat, she would be purring.

"I was, but your loud thinking woke me up."

"My loud thinking?" Eva asked.

"Hmm. Your body tenses when you are nervous. Do I need to ask what you are thinking about?"

"How am I going to pull this off, Zo? Greta knows me."

Zoe hitched herself onto her elbow, placing her hand on Eva's chest and looking at Eva's worried face. "She doesn't know you. You told me that you are not the same person you were back then, so how does she know you?"

"Zoe, my personality may have changed, but not how I react when I'm..." Eva found she was a little shy, which was ludicrous since Zoe knew her body intimately.

"Aroused?"

"Uh...yeah."

"I like it when you're aroused," Zoe joked, trying to relax her wife, who was wound up tighter than a watch. "Your eyes go deep blue and you get a pink flush that travels up your chest." Zoe found she was getting rather warm herself by thinking about it, which got Eva shaking her head and chuckling. "You are an incredibly sexy woman, Mrs H," Zoe whispered as she nuzzled Eva's neck.

"Oh, that's nice," Eva responded, letting her hand roam Zoe's bare back. "Uh, Zoe...that's my problem."

Zoe sighed. She thought she could take Eva's mind off the encounter with Greta the next day, but it was obvious that Eva's mind wasn't on making love to her at the moment. "What's the problem?"

"Greta will know I'm not aroused...I mean, she will *know*," Eva stammered. She found she couldn't say the words to her wife.

The younger woman put her head down on her lover's shoulder and let her finger trace around Eva's nipple. She grinned when Eva responded to her touch, and she continued the slow tease. "I think you've had enough time to think about this," Zoe whispered, as she rolled on top of Eva's long body and stared into her wife's eyes. "I love you, Evy, and I know you are going to have to let yourself go so you can convince the Nazi bitch that you are for real, but for now I want to make love to you." Zoe leaned down and kissed her passionately, wanting her kiss to erase the thoughts of that woman from her wife's mind. The kiss deepened, and they both let out a low moan.

"I think you talk too much," Eva said breathlessly as she reversed their positions, her hands roaming over Zoe's body. She looked into Zoe's smiling eyes and let a sexy grin steal across her face. She was about to say something when Zoe put her finger to her lips.

"Make love to me. Don't talk," Zoe whispered, as she reached up and entangled her fingers in Eva's dark hair.

Eva lowered herself, passionately kissing her wife. She stretched the length of her body out alongside the young woman and ran a strong, yet delicate hand up the span of Zoe's figure, stopping at her face to gently brush her fingers across soft, full lips. Eva smiled, reaching down once more to capture her wife's mouth. The young woman moaned into Eva's mouth at the gentleness of the kiss.

"Is this what you want, my love?" Eva asked, her lips moving down to Zoe's neck. "Hmmm?" she prodded, bringing her hand to the underside of a soft breast, brushing her thumb across the nipple, the flesh hardening under her caress.

"Yessss..." Zoe tried to say, but it came out as more of a strangled groan.

Eva continued to tenderly kiss and stroke the young woman's body. She moved over the smaller woman and lowered her body down onto Zoe's, her weight resting on her arms. Zoe moaned in pleasure at the feel of her wife's body. Eva reached in, covering the inviting mouth with her own. She loved kissing this woman, always feeling as if she would never get enough of it. She reveled in the taste and the different reactions every touch of her own lips produced in her young wife.

Softly, breathlessly, Eva whispered, "Remember what I promised you that night you were painting? You had to stand outside in the rain just to cool the heat of the fire from my promise, didn't you?"

Zoe was beyond answering and simply nodded her head in response.

Eva lowered her voice even more. "You will want for... nothing. My tongue...my lips...my voice...everything I have, Zoe...all of it...will only ever be for you."

"Oh, Eva!" Zoe finally cried out.

Zoe's nipples tightened with arousal as Eva slid down the young woman's body, allowing her skin full contact with the woman beneath her.

"Please, Evy..." Zoe whispered faintly, arching her back as Eva permitted her fingertips to brush across very erect nipples.

Sliding up against the overheated skin once more, the tall woman slowly enclosed one of the hardened nubs with her mouth and sucked gently. Using her knee, she spread Zoe's legs apart and moved her thigh in to press against the warm wetness she found there. Both women moaned simultaneously.

Eva couldn't help the delighted whimper that escaped from her throat at the feel of her own wetness as she pressed her center harder down onto Zoe's thigh. The older woman pressed her leg against her wife's center, feeling Zoe unconsciously begin to rock her hips against her.

Eva took her time, moving slowly downward, her lips and tongue causing Zoe to shiver in anticipation. Eva tenderly kissed her lover's belly, just above the soft brown curls. Settling her shoulders between her wife's thighs, Eva breathed deeply, savouring the delicious musky scent that was so Zoe. The brunette's mouth watered at the perfume of her wife's ardor, her own body tensing in delightful anticipation at the thought of tasting that sweet wetness.

"Please, Evy," Zoe raised her hips slightly. "I can't wait."

Eva smiled at her wife's plea. Everything was life and death and impatience with this woman. That was one of the reasons she loved her, however. With Zoe, every day was new; every experience was as though she were living it for the first time, no brakes, just flat out. That's what this small woman brought into Eva's life...passion. Once again, Eva was able to experience an enthusiasm for life, and all because of the woman who now lay, breathless, underneath her.

Eva slipped her hands under Zoe's hips, pulling her closer to her waiting mouth. She ran her tongue lightly along the drenched folds, feeling her wife's hips rise up in response. Zoe spread her legs wider as Eva grazed her tongue across the sweetness. She took the warm folds into her mouth, letting her tongue investigate every curve and crease. She allowed her tongue to explore, delighting in Zoe's moans of pleasure. She slowly began stroking the hidden nub, now swollen with need. Eva felt her own desire increasing and the sound of Zoe's breathless moans, combined with the feel of her wife's hands entwined in her hair, caused Eva to practically hum into the flesh under her tongue.

"Oh, God, Eva...please...oh, please, don't...stop," Zoe begged, her hips rising off the bed, thrusting harder against her wife's insistent tongue.

Eva held her lover's rocking hips still, pressing deeper, sucking harder, while her tongue flicked across the swollen nub. Zoe cried out her lover's name, her fingers clenching in the dark locks, pressing her lover to her. The young woman's body convulsed, her back arching into her release.

As Zoe lay basking in the last few shudders of pleasure, Eva moved up, wrapping strong arms around the beautiful woman. Zoe found herself on the receiving end of a deep and passionate kiss, tasting her own essence on Eva's lips and tongue. She lovingly let her hands roam, massaging and caressing the tall brunette's back, reveling in the feel of her wife's body pressed against her own.

The feel of her wife's hands on her skin, touching her, caressing her lovingly, drew a soft moan from the older woman. Eva could feel her own need upon her. Making love to her wife could be so satisfying, but right now, she knew she needed more.

"I want you, my wife," Zoe said with an intensity that seemed to surprise the older woman. Zoe pressed against her wife's body, Eva rolling them both over. Sliding her hand down the soft skin of Eva's stomach, Zoe swirled her fingers with a teasingly light touch into the dark curls between long, quivering limbs.

"Zoe, I love you so much. I don't ever want to lose you," Eva whispered passionately.

"I'm not going anywhere, love," Zoe responded reassuringly. "Ever," she added just before her lips covered the tall brunette's in a fiery kiss.

"Zoe..." Eva moaned, her voice low and rasping. Pulling away to take a much-needed breath, her wife kissed her again, brushing the tip of her tongue along Eva's lips, then Zoe's tongue slid into her mouth. The feel of the young woman's tongue, exploring, commanding, stole her breath away. Zoe's hand slipped lower, teasing the inside of Eva's thigh with her fingertips, as the smaller woman's tongue excited her wife in ways she knew no other would ever be able to.

"Zoe...please...oh, Zo...I need you so much." Long legs quickly parted in a silent plea for more.

The young woman slowly slid her fingers into the silky wetness. Eva gasped and her eyes closed at the pleasurable sensation, exhilaration and enchantment visible in her face. She arched her back into her lover's touch, a throaty sound of satisfaction rumbling forth from deep in her chest.

Eva could feel her body being taken to the very precipice by the breathtaking contact with her young lover's body. She felt her inner muscles contract around two fingers as her lover gently entered her, releasing as they felt the fullness sliding out, only to contract again when the digits were pressed in once more.

Slowly, relentlessly, Zoe matched her rhythm to the cadence her wife's hips set, all the while their tongues danced together. Eva surrendered her mouth to her wife's loving assault, the sensation drawing long moans from the older woman.

Zoe's actions managed to drive any logical thought from Eva's brain. The dark-haired woman began to moan louder, her hips picking up the pace. Breathlessly, Zoe wrenched her mouth free.

"Eva, look at me," the young woman panted.

Eva opened her eyes, the blue irises disguised by a passionate haze. Finally, she was able to focus on the beautiful young woman above her.

"I want you to see me, Eva. I want you to know who this is loving you, know who touches you this way, know who alone can make you feel this way. It's me, my love...only me."

Zoe reached down one last time to capture her wife's lips. She felt the woman beneath her groan into her mouth, as Eva's climax took control of her long-limbed figure, her muscles jumping and quivering in irrepressible spasms of delight.

When at last the older woman's body stilled, the smaller woman planted a soft kiss on the sweat soaked brow, short dark locks plastered against Eva's satisfied face.

"I love you, Evy," Zoe whispered.

Long arms wrapped around the woman above her, pulling the small figure tightly against her body. "I love you too, Zoe. More than you will ever know."

❖ ❖ ❖ ❖ ❖ ❖ ❖

The next morning, she rang the number Greta gave her and left a message for the woman to contact her. It didn't take long for her former lover to return her call; she received it at 10 a.m.

Eva looked at the phone that was ringing and took a deep breath, picking up the receiver. She hoped she wouldn't sound nervous and give the game away. She answered the phone in a calm voice, surprising herself that she could do so.

"Eva, darling, how nice to hear your voice again," Greta said, sounding very cheery. "So when can I see you, or is your 'wife' not going to let me near you?"

She could hear Greta laugh. "Eta."

"Oh dear. I haven't heard that nickname in a long time. It must be at least 9 years."

"Things have changed...love," Eva said, rolling her eyes at the endearment and mentally shaking herself to keep her mind on the job.

"How so?" Greta asked. Eva knew Greta was very much interested in resuming their relationship, but was playing it cool.

"Zoe and I have been having some problems...I mean, ever since you came back, I haven't been able to stop thinking about you. Debbie gave me your telephone number, and I wanted to call you..."

Greta laughed. "Oh, I don't doubt it. That little spitfire of a wife of yours must have you firmly under her thumb!"

Eva had taken the receiver and looked at it with a shake of her head. "She is rather..."

"Domineering?" Greta offered and chuckled, which was beginning to annoy Eva a little.

"Bossy is the word I would use. She isn't tall enough to be domineering." Eva cringed at what she had just said and was grateful Zoe wasn't around to hear it.

"So, what would you like us to do, *meines kleines eichenkaetchen*?"

My little squirrel. Eva shook her head at the nickname. "Can I meet you here?"

"Ah, afraid the little woman would catch us?" Greta asked.

"Well, what she doesn't know won't hurt her. I mean, if you are interested."

"Interested in making love to you, *meine liebe*? Of course! I want to feel your body under mine and hear your passion. I would be stupid to pass up that opportunity."

Eva grunted, which Greta mistook for arousal, which suited her purpose at that moment.

"Not now, *meine liebe*, wait until I get there." She chuckled over the line. "I will make you forget that little child."

"Can you come?"

"I can come any time you want me to," Greta interjected and laughed at her own crude joke, much to Eva's disgust. "What time do you want me there?"

"Well how about 5:00 p.m.? Zoe has classes until 6:30 at university, and she won't be home 'til late," Eva said, hoping that Greta would take the bait.

"Perfect. It's been a long time, *meine liebe*, and I am looking forward to getting reacquainted with that gorgeous body of yours."

"I would like that."

Greta chuckled. "I'll see you at 5:00. Goodbye, *meine liebe.*"

"Goodbye," Eva whispered.

Eva spent the rest of the day going through the motions of interviewing clients, and watching the clock. She was sitting at her desk, looking at the files in front of her but not paying much attention. Around lunchtime, Friedrich and David came to see her to finalize the arrangements. They were going to be waiting in Eva's flat. The plan called for Eva to take Greta to her flat, and then they would take over.

❖ ❖ ❖ ❖ ❖ ❖ ❖

Eva jumped a little when she heard a light knock on the door and looked hurriedly at her watch, which read only 4:00. Eva stood as the door opened and, much to Eva's relief, it was Zoe's dark head that popped around the door.

"Hi there," Zoe said as Eva opened her arms and her wife embraced her in a tight hug. "Did you do it?"

"Hmm. She's coming at 5:00. Is Earl with you?" Eva asked and stroked her partner's cheek.

"Sure is. He's waiting outside, chatting to Debbie and charming her."

"Is there anyone in the waiting room?"

"No, it's quiet."

They stood like that for a few moments, enjoying their closeness, and were a little startled when the phone rang. Eva leaned back and picked up the receiver. She listened for a few moments, her face going a little pale.

"What's wrong?" Zoe asked.

Eva shook her head. "Um...tell her I'll be ready to see her in a few minutes." She put the receiver down and swore.

"What's wrong?" Zoe demanded as Eva sighed loudly.

"Zoe, I think we need to change the way we are going to do this. Greta is early."

"Stupid bloody bitch," Zoe swore.

"Zoe, we need to have an argument. Um, I told her that you...uh...sometimes hit me."

"What!" Zoe exclaimed. She wasn't going to hit her wife, no matter what the situation. The last thing she wanted to do was hurt her wife. "No way!"

"Please, Zoe, this could unravel right this minute. When Greta comes in, I want you to yell at me and slap me, then storm off. Get yourself and Earl back to the flat and make sure Friedrich and David are in place!"

"Stupid bloody bitch, I'm gonna kill her." Zoe continued to swear as Eva tried to get control of herself. She heard a soft knock on the door and gave Zoe a quick kiss before the curtain went up.

The door opened, and a smiling Greta entered to find Zoe shoving Eva in the chest and yelling in Greek, which she couldn't understand; but she understood that Zoe was extremely upset. The German woman stood watching them for a moment before clearing her throat to announce herself.

Zoe turned when she heard her and directed her anger at Greta. The older woman took a step back in surprise at the hatred in Zoe's eyes, which she wasn't expecting. She wasn't used to being intimidated and quickly covered up her backward step, a tiny smile playing on her lips, and made a big show of removing her gloves.

"Hello, *meine liebe*," Greta greeted Eva. Zoe's eyes narrowed on the use of the German endearment "my love." Greta turned her attention to the angry young woman. "We meet again, little Zoe."

"Shove it up your arse," Zoe angrily spat out.

Zoe turned to Eva, reverting to German for Greta's benefit. "So you were planning a little rendezvous with the Nazi bitch from hell?"

"Hey!" Greta advanced towards Zoe, wanting to stop the tirade against her lover.

Eva stepped in between Zoe and Greta, who glared at each other.

"Shut the fuck up!" Zoe screamed at Greta. "You steal my wife, and I'm supposed to sit here and take it?"

"Your 'wife' would like a real woman making love to her, and you're not it," Greta replied with a smug expression on her face.

Zoe turned back to Eva, who sat on the edge of her desk, arms folded, looking quite nonchalant and aloof. From Eva's stance, Greta assumed she had gone through these tirades before, and she pitied her lover.

"I thought you loved me, but as soon as the Nazi slut comes back, you just have to run off."

"Loved you?" Eva chuckled. "You were a means to an end," Eva's heart ached as she spoke those words, but she had to go through with the charade.

"Well, little one, I don't think it's much of a contest now, do you?" Greta was enjoying the show. She hadn't seriously believed that Eva would fall for the naive child, and she was right.

"What does that mean, you Nazi whore?"

Greta chuckled at Zoe's reddened face, her whole body ready to pounce on the German. "It means, little Zoe, that I'm going to be making love to her tonight. She will be screaming *my* name, and you're just a little footnote in the life of Eva Muller."

"You were a way to get out of Greece." Eva looked up at Greta and gave her a lopsided grin. "You know how it is, Zoe, you were in the right place at the right time."

The words stung. Zoe knew they were a lie, but they hurt nonetheless. Silent tears tracked down Zoe's face as she looked at Eva. She pushed her way past Eva and then stopped. "May you and your slut burn in hell."

Zoe felt as if she were watching someone else. Time seemed to slow down as she lifted her hand and slapped Eva hard.

"Bye bye, Zoe." Greta taunted her as Zoe flung the door open and marched down the corridor to where Earl was waiting. She didn't bother telling him to come after her. Earl looked at Zoe's retreating back and then back up at the corridor at Eva's office for a moment, before following Zoe down to the car park.

"Zoe?" Earl asked with concern as he caught sight of his friend doubling over near the car, throwing up.

"Earl, take me home, quickly," Zoe said through clenched teeth as she wiped her mouth.

❖❖❖❖❖❖❖❖

Eva put her hand up to her cheek, and her eyes misted over as Zoe stormed out. Her heart ached. The pain she felt was as if someone had cut her and let her bleed—not because of the slap, but from having forced her wife to do it to make this charade look real to Greta.

Greta put her arms around her new girlfriend. "Are you all right, darling?"

Eva nodded and brushed away the tears.

"Well, you don't look all right." Greta turned Eva to face

her and cupped her face. "Sit down and I'll bring you a glass of water." She directed Eva to sit down on the visitors' chair, went to the pitcher of water on the desk, and poured her a glass.

Eva took the glass and cupped it with both hands. She was tired and wanted to get this crazy and idiotic plan over and done with. She wanted to go and comfort her wife, who needed her more than ever.

"I want you to come home with me, *liebchen*."

"Can't," Eva whispered and then cleared her throat. Eva needed to stall to give Zoe and Earl a chance to get back, to warn Friedrich and David that they were headed to the flat an hour earlier than planned.

"Why? That she-demon is going to be at your place, and frankly, I don't feel like going another round with her. I think even the Gestapo were gentler."

Eva forced herself to chuckle at Greta's joke about Zoe's temper. "I have some papers I need to retrieve before Zoe finds them."

"Oh, of course," Greta said and got to her feet. "How about I relax you a bit, and then we can go back to your flat and pick up your papers and clothes? I have my own house, and I would love for you to live with me."

"You have your own house?"

"Yes, a lovely federation house; you'll like it." Greta went around behind Eva's chair and began to massage her neck.

Eva groaned slightly as the pressure was released under Greta's ministrations. Eva slumped forward, enjoying the massage.

Greta smiled at her lover's acceptance of her offer. She slipped her hands inside Eva's shirt and began to massage her neck and shoulders. She frowned when she looked down and saw the faint scars. "Eva, did Zoe cause these?"

Eva was wondering when Greta would notice and sighed. "No, that's my stepfather's legacy," she said quietly.

"Ach, my *meines kleines eichenkaetchen*, why?"

"Because I loved you," Eva replied quietly.

"That brute." Greta was angry, angry with Muller that he had disfigured such a beautiful woman. "Zoe didn't hurt you, did she?"

"Not often," Eva continued the lie. "She hated touching my back, though."

"Stupid fool." Greta pulled Eva to her feet and looked onto

her eyes. "I have always loved you, Eva, and I'm sorry you were taken away from me."

"I love you, too. I didn't realize until you came back that I am still very much in love with you."

Greta smiled as she leaned down and kissed her lover with as much tenderness as she could, her kisses becoming more demanding and passionate as she held Eva's hands behind her back. Eva moaned a little, much to Greta's delight. "We have a lot of catching up to do."

"Hmm." Eva hugged her former lover and let a little sigh escape.

"But first, we have to go to your flat and get this mess over and done with, okay?"

"I'm looking forward to it," Eva replied, and for the first time since Greta had arrived, the truth was spoken.

❖ ❖ ❖ ❖ ❖ ❖ ❖

Earl drove at a high speed and stopped just around the corner from the block of flats. He followed Zoe inside as Elena opened the door, waiting for them. She watched as Zoe rushed past her and into the bathroom.

Earl shrugged and went to Eva's flat, letting himself in. He was pleasantly surprised to find both men in the flat, getting ready for Eva's arrival.

"She arrived early," Earl looked at his watch and turned to the men, "I would say, expect them here in about half an hour. Eva is going to try and stall her, but I'm not sure how successful she's going to be."

"Okay, we're ready." Friedrich indicated the bedroom where five police officers, David, and himself were going to be when Eva and Greta entered the flat.

"Okay, if you need my bat, let me know," Earl joked. He closed the door to the flat and entered Elena's flat, closing the door quietly.

"Where's Zoe?" he asked Elena, who pointed to the bathroom.

"What happened?"

"I don't know. Greta arrived early and they had to improvise, so I'm not sure what happened, but Zoe was very upset."

Zoe had rushed to the bathroom and sunk to her knees. She felt sick to her stomach, leaned over, and threw up into the toilet bowl. She sat on the cold tiles, placing her head on her knees, and cried bitterly at what she had been forced to do to the woman that she loved more than life itself. The look of shock on Eva's face caused a pain so deep in Zoe's heart that her world seemed to shatter.

Earl knocked on the door and entered. He knelt down beside his distraught friend and held her as she cried on his shoulder. "She's going to be all right, Zo..."

"You don't understand."

"Zoe..."

"You don't understand, Earl. I made a promise never to hurt her, and I just did."

Zoe felt heartsick All she wanted was to love her wife and hold her and apologize. "She's been abused before by people she thought loved her, and now me. I hit her. I hit my wife," Zoe cried and dissolved into tears.

Earl didn't know what to do or what to say. He hoped Friedrich and David would finish the job and let the two women come together again soon, because it was like watching a slow death.

Chapter 20

The car turned the corner at Glebe Point Road, the driver putting the vehicle in park and turning off the engine. Dieter looked up at his mirror, watching for a few moments as Greta was all over the other woman. It surprised him when Greta informed him that she was going to bring home her former lover. His first thought was that he might have a chance with the tall woman, but his hopes were dashed as soon as Greta returned.

To his complete astonishment, Greta had entered the car with one of the most beautiful women he had ever seen. The tall brunette was quite striking, short dark hair framed her gorgeous face, but it was the blue eyes that captured him. He was about to ask what had happened, when Greta had introduced Eva as her lover. His mouth hung open in surprise, causing Greta to laugh at him.

He was enjoying the ride home, sneaking occasional glances in the mirror to see Eva snuggling up to his employer. Greta whispered to her as she stroked Eva's face and ran her hands over the lithe body. He nearly lost control of the car when Greta made sucking noises, and he couldn't help himself and looked back. Greta caught him looking and cuffed the back of his head, which only got him more interested. He didn't think she was too upset, since she made a comment about him joining them later. He was looking forward to that a great deal.

"Stay here, I don't think we will be long," Greta ordered as she stepped out of the car and took Eva's hand. "Are you okay?"

"Yeah, I hope Zoe isn't there," Eva replied taking a quick look up at Elena's balcony where she spotted her friends. She hid a smile at the sight of Earl and Elena in a lover's embrace. To any casual observer, it looked like two lovers enjoying the warm day outside.

"Don't worry, my love, I can handle that little peasant," Greta replied. Taking her hand they walked up the walkway, leaving Dieter to watch them with a smile on his face. He was looking forward to going up to the flat and joining in the fun.

❖ ❖ ❖ ❖ ❖ ❖ ❖

Elena was anxiously watching the road from her balcony, hoping to see Eva and Greta. Her friend Zoe was crying her eyes out and there was nothing she could do to help her. She felt helpless, which brought back memories of her time in the camps when she was powerless to keep her mama from dying. Elena took a deep breath and leaned over the railing, hoping if she wished it hard enough they would materialise. She smiled grimly as a car stopped outside the building. "Hey, Earl, they're here!"

"About bloody time," Earl muttered as he walked out. He held Elena in his embrace so as not to arouse suspicion. Earlier they had worked out a plan which enabled Earl to watch the road. He prayed that this whole plan worked out or else he would take his gun and start shooting.

"Are they all in place?" Elena asked.

"Yeah, the authorities are in their bedroom. They found the right flat." Earl said sarcastically.

"You're not going to let them forget that, are you?" Elena asked, a little annoyed at Earl for mentioning the mix-up. "Friedrich feels really badly about that."

"El, mate, it was only blind luck that we got out of that mess," Earl said as he watched Eva and Greta walking towards the units. He snarled when he saw Greta pawing Eva. "That bloody demon! I swear I could wring her neck."

"I think you would have to get in line, Wiggy," Elena muttered as they lost sight of the two.

❖ ❖ ❖ ❖ ❖ ❖ ❖

Greta was happy, the happiest she had been since she'd left Auschwitz. Her future looked anything but secure, but she was determined to enjoy her life. She'd never believed in coincidence, so when she saw Eva again after so many years, she took it as a sign from God. She was a good Lutheran, and this was her reward.

"Are you happy, my love?" Greta asked and leaned in towards Eva as they walked up the stairs.

"I am now," Eva responded, giving the older woman a smile. They passed Elena's flat and Eva gave it a quick look before stopping in front of her own. She hoped Earl and Zoe had managed to come back quickly and let Friedrich and David know about the change in plans. She certainly wasn't looking forward to another miscue like the one they had experienced with her stepfather.

She opened the door and let Greta inside, taking a look around to see if Friedrich had overturned a book, which was to be the sign that they were indeed ready. She smiled when she saw the overturned book on the low table, a single flower resting on top.

Greta spun her around and pinned her against the door holding both her hands. "You know, I know what you are up to," Greta leaned in and whispered. She began to nibble on Eva's ear, which caused Eva to tremble slightly. Greta took that as a sign she was getting her lover where she wanted her.

Eva took a deep breath to calm herself, giving Greta a sexy grin. "You do?"

"Oh yes, indeed. You haven't had someone to make love to you the way you deserve. That child probably didn't know how to please you or what turned you on. I know what you need. My mere presence turns you on, doesn't it, my little squirrel?"

Eva grinned back as Greta pulled her shirt out of her skirt and began to run her hands over Eva's back, bringing her closer, nuzzling her neck.

"Hmm," Eva agreed, not trusting her voice at this point, nauseated by Greta's attempts to excite her. She closed her eyes as Greta unbuttoned two more buttons of her shirt pulling it slightly off her left shoulder, Greta kissed her shoulder and then returned to her neck.

"You brought me up here to drive me mad with desire." Greta let her go and unbuttoned the remaining buttons of Eva's shirt. "You know I don't mind if I make love to you, right here." She pulled Eva to her, cupping her breasts and squeezing them a little, causing Eva to whimper. "I am going to enjoy getting to know the grown up body..."

Eva wanted to push the woman away from her and get this over and done with. She hoped David and Friedrich were indeed waiting in the next room as the overturned book indicated. She caught Greta hands and leaned in. "What about we go into the bedroom and continue this sexy game?" Eva whispered seductively, taking Greta's hand.

"Ah, you've outgrown making love in unusual places?" Greta laughed remembering the first time they had made love, Eva's first time ever, out in the park. It was a glorious day, and she had spent so much time preparing to make the day special. They had found a clearing with a huge chestnut tree, which afforded them privacy, and had spread the blanket out. Greta took her time in letting the young woman know how much she loved her. She was rather proud of herself for being Eva's first lover, and she grinned every time she passed a chestnut tree.

"You don't have any squirrels in there, do you?" She smiled as Eva turned and gave her a huge grin.

"Oh, much better than that, my love, much much better," Eva said and turned the knob of the door and entered. She saw David crouched, ready to pounce, and she turned and brought Greta's dark head down for a sensual kiss as they entered the room.

Friedrich's eyebrows went up at Eva's state of undress, but he concentrated on backing David up and not screwing this up. He got quite a shock as Eva pulled Greta inside, blocking her view of David and the other officers. He watched slack jawed as Eva's long sensual kiss caused the other woman to moan out loud.

Eva decided to end this charade and took Greta's hand on the pretence of kissing it. Greta's arm was yanked behind her back, and she was shoved up against the wall. Eva's knee connected with her back, pinning her.

"Ohhh, Eva, you like it a little rough?" Greta muttered as her face met the wallpaper of the bedroom wall.

Eva leaned in and whispered into her ear, "After what you put my wife through, I could kill you." She turned her head towards David who was watching open mouthed. "She's yours."

"Hey!" Greta yelled, as David took over from Eva. He pulled Greta's arms behind her back and kicked her legs out from under her, letting her drop to the floor.

For a few seconds, Eva watched the prone woman who was

yelling expletives. She buttoned her shirt and stepped over Greta, leaving the bedroom. She was about to run out of the flat, but stopped and turned. She went to the bathroom and let the water run before picking up the soap to wash her face and neck.

She held the towel in her hands and patted her face dry. They had done it. Eva couldn't believe that they actually had caught the woman, but at what cost? Zoe had been hurt, and for that she would never forgive Greta or herself for agitating her wife to the point where she raised her hand against her. Eva brought up her hand and cupped her cheek where she had been slapped. She would make it up to her partner, hoping it was going to be enough to rid the young woman of any lasting effects.

Eva sighed as she put the towel back. Taking another look at the commotion in the bedroom where the expletives from Greta were still ringing out, she closed the door to the flat and went to Elena's.

Just as she was about to knock, the door opened and a very concerned Earl stood at the threshold with a bat in his hand. A smile spread across his stubbled face as he dropped the bat and yelled at the top of his voice "*Eureka*! You little bloody beauty." He hoisted Eva in a bear hug, taking her inside and twirling her around the room. He gave her a kiss on the cheek as he put her down.

"Earl, you're crushing me." Eva cried out, hitting the big man across his broad shoulders.

"I am so glad to see you. Zoe's in the bathroom, and she needs you, my friend..." Earl didn't finish as Eva left Earl and Elena and raced into the bathroom to find her wife kneeling doubled over on the floor, crying.

"Zoe, love," Eva whispered as her heart broke into a thousand pieces at the sight. She dropped to the floor next to her partner.

Zoe looked up at the sound of her wife's voice. Eva knelt next to her. Tears ran down her face as she opened her arms in invitation for her wife. Zoe hiccoughed, letting fresh tears fall as she melted into Eva's embrace. The older woman scooped her into her arms as Zoe began to cry anew.

Eva held onto her and rocked her back and forth. "I'm so sorry, love," Eva whispered. "I'm so sorry." Eva kissed the top of her head and caressed her cheek.

"I...hurt you," Zoe stammered in between hiccoughs.

"No, you didn't. You could never hurt me, love."

"I did," Zoe repeated and looked up. She cupped her hand over the cheek she had slapped only an hour ago. "I hurt you,"

Eva closed her eyes and shook her head. "No, you didn't. I love you so much, Zo. I want you to listen to me, okay? You didn't hurt me. I should never have asked you to slap me." She brushed away Zoe's tears with the back of her fingers. Lifting Zoe's face, she leaned down and gently kissed her wife. The kiss deepened as Zoe put her arms around Eva's neck, tangling her hands in Eva's hair.

"I promised you I would never hurt you, Evy, never," Zoe murmured. She held Eva's face and looked into her eyes. "I don't ever want to hurt you."

"I know, love, I know." Eva let her own tears fall unhindered while she held Zoe in her embrace. She sat down on the floor with her back against the wall and cradled her wife, whispering to her, reassuring her of her love. "We did it, love, we did it."

"Did she hurt you?" Zoe asked, putting her hand on Eva's chest.

"I let her kiss and grope me, which made me sick," Eva sighed. "I washed myself before I came here."

"Is that why you smell all nice?" Zoe murmured as she relaxed in Eva's embrace for the first time in hours.

"I didn't want to have even a trace of her scent on me."

They sat on the floor holding and touching each other until the door opened slightly to reveal a very worried Earl sticking his head around the corner. "David said they are ready to leave. Do you want to say anything to the bitch from hell?"

Eva looked down at Zoe, who nodded. "We'll be there in a few minutes."

"No worries," Earl replied.

"Earl?"

"Yeah, mate?"

"Thank you," Eva said. Zoe looked up as well, giving Earl a tiny smile.

Earl smiled. He didn't have the words to express how much he loved his two friends. They had always been there for him in the last nine months; he wanted to be there for them as well. "Anything for you two."

The door closed as Eva stroked Zoe's cheek. "Are you feeling up to it, love?"

"No, but I'm not going to let her think she's beaten me," Zoe mumbled.

"That's my Zoe," Eva whispered, giving her wife a kiss. "Come on, let's go and stick it up her." Zoe got off her lap as she was helped up from behind. "I love you, Zo."

Zoe looked up. Closing her eyes, she put her arms around Eva's slim waist and began to cry again.

"Hey, I didn't mean for you to cry. Come on, love, it's okay." Eva held her partner. "I won't let her hurt you again."

Zoe sniffed back tears. "It hurts, Evy."

"I know, love, but the sooner we do this, the sooner we can go and rest, okay?"

Zoe nodded. Eva opened the bathroom door, leading Zoe out to where Elena and Earl were waiting. Elena stepped forward and embraced the both of them. "Thank you," Elena said quietly. "I know it hurt both of you, and I want to thank you for getting her here. And I think all those that she helped kill would thank you, if they could."

Zoe's tears started anew at Elena's heartfelt words. Eva brushed away her own tears and held Zoe closer.

She led Zoe outside where the police were milling around in the corridor. Eva rolled her eyes when she caught sight of Mrs Jenkins talking to her father. She hoped he would handle their landlady since she was in no mood to explain everything to the older woman.

David spotted them immediately, but finished speaking to an officer before walking towards them. "Thank you," he said earnestly, offering his hand.

Eva took his hand and shook it. "I don't mean to be rude, David, but I hope I never see you again," Eva said as she held Zoe closer to her.

David nodded. "I want to apologise for my behaviour. I, um...I've been trying to trace this woman and Mengele since the war ended. I made a promise to a young woman and..."

"There's no need to explain, I understand," Eva said, catching sight of Friedrich leading a dishevelled looking Greta towards them.

"You betrayed me," Greta said hoarsely. She was incredulous at how Eva had fooled her. She had been so certain she had outsmarted these idiotic little fools with her faked death. Of course, she should have followed up and made certain Dieter got the right information. Stupid fool. "I could have given you so much…Why?"

"You are truly blind, aren't you?" Eva said and shook her head. "You killed thousands, and you want to know why I helped to arrest you?"

"Good God, I was just doing my job. I was following orders. And I am so sick of saying that. Don't you people understand?" Greta sighed and turned her attention to Zoe. "I know Eva loves me. She loved my touch." Greta grinned, determined to get in the last word.

Zoe rolled her eyes. "Not only are you a bloody idiot, you are deluded!" Zoe put her arm around her wife's waist and squeezed. "She's mine, and you had a snowball's chance in hell."

Greta snorted.

"Zoe is the best thing to happen to me; she is my life," Eva said quietly to her former lover. "You never owned my heart. Zoe does, and always will."

"You are the deluded one, Eva darling. A peasant has—"

Zoe's anger got the better of her as she let go of Eva and swung with all her might. She hit Greta in the face, breaking her nose and sending her falling back into Friedrich's arms. Her blood ran down her chin and onto her white shirt as she cried out in pain.

"A peasant that packs a wallop," Friedrich said, leading the woman off before Zoe got another shot at her. He was tempted to get in a lick of his own, but that thought soon passed. He looked down at his once white shirt to see the woman's blood spattered there and sighed.

Zoe turned to a mildly amused Eva and looked up. "Ow," she cried out as she held onto her injured hand. Eva took it and kissed the skinned knuckles.

"Come on, love. I think we've had enough excitement for the day." Eva was about to lead her wife inside their flat when she spotted her father coming towards them. "Father."

Panayiotis hugged his two daughters. "Are you okay?"

"A little fragile at the moment," Eva said quietly, "but we're going to be all right."

"I'm proud of both of you." Panayiotis leaned over and gave Eva a kiss and then Zoe, who hugged him back. "Go, I'll deal with everything out here."

"Thank you, Father," Eva said and led her wife inside, closing the door to their flat.

Chapter 21

They stood in the middle of the living room holding each other, not saying anything—for there weren't any words that could convey what Eva was feeling. She tried, but stopped. She wanted to tell Zoe how much the young woman meant to her, but the words were inadequate to express her deep feelings. She had to try and convey her thoughts to her loving spouse.

"What's going to happen to her?" Zoe asked. She put her head on Eva's chest and sighed, feeling safe in her wife's arms.

"If she is found guilty, a death sentence or life in prison," Eva replied as she looked down at the dark head thoughtfully. She had said some hurtful things in the office. "Zo, um...what I said in the office..."

"Evy, I know you didn't mean them." Zoe put her hand on Eva's chest and looked up into her lover's face.

"God, I love you," Eva whispered and she picked up her wife, cradling her in her arms. "If any good has come from the war, it's been you."

Zoe stroked Eva's face, tracing with the tip of her finger the pronounced dimple in Eva's chin. "I would go through everything again if it meant I was to fall in love with you." Zoe put her arms around Eva's neck and laid her head on her shoulder.

"Amen," Eva whispered as she took her wife into the bedroom.

❖ ❖ ❖ ❖ ❖ ❖ ❖

Elena leaned over the balcony, watching the police and the crowd that had gathered outside the flats. Somehow the local media had arrived. *Like vultures*, she thought to herself. She watched with satisfaction as Greta was taken away in a police car that was tailed by several other cars.

"Hi."

Elena turned to find Friedrich smiling at her—his hat slightly askew, his shirt bloodied—but a very happy man.

"You were wonderful," Elena gushed as she unbuttoned his shirt. She frowned when she realised his singlet was also stained. Friedrich looked down and gave her a crooked grin. "Zoe popped her one."

"Did she?"

"Oh yeah. Remind me never to get Zoe angry with me," Friedrich joked, removing his undershirt and handing it to Elena. Elena admired his bare chest with a grin before going inside to the soak them in cold water.

"What happened when they arrived?"

"Ah, well, they were in the lounge room and took forever to get in to the bedroom. David thought that we would need to go out there instead. Eva finally brought her inside. She scares me."

"Who does?"

"Eva," Friedrich replied. He wasn't ashamed to admit he was intimidated by the tall woman.

"You're kidding, right?"

"No," Friedrich replied shaking his head. "When I first met them, I couldn't figure them out."

"Eva is one of the most gentle women I have ever met, sweetheart. She absolutely worships Zoe, and she would do anything for her friends. I should know. It does take a little time for her to warm up to you, but she was trying at the BBQ yesterday."

"Yeah, I know. Maybe it's because she's so tall," Friedrich joked.

Elena smiled. "Well, I don't think she can help that."

"Hmm," Friedrich leaned on the balcony with a smile on his lips. "So do I get a kiss?"

"You want a kiss?" Elena teased. "Just a kiss?"

"A cuddle would be nice as well," Friedrich replied, opening his arms to his fiancée. Elena snuggled up against his chest and closed her eyes.

❖ ❖ ❖ ❖ ❖ ❖ ❖

Ally looked around the dishevelled flat and began to clean up, putting things back to normal. Earl had volunteered to cook them all a dinner, and he was busy in the kitchen, while Panayiotis was getting Elise Jenkins' feathers unruffled.

Ally quietly opened the bedroom door and winced when it squeaked a bit. She hoped it hadn't woken her two daughters from their rest.

She wasn't surprised to find Zoe sprawled on top of Eva's body as if she was a mattress, with Eva's arms wrapped around her small body. Satisfied they were indeed sleeping soundly, she turned to leave.

"Ally?" a sleepy voice came from the bed.

Ally turned to find two very tired blue eyes looking at her. "Oh, sorry I woke you," Ally said quietly so as to not disturb Zoe, who was still asleep.

"No, that's okay."

"How are you feeling?"

"Relieved at the moment, though I'm angry that I let her get to Zoe." She ran her fingers through Zoe's dark hair that was resting on her chest. "I'm glad it's over, I can't sleep."

"You're still hyped up. Do you want me to call Dr Theophonous to give you something to sleep?"

Eva shook her head. "No, it's okay. I'm just going to try and rest. How's Dad?"

"Well he's trying to soothe Elise. I don't think this building has seen this much excitement since Mr Jenkins' toupee went flying in a southerly," Ally joked.

Eva wanted to laugh at the mental picture of their landlord trying to hold on to his toupee in the Sydney southerly winds that were quite common during summer.

"Once the excitement dies down, everyone will be happy. Now, young lady, I want you to rest. Earl is cooking up a storm in the kitchen, so if you feel up to it later, come out and have a bite. I think it would be good for both of you to eat something. I know Zoe hasn't eaten all day."

"I couldn't eat either; my stomach was in knots."

"I don't doubt it, but you have to eat something later."

"I will. Thanks, Ally."

"You're welcome. We'll talk later, get some rest." Ally leaned down and kissed her daughter on the head, tucking the sheet around her.

Eva watched Ally leave. She looked down at her best friend and found a tiny smile on Zoe's face. She murmured something that Eva couldn't hear and burrowed deeper in Eva's embrace.

Eva closed her eyes, wanting to catch up on the sleep she hadn't gotten the previous night. She was too restless to sleep, her mind too active.

"You're thinking too loud again," Zoe murmured.

"Sorry, did my loud thinking wake you?"

"No, but I'm glad I woke up. I had this most wonderful dream."

"What were you dreaming about, us on a deserted island, no Nazis, no excitement?"

"No."

"No? Couldn't have been that nice a dream, then. I know that's my dream," Eva teased.

"Really?"

"Oh yeah," Eva grinned. "What were you dreaming about?"

"Hmm, I was driving this huge American tank. You know how big they are. I couldn't see over the top, but I was driving it. Greta was standing on the road waving that blasted Nazi broach of hers. I got so mad I ran her over a couple of times just to make sure, but the funniest thing was that I could hear Hymn of Freedom playing."

"Hey, musical dreams—that's different, and patriotic," Eva chuckled. "I bet that stupid pin survived."

"Nah, I made sure it got pummelled," Zoe replied letting her head rest on Eva's chest. "I wish life was like a good dream."

"It is," Eva replied. "Sometimes, it's even better."

"Aww, that's so romantic," Zoe grinned up at her partner.

"I'm just a romantic kind of gal," Eva replied, getting a giggle from her wife. "I've been thinking of taking a few days off work. Would you like to go to the mountains?"

"Hmm, sounds good," Zoe said sleepily and patted Eva's belly. "You have to sleep. You've been awake for too long."

"Yes, mum," Eva teased and closed her eyes.

❖❖❖❖❖❖❖

Earl wiped his hands on a towel and draped it over his shoulder. Ally had told him that the girls might be coming out for dinner, but it was late. He closed the doors to the balcony and shut off the lights before retiring to the spare bedroom. He turned to switch off the light of the lounge room when the bedroom door opened and Zoe came out quietly.

"Hey, Wiggy," Zoe greeted her friend. "Come here, big guy, I want to give you a hug." Zoe put her arms around his waist and hugged him. "Are you okay?"

"Me? Oh yeah. How's Eva?"

"Tired. She didn't sleep at all yesterday. Um, Earl, do you remember you were telling me about that jeweler friend of yours?"

"Yeah, Jack. He does some nice pieces."

"Do you think he can do something for me?"

"Sure, what is it?"

Zoe smiled. She took off her ring and handed it to Earl. "I want one similar to this for Eva."

Earl twirled the ring in his hand. "Exactly like it?"

"Yeah."

"Not a problem, Stretch. I'll see him tomorrow and give him the specs. This is for your anniversary, huh?"

"Yeah. With everything that's happened, I don't think Evy has remembered..."

"Hello? You're kidding, right? Eva's booked...er...oh shut up, Earl!" He clasped his hand around his mouth. Eva was going to kill him.

"She hasn't forgotten?"

"No, and that's all I'm going to say!"

"That sneaky, drop dead gorgeous wife of mine."

"You didn't hear it from me."

"You have a big mouth, my friend." Eva leaned against the door frame grinning.

"Aw hell, I didn't tell her about the Timb...er...I'm going to bed. Good night."

"Good night, Earl." Eva grinned as the tall man shut the door.

"What are you doing up?" Zoe demanded.

"Wondering where you got to. I can't sleep without you."

"Saved once again by your mushy streak. Let's go to bed, Miss Evy. I think I've had enough of today."

"I agree, Miss Zoe." Eva put her arm around Zoe's shoulders and led her back into the room.

Epilogue

"Oh, Evy, don't stop."
"You like?"
"Uh huh,"
Eva smiled down at the young woman who was sprawled below her on the beach towel. Eva spread the warm suntan lotion, massaging the liquid into her back, eliciting moans of pleasure. Zoe hummed, feeling her wife's soft hands spread the warm liquid over her back. She was feeling very relaxed and a little sleepy.

It was another hot and sultry Sydney day, the heat making the sand burn. The beach was packed with sunworshippers in various states of undress. Young children played near the water's edge while their protective parents looked on. Eva looked up from her enjoyable duty to see Earl coming towards them, dripping wet from the surf, holding his surfboard in one hand and seaweed in the other.

Earl put his finger to his lips to stop Eva from telling her wife that he was heading their way. Eva shook her head, grinning as Earl came near and dropped the wet seaweed on Zoe's back.

"Arghhhh!" Zoe screamed as she sat up and glared at Eva, grabbing the offending seaweed and throwing it at Earl.

"Hey, don't look at me!" Eva put her hands up in protest and then pointed to their friend who had wisely chosen to stand back.

"You are in big trouble, mister." Zoe got up and chased Earl down to the surf, squealing when Earl stopped and picked her up, putting her across his broad shoulders and walking purposefully into the sea.

Eva watched them having a mock fight in the water. Zoe's yelping at being dunked caused Eva to grin as she sat back on the low chair, extending her long leg and digging her toes into the hot sand.

Zoe had bought her a pale blue swimming costume, which she was wearing under a light cotton shirt. She put on her dark sunglasses and sat back to enjoy the day. It had been a few days since they had gone through one of their most traumatic times together.

Eva had chosen to take a few days off from work to take care of Zoe—to reassure her of her love and to be with her. Their first year wedding anniversary was coming up on Saturday and she wanted to make it extra special. She had booked a room at the Hydro Majestic Hotel where they could just enjoy each other's company. She was looking forward to spending time with her wife.

Eva picked up her book, intending to read, when she caught sight of Earl trying to teach Zoe how to swim. She fingered the light cotton shirt she wore and sighed. She thought back to how courageous Zoe had been when she was going to confront the woman who taunted her. "*I'm not going to let her think she's beaten me,*" Zoe had said.

Eva decided it was time to stop letting Muller dictate to her, time to stop being afraid. She pulled off her cotton shirt, putting it with the rest of their clothes. Setting the book down, she got up and walked towards the sea.

Earl brushed back his wet hair as he held Zoe, who was making a valiant attempt to float but kept squealing when Earl tried to let go of her. He glanced up to find Eva walking towards them. His mouth fell open as he realised that she wasn't wearing the shirt, just the swimming costume.

Eva put her finger to her lips to prevent Earl from letting her wife know she was there. Coming around Earl, she replaced the tall man's hands keeping Zoe up with her own. She leaned down and whispered, "I've got you."

Zoe's eyes flew open to stare into her wife's smiling deep blue. "Eva!"

"Hmm?"

Zoe touched bottom and turned to her partner, who was standing in the water with a smirk on her face. She approached closer, putting her arms around her waist. "Your shirt?" Zoe asked, referring to the ever-present shirt that covered the scarring on Eva's back.

"I left it with our other stuff," Eva grinned. "It's time I stopped being scared. I remembered what you said about not allowing Greta to think she'd beaten you. It made me think that I've allowed Muller to do that to me for too long."

"Oh, Evy!" Zoe cried as she hugged her partner, knowing the courage it took for Eva to expose her back. "You're going to get burnt now."

"Well, would you blow on my back to cool it down if I do?" Eva asked, causing Zoe to look up at her with a sexy grin, nodding vigorously. Eva chuckled.

"Kiss me," Zoe demanded.

"Out here?" Eva asked, indicating all the people in the water and out on the shore.

"Yeah," Zoe replied, jumping into Eva's embrace and wrapping her legs around Eva's waist. "I don't care what people think. I love you, and if I want to kiss you in the sea, then I'll kiss you in the sea."

"Zoe?"

"Hmm?"

"You talk too much." Eva kissed her wife, letting her hands roam under the water, causing Zoe to moan.

"Oh, this is much better than learning to swim."

Eva laughed as she went into deeper water, her wife still wrapped around her. She hadn't gone swimming in years, and the feel of her wife nuzzling her neck out in the surf was making the experience all the more enjoyable. "Zo, we're going to the mountains next week."

"Hmm, climbing." Zoe waggled her eyebrows, which got a sexy growl from her wife.

Earl watched from the shore, grinning broadly. He shook his head and, hefting the surfboard, turned to find a good place to catch some waves.

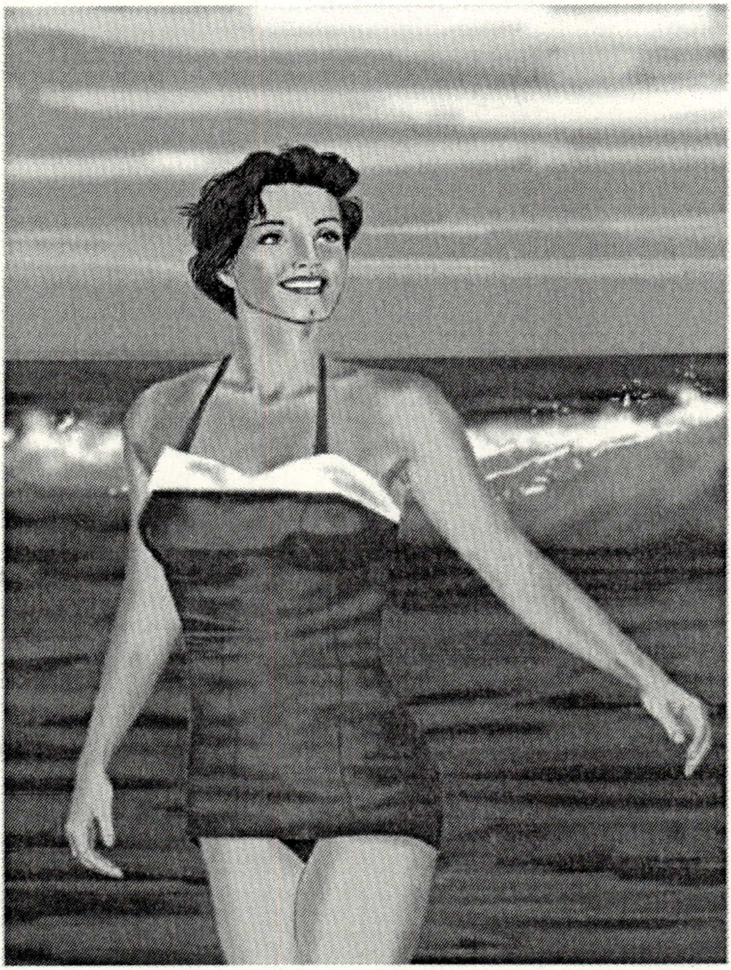

Available soon from
Renaissance Alliance

Jacob's Fire
By Nan DeVincent Hayes

Jacob, a university professor/scientist has found a formula to cure AIDS—a formula that causes mass destruction if improperly used. The government and a private pharmaceutical firm want Jacob's formula, and go to brutal, vicious, murderous means to get it. But Isleen, the pharmaceutical rep who is assigned to cajole him into selling the formula to her firm, refuses to exert unethical means, and, instead, she and Jacob eventually become friends and allies who try to fight "Big Government." Isleen tries convincing Jacob that world events are following biblical prophecy, the end time is near, and that he should reconsider his staunch Judaic position. She wants him to believe that the Second Coming of Christ is at hand.

Mystery, intrigue and suspense intertwine with secret societies and politics while the global leaders attempt to form a "New World Order" on the political, religious, and economic levels. Jacob innocently gets caught up in this web of shadow organizations and soon finds himself trying to find an antidote for the plague that has been unleashed on the world, all the while watching as the prophecies Isleen told him about continue to unfold. In the end, Jacob must make a decision on the Truth before it is too late.

Other titles to look for in the
coming months from
RENAISSANCE ALLIANCE

Full Circle By Mary D. Brooks

Bleeding Hearts By Josh Aterovis

New Beginnings By Mary D. Brooks

A Sacrifice For Friendship By DS Bauden

Printed in the United States
2245